PEACE

"Denise, I want to get to know you better."

"I don't think that's possible." She attempted to sound serious. "In case you've forgotten, you're the enemy. I shouldn't even be here with you."

Brother Jahid-Ali's eyes twinkled. "Ah, but you are."

He was right. She was sitting in Norm's with him. In fact, this was the best she'd felt in three days. Denise wondered what it was about him that made her feel so good . . .

"Thanks for the lift and the dinner," Denise said.

"Hakuna furaha bila upendo. That's Swahili for 'there's not joy in this world without love'," he said seductively.

Denise blushed. "Thanks again."

"Maybe I'll see you on Tuesday."

"Maybe you will, maybe you won't," she smiled coyly.

TIMELESS LOVE

Look for these historical romances in the Arabesque line:

BLACK PEARL by Francine Craft (0236-0, $4.99)

CLARA'S PROMISE by Shirley Hailstock (0147-X, $4.99)

MIDNIGHT MOON by Mildred Riley (0200-X; $4.99)

SUNSHINE AND SHADOWS by Roberta Gayle (0136-4, $4.99)

ABANDON

Neffetiti Austin

Pinnacle Books
Kensington Publishing Corp.

http://www.pinnaclebooks.com

Though ABANDON is fiction, my sentiment that there is not enough written about women in the Black Panther Party is sincere.

PINNACLE BOOKS are published by

Kensington Publishing Corp.
850 Third Avenue
New York, NY 10022

First Printing: November, 1996
10 9 8 7 6 5 4 3 2 1

Printed in the United States of America

I dedicate Abandon *to Professors' P. Von Blum, and R. Daniels for allowing me to submit portions of my manuscript in place of research papers. I must also thank W. Johnson for letting me keep my job, even though I was late to work almost every day. Further kudos go to Professor R. Hill, T. Sheehee, S. Graham and R. Yarborough at the Center for African American Studies at UCLA for extending deadlines, so that I could graduate on time.*

Last, but not least, I dedicate this story to my mother, Diane; late father, Harold, and my Aunt Carolyn for sharing the intimate details of their real life adventures (and poetry) in the Black Power Movement.

Acknowledgments

Space prevents me from naming everyone, but as always, I thank my grandparents: A. & H. Hawthorne; J. & D. Austin; S. Austin; C. Wimbush; and the rest of my many dear friends for their support and encouragement. Special thanks to T. Adams, N. Austin, and L. Bobbitt. Finally, thank you Monica Harris for giving me the opportunity to turn my dream of becoming an author into a reality.

Also thanks to my life long supporters: M. Archie-Hudson; K. Earl; L.&C. Williams; H. Newbon; T. Smith; P. Means; E. Wilson; M. Doby; H. Dixon; B. Rollins; The Flanagans; The Andersons; The Smiths; The Adams; Mallory & Brown-Curtis; and Community Build, Inc.

To my pre-editors—when I thought all I had was a short story, you encouraged me to continue writing: L. Warren; R. Lyles; D. Tarkington; J. & C. Kirkland-Andrews; K. Rickett; The Hinkles; M. Lee; L. Engleskirchen; The Hookers; L. Kirtman; L. Appleberry; L. Dickey; D. Flanagan; B. Soria; S. Farr and M. Saoud.

If I omitted anyone, please forgive me. I'll name you in the next book!

Part 1:

Are You Part of the Problem or Part of the Solution?

Prologue

1969. The UCLA Bruins' Basketball Team was the number one team in the nation; the United States was in conflict with Vietnam; and Motown was the place to be if you were Black and could sing.

"Good morning, sista."

"I am not your sister." Denise Davis rolled her eyes at the black giant who, standing six feet five inches tall, was wearing a black leather jacket, black chinos, light blue denim shirt, and a black beret on top of his bushy 'fro. To complete his ensemble, he wore black wayfarer sunglasses and combat boots. As usual he was in her way, but she continued her journey to her eleven o'clock class, up Bruin walk.

Denise had just left her room in Heisman Hall at UCLA. Heisman Hall, named for the past chancellor of the campus, housed most of the juniors and seniors. It was the northernmost dormitory, and rumored to have the best dorm food on campus. UCLA was the cornerstone of Westwood, an all white exclusive suburb of Los Angeles. The campus was nestled among green foliage, beautiful trees, and brick buildings. It had a flavor all its own.

"All oppressed people are related, sista." Kweli fell into step with Denise. He was trying his best to put a purple colored leaflet in her hand. Kweli was the latest in a long line of militant activists trying to recruit Black students to join the Black Panther Party. UCLA seemed to be prime ground for different factions of the Black Power Movement, the Stop the War movement, Flower Power, and the ERA. Each organization had its own agenda for the best way to recruit the students on campus.

Denise accepted the leaflet, took one look at the picture of Mao Tse Tung with the words: "Are you part of the problem or part of the solution?", and threw it to the ground.

Denise was twenty-one years old, majoring in social welfare with her whole life planned out for her. As soon as she graduated from UCLA, she was going to marry her boyfriend, Charles Jackson. They would live in a three-bedroom house and have two children, a boy and a girl. The last thing she needed was for something or someone to get in her way.

The campus was charged with student protests and had been for the last few years. The conflict in Vietnam had particularly hit home for many students who carried signs that read HELL NO! WE WON'T GO! Although she had not participated in any rallies, Denise did sympathize with the protesters. Her second cousin, Leon, was over in Vietnam. So far he was okay, but her Aunt Johnetta seemed to die a little each day that he was gone.

The latest campus uproar was over whether or not to have a Black studies program added to the college curriculum. Denise thought it was a good idea, but was doubtful that the university would agree to the idea, at least as long as she was a student there.

Accustomed to the mentality that pervaded the Negro students at UCLA, Kweli was undaunted by Denise's apathy. "Sista, what class are you late to?" His narrow face and small features gave him a mousey look. Though only twenty-four years old, his sad eyes caused him to look older.

"Who said I was late?" She switched her purse from her left shoulder to her right. The book Denise was carrying was heavy and her left hand was cramping. Her face turned red, darkening her smooth café au lait complexion. Denise's hair was the color of dark honeysuckle, and her amber eyes changed color with the seasons. Today, they were a fierce brown.

"Well, you are at the bottom of the hill, there is sweat on your forehead and you are breathing heavily, ya dig?" Kweli tugged on the bottom strap of her orange backpack. "Your backpack doesn't feel very heavy, Sista," Kweli was staring hard at her, "why don't you just admit that you're late?"

Spring semester 1969 had just started and Denise was already off to a poor start. She couldn't seem to get to class on time. She daydreamed in class, and to be truthful, Denise was beginning to feel anxious. Her mother believed that she was suffering from senioritis; her father agreed with her mother—as usual. Shelly Taylor, her best friend, thought that Charles was her problem. Charles was a medical student whose studies often interrupted their time together. Denise believed that her lackluster attitude was a combination of all of those things.

She was also feeling disconnected from the broader world. Denise thought about joining the Black Student Alliance or BSA, but decided against it when she heard that they didn't want people who belonged to Greek letter organizations. She was considered a "handkerchief head" because she had joined the Alpha Kappa Alpha sorority. It bothered Denise that the BSA allowed three little letters to stand between them and her. Denise pledged a sorority, not in order to become somebody, but because she admired the qualities in the women who belonged to the organization. These women inherited the legacy of being the first Black sorority in the United States, not to mention they provided Denise with a deeper commitment to scholarship, leadership and community service. These were also the same virtues instilled in her by her mother, and joining a sorority was a natural extension of her dedication to others.

Though Denise did not know Kweli personally, she had seen him on campus many times before. Nevertheless, she also had no desire to talk to the pesky militant standing next to her. She really *was* late to her American history class, "The Reconstruction Era: 1865–1890," and he was slowing her down. Denise ignored his question and continued up the hill to the main campus.

"Let me guess, a white man is teaching your history class." Denise thought that was more of a statement than a question.

"Yes, so?" Kweli's question surprised her because he wasn't a student at UCLA. If he was, she would have known. There were so few Black students, and they all knew each other.

He pointed to the textbook entitled *The Newly Freed Slaves* in her hand. "He's the only professor who teaches Negro history at this institution of *supposed* higher learning." He snorted. "You should know that, sista', but I guess field hands aren't privileged to the truth . . ."

"You are so rude." Denise stopped walking and looked at him.

Kweli continued his diatribe: "It's the so-called educated Negro like yourself who are obstructions to the movement. When you niggas get tired of whitey telling you about yourself, call me." He turned and headed back down the hill.

"Listen, you aren't even a student here or anywhere as far as I can see." He stopped in his tracks. It was her turn to walk away.

Pretending to be shot, Kweli clutched his heart. He removed his wayfarer glasses in a dramatic motion. "I see that you have been effectively brainwashed into believing that this university is the mecca of knowledge. But that's alright, I know your pain. See, sista' I was once like you. I was an honor student at another institution like this one, and I was being programmed to be a productive member of whitey's society." Kweli took one giant step and was standing directly in front of her. Denise tried not to look at him, but had a choice between staring at his collarbone and looking into his eyes. Denise chose the latter. "My spirit was divided and I was being lulled to sleep by the racist, fascist indoctrination of nonviolence . . ." He picked the leaflet up off the ground and dusted it off. "Anyway, one day I found the truth and never looked back. I stopped diggin' Mr. Charlie and discovered that Mao is the truth and revolution is the key. And another thing sista, I wish that you wouldn't castrate me. What you need is—"

"What I need is for you to first, call me by my name; second, stop harassing me with your communist leaflets every day; and third, get a damn job!" Denise tried to step around him.

"Such a foul mouth for such a beautiful princess." Kweli was trying to press her buttons. Even in her pink and green sorority sweater, white turtleneck, bellbottom levi's, and beige, yellow and black platform shoes, Denise was able to shine him on. Her hair, which reached the middle of her back, was parted down the center of her head and tucked neatly behind her ears on both sides. She wore huge silver hoop earrings and a matching silver bracelet. Denise was especially dressed cute because it was "Black Day."

It was Wednesday and that was the day that some of the Black students congregated in the Cooperage, which was located inside Ackerman Union. She didn't know how or why Wednesday was the chosen day for the Black students on campus to congregate, but it was. The Ackerman Union housed the student store, the bowling alley and, of course, the Coop.

Very few revolutionaries ventured into the Coop. It wasn't relevant as far as they were concerned. They spent their time at Meyerhuff Park, which was the grassy area located directly in front of Ackerman Union. The conscious Blacks attended the many rallies held at the park, or they hung out at the Gypsy Wagon. This food cart, which was parked in front of Campbell Hall, held its own series of debates about politics and war.

The Blacks who hung out in the Coop played bid wiz, spades, and exchanged fraternal and sororal handshakes. There were other Blacks there, but they tended not to belong to any group at all. Denise did not know how to play wiz, but enjoyed watching the competitors play the dozens, in order to rattle their opponents.

As Denise continued her trek up the steep hill to Moore Hall, Mr. Revolution walked along side of her. "By the way, my name is Kweli." He returned his sunglasses to his face. "What is your name?"

Her best friend, Shelly, had a crush on him and already told her his name. Shelly had spotted him on campus a few times before and somehow discovered his name. Denise pretended that this was the first time she had ever heard it. "Kwe—what?" She knew that his mama did not name him that.

"Kweli pronounced Kway-lee. That's my traditional name. It's Swahili for "Truth." And your name, queen?"

"Denise," she huffed. The hill seemed to be growing steeper.

"That's too bad. I thought you were going to say something beautiful like Lamachosie. Denise is so . . . white." He made a face as if he had swallowed something bitter.

"I am told that I am the reincarnation of my grandmother, Denise Marie and I'm named for her." *Why was she explaining this to him?* Denise stopped dead in her tracks and put her empty hand on her hip. "Look Kwazimoto—"

"Kweli."

". . . Whatever your name is, I'm tired of talking to you and if you don't leave me alone, I'm going to call the campus police and have you arrested." Denise tried to run away from him, but her platforms were too high.

"Wait sista', I wasn't trying to offend you. Lamachosie is a South African name that means 'one who is loved by the gods'." For the second time that morning, he removed his sunglasses and stared at her. His look was that of approval, but Denise felt a chill run down her spine. "And I see that the gods have loved you a whole lot." Kweli winked and bowed to her, while sliding his shades back on. "You go on to class and continue to hear the lies. I promise he will never tell you the truth about black history or any history for that matter."

Denise started to say something smart to remove that smug smile off of his face, but couldn't think of anything; so she continued her sojurn to class.

Late as usual, Denise sat down in the third row of the lecture hall. The room had a seating capacity of five hundred students, but only half of it was ever used. Whenever class was boring, which was most of the time, Denise pretended she was sitting in a huge movie theater. The desks formed a huge "U" and were joined together on the right side. The writing desks were collapsible and also stored on the right side of each seat, which made it nearly impossible to write if one was left handed, like she was. There was nothing spectacular about the room, other than the fact that the seats were covered in the same brown material that doubled for carpet.

Denise tried hard to forget what Kweli said, but her mind kept wandering to the leaflet—"Are you part of the problem or part of the solution?" Instinctively, she knew that she was not part of the problem. No, not her. Kweli was the one with the problem. Denise was in college and studying to be a social worker, not some low life spouting rhetoric for a living. While there was some truth in what he had said about the watered down history they were being taught, there was nothing Denise could do to change the system.

Denise eventually forgot about Kweli and focused on the ongoing lecture about the numerous senators and congressman who held office in the former slave states. A hand went up toward the back of the lecture hall.

"Professor, why did the ex-slaves think they were smart enough to hold office?" A couple of students nodded in approval. Noting this support, the student continued matter of factly. Jason was the student body president and captain of the debate team. "I guess some of them were qualified to be senators, but most of them weren't educated."

"You're right," Professor Beale answered. "Some historians purport that Africans were mainly agrarian people. Their use in the New World was useful in the cultivation of rice and slave labor. Otherwise we don't know too much

more about their technical skills and analytical skills."
Denise stopped writing in mid-sentence and raised her
hand. "As many of the Africans were animists and poly-
theists, with obvious exceptions where conversion to Ca-
tholicism and Christianity occurred. Also—"

Denise couldn't stand anymore. Before she knew it, she
was on her feet. "Excuse me, professor." Jason was such
an arrogant bastard. She remembered him from the Sociology of Education she had taken the previous Fall quarter.

"Not now, Miss Davis." Professor Beale saw the anxiety
on her face, but did not want to hear her comment. "This
is a lecture, not a debate team."

Denise was not moved. Her parents paid tuition just like
all the other students' parents, and she had a right to be
heard. "I have something to say." Also as the only Black
student in class, it had been an unwritten policy that she
be allowed to speak. At least that is what the professor told
her during her visit to his office hours. Speaking out of
turn, Denise said, "The Africans built the pyramids, started
civilization, mathematics and studied the stars . . ."

"Be quiet, Miss Davis." Professor Beale repeated loudly.
He feared losing control of his lecture.

"I would like to finish making my point." Until today,
Denise had never behaved this way in front of a professor.
Her grade point average was a three point five yet she knew
that defying the professor was the quickest way to ruin a
near perfect academic career.

"If you're unable to deal with rational discourse, I suggest that you go outside until you can contain your emotions," Professor Beale said blandly as he pointed toward
the wooden double doors.

Two hundred eyes stared at her. Denise was hurt and

embarrassed. "Professor Beale, why are you agreeing with Jason?"

"Get out now!" Professor Beale yelled. He knew that he was overreacting, but he didn't know what else to do. Ever since the summer of 1966 when the slogan 'Black Power' became popular, there seemed to be an incredible tension on the campus and in the street between Blacks and whites. He didn't understand what 'Black Power' meant and, the last thing he was going to do was be up-staged by a young Negro girl in front of his students in his classroom.

Instinctively, Denise felt a need to protect the slaves, her slaves, her ancestors who died so that she and a handful of other blacks could sit so proudly among the master's grand-children. Defeated, she returned her books to her backpack. Feeling heat spread across her face, Denise went outside and cried. In the haze of anger, Kweli flashed through her brain. She hated to admit it, but he was right. She had to do something!

In a few short minutes, Denise had become the object of a surrealist dream, and couldn't break the trance. She began to question whether or not she had adequately stood up for her ancestors in her class. Dang, she thought to her-self, Kweli was right again—she was part of the problem. By allowing herself to be aggravated and then dismissed by ignorance, Denise let racism get the better of her. She continued to berate herself until Shelly found her after class. Shelly reached for her hand so that they could ex-change their secret sorority handshake, but Denise couldn't do it. She was unable to move.

Shelly saw the tears welling in Denise's eyes. "What's wrong? Did you and Charles break up?" Shelly asked, con-cern all over her face. She had smokey-brown eyes, a slight gap between her front teeth and was the color of toasted almonds. She was average height for a woman and a little on the thick side. Most of the brothers on campus called her "H.G." because she was shaped like an hourglass.

"Breakup?" Denise forgot she was angry and smiled. "Girl, Charles and I are going to get married. Did you forget?"

"Yeah, yeah, yeah." Shelly had heard this drill before. Though Denise and Charles looked like the perfect couple, Denise had too much personality for him. Charles was dry in the truest sense of the word. He wore too thick glasses and looked as if he did not eat enough. He dressed very conservatively—slacks, madras shirts, and a different sweater everyday. "If everything is okay with Charles, why are you crying?"

"I got kicked out of Professor Beale's class today." Denise began to take control of herself.

Shelly gasped and then sat down next to her. "What happened?"

Denise cleared her throat. "I raised my hand to make a point about the former slaves during the Reconstruction Era, and he wouldn't let me speak."

"Niecie, why do you get so worked up about the slaves?" Shelly shook her Mario Thomas flip and handed her a tissue. "I mean, that was a long time ago. It's 1969, not 1869, get over it."

"Look Shelly, I know that those people are dead, but the professor let this guy in my class say that the slaves were lazy, ignorant, and stupid. I don't know about you, but that makes me mad."

"It makes me mad too, but what can we do about it?"

Denise blew her nose. She was finished crying. "I don't

know, but something really needs to be done to eradicate the ignorance on this campus."

"Alright, Ella Baker, why don't you put your money where your mouth is and go to the Black Student Alliance meeting today?"

"For what?" Denise wiped her eyes. "I'm not about to waste my lunch break listening to some African mumbo jumbo, from a bunch of pseudo-intellectuals."

"Ordinarily, I wouldn't go either, but one of the speakers is a fox and I have got to meet him!" Shelly clapped her hands together.

"Oh Lord." Denise shook her head. Shelly's sole occupation was chasing men. "You are willing to sit through an entire hour about 'The Revolution' just to get close to some man?"

"Well . . ." Shelly smiled mischievously.

"I knew it!"

"Niecie, that's not the only reason I'm going," Shelly said defensively.

"Okay, I'm listening. Tell me the other reason?" Denise smiled, calling Shelly's bluff.

Shelly shrugged her shoulders "Why are you so down on the BSA, anyway?"

"When did *you* become so interested in them?" Denise raised her left eyebrow. She was a lot of things, but Denise wasn't crazy. Shelly had a hidden agenda and Denise wanted to know what it was.

Shelly looked around conspiratorially. "I hear that they've invited the executive vice chancellor to have an open forum about the petition to get a Black Studies Department and more Black faculty on campus."

"Really? It's about time." Denise was impressed. "Ordinarily, the BSA spent their time high-signin' and cosignin' with one another about who's Black and who's still a Negro."

"Right on," Shelly said.

Denise continued, "It is enough to make me shine the BSA and every other fake revolutionary on." The whole subject of supporting Black people on campus made her so mad. Even at the college level, so many Blacks acted like crabs in a barrell, always pulling and putting one another down. She really wanted a Black studies department on campus, but as long as she was a member of a sorority, no one would take her opinion seriously. "Who is speaking today?"

"Kweli Hasan."

"Ugh!" This morning's conversation came back to her with a vengeance. "He makes me so sick."

"I didn't know you knew him, Niecie." Shelly had been trying to meet him, since before Christmas break. So far, Shelly had been unsuccessful.

Denise rolled her eyes so hard Shelly thought they were going to get stuck in her head. "I met him this morning."

Her face brightened. "Good, then you can introduce me to him."

"Shelly, I am not going near him." Denise took her mirror out of her purse. "And anyway I'm meeting my man at noon, so I'm not even going to see Kweli."

"Where are you meeting him?" Shelly asked though she knew the answer to her question.

"The Coop." Denise reapplied tangerine colored lipstick to her full lips and then blotted them. "You're not going to the Coop today?" Denise gave Shelly an exaggerated flutter of her eyelashes.

"I'm going to go after I leave the BSA meeting. Niecie, please come with me. Just come for one hour."

"No." Denise was adamant. She had had enough of Kweli, Professor Beale and everybody for one day.

"Please, please go with me," Shelly was begging. "Just think if we do get a Black Studies Department on campus, you won't have to deal with the Professor Beales of the world. And if you go with me, I will go with you to meet Charles."

Denise hated it when she begged. "Oh, okay, I'll go, but I'm not introducing you to Kweli—and I mean that." Denise shot Shelly her most serious look and put her lipstick back into her purse.

Shelly made Denise hold out her hand and give her five. "You are definitely my ace!"

"Yeah, yeah." Denise half smiled, "I hope that I don't live to regret this."

"You won't, Denise, I promise!"

"Shut up!" Beverly Smith screamed. She had been trying to quiet the room for ten minutes. They were in a small classroom on the second floor of Campbell Hall. It was hot and the room was overflowing with students.

Beverly was the recording secretary for the Black Student Alliance. In addition to taking the minutes at the meetings, she was in charge of inviting guest speakers to campus. Today she was really excited because she was able to get Brother Jahid-Ali, Maulana Imhotep's representative from the We Belong to Africa organization, popularly known as WEB; Kweli Hasan, Captain of the Black Panther Party, Southern California Chapter; and Executive Vice Chancellor of Curriculum Development, Vincent Brinkley on the dias together to discuss the development of a Black Studies Department at UCLA.

The crowd rumbled on. "Sh! Sh! It is eleven-twenty and this meeting should have started twenty minutes ago!" Beverly stopped hollering and looked around the room. Her eyes settled on Sean Brown, the BSA president. He was gangly and loose limbed like a basketball player. Most of the girls thought he was fine. Sean was a true fox with his five-inch afro, brown love beads, powder blue suede blazer, white turtleneck and blue eyes. His tight jeans hugged his butt just right, and his three-inch platform ankle boots made him more of a giant than he already was.

Sean reached Beverly's side and bellowed, "Brothers and sisters! This meeting has officially been called to order!" He banged the gavel three times upon the podium and a hush fell upon the room.

"Brothers and sisters, thank you for your cooperation. On this most auspicious occasion, I am honored to be in the company of Brother Jahid-Ali." Sean turned in Brother Jahid-Ali's direction. "We are delighted to have you speak at this university where Greek thought and methodology are touted as the gospel, rather than the fakes that they really are! . . ."

"Right on!" a high-pitched voice screamed out from the back of the room.

"As Black students in America, we need authentic carriers of the truth and not white professors who begrudgingly teach us about our ancestors. Those of you who have ever taken Professor Beale for history know exactly what I'm talking about."

"THACK!"

Denise ducked, thinking someone had thrown a fire cracker. Shelly tapped her on her shoulder and pointed to Sean. He had slammed his textbook, *History of the Americas* onto the podium and that had caused the loud noise.

He pointed to the book. "This is what I'm talking about. This, brothers and sisters, is three hundred pages of lies and watered down truths!" Sean lifted the book high above his head so that everyone could see the object of his disgust. "In this false testimonial about the native peoples of the world, it says that the Africans had no religion and needed saving from themselves; the Indians were children and needed the white man to help them control their land; the Asians were docile; and the Mexicans were backward. Brothers and sisters, we can't allow this nonsense to continue! And just as Marcus Garvey proclaimed Africa for the Africans, we, the Black Student Alliance proclaim Black studies for the Black students!" A huge roar went up from the floor. Sean revelled in the spotlight and then lowered his arms to silence the room. "Brother Imhotep, though you will not be speaking today, will you please rise?"

Instead of rising, Maulana Imhotep, who was a short, bald headed man, was wearing a crimson and gold dashiki dress, nodded to one of his Lions. Instantly, Brother Khalid rose, as did Brothers Sphinx and Ivory. They all wore elaborate dashiki's, dark glasses, and bald heads. Khalid wore a thigh length dashiki of royal blue; Sphinx's tie-dyed emerald-green dashiki had a V-neckline that revealed a hairy chest; Ivory, the smallest of the three Lions, wore a beautiful alabaster dashiki that provided a striking contrast to his creamy brown skin.

Sean gave a brief rundown of Maulana Imhotep's ever vigilant Lions, these were men who provided protection for him. Sean said that the Lions were trained in martial arts, firearms and explosives. Denise noticed the Lions did not speak unless spoken to. They were as disciplined and rigid as the Royal Guard that protected Buckingham Palace. She couldn't believe her ears. Could one man be that important? Whether he was or not, she was unimpressed. The Lions looked like robots and Maulana Imhotep looked like a marshmallow.

While the other students appeared to be in awe of the military-like precision of the Lions, Shelly and Denise couldn't stop giggling to each other. After the Lions were in place, Brother Imhotep rose and bowed before the members of the audience while his men looked on.

"Niecie, look at all of that fat on his neck. Yuck!" Shelly whispered. His perfectly round brown head ended in three thick rolls. This time Denise laughed so hard her shoulders jumped up and down.

"Shh, girl, you are going to get us put out of here!" No sooner had the words left Shelly's mouth did Yvonne Walker turn around and tell them to be quiet. Denise apologized. Shelly gave her a defiant look and rolled her eyes.

"Humph. She thinks she's cute just 'cause she's dating Sean." Sean was Shelly's ex-boyfriend. "I hate her." Shelly said in a normal tone of voice. Shelly was so loud, Denise just knew Yvonne was going to turn around again.

"Comrades, I have someone else to introduce to you. Many of you have seen this brother passing out leaflets and sharing heavy knowledge around campus." Sean pointed at Kweli.

Kweli stepped from out of the doorway. He was an imposing figure in blue jeans, a chambray shirt, black sunglasses and combat boots. Shelly elbowed her in the ribs, "You can't tell me that he ain't fine!"

"He looks like a mouse to me—"

"A mouse? You mean, like a rodent?" Shelly couldn't believe her ears.

Denise looked at Kweli a little harder. "Well, I guess he

looks alright." She was unable to get past his rhetoric to see if he was cute or not.

Shelly poked her again. "I forgot that you like dorks."

"Charles isn't a dork! He's a little stuffy, but that's because he is so intelligent," Denise responded.

They had missed Sean's entire introduction of Kweli. Once again, the room erupted into wild cheers.

After Kweli took his place upon the dias, Sean made his final introduction. "I know that all of you know my next guest." He motioned toward Vincent Brinkle who was wearing a gray and red checkered leisure suit.

Boos resounded throughout the classroom.

"Mr. Brinkley is the Executive Vice Chancellor of Curriculum Development. He has graciously agreed to meet with us today to discuss the creation of our Black Studies department," Sean said condescendingly. "Today, brothers and sisters, we will see if the esteemed Executive Vice Chancellor has come in peace or if he is prepared to do battle."

Apparently weary of all the tension swirling around this issue, Vincent Brinkley looked hopeful and took his seat upon the dias.

Ten students filed loudly into the room. Sean continued, "For those of you who just came in, we are discussing . . ."

While Sean was running down the meetings agenda, Denise focused her attention on a bald-headed brother seated on the dias, two seats over from Kweli. Now, that was a man. She couldn't see how big he was under his rust colored Kente embroidered robe, but he appeared to be stocky, like a wrestler.

Denise caught the last of Sean's comments. She looked in the direction of Brother Jahid-Ali. ". . . I will act as moderator for today's panel discussion. Once again our guests

include the Brother Jahid-Ali and Comrade Kweli Hasan."
There was wild applause and screams. Simultaneously,
Brother Jahid-Ali and Kweli stood up. Brother Jahid-Ali
bowed to the audience, while Kweli raised his clenched
fist raised high in the air, and lowered his head. "And Executive Vice Chancellor Brinkley." The entire room booed.
He didn't even bother to stand. Sean appeared not to notice.

"Now that the panel is assembled, let's begin." Sean
moved the podium to the right of the stage and sat down
next to Kweli.

Brother Jahid-Ali spoke on behalf of Maulana Imhotep.
Maulana Imhotep was a self-proclaimed prophet whose
mission was to bring Africa to middle-class Blacks. The
Temple was home to young Black men and women, whom
he had renamed with African names and taught Swahili.
WEB was a cultural nationalist organization. His home-
made African village sat smack dab in the middle of the
Vermont Knolls. This area was primarily residential and
home to middle-class Blacks, who had migrated to California from the South after World War II.

Denise sat intently and listened to the ongoing discussion. While she agreed that the university was in dire need
of Black professors who would teach history, English and
other courses, she didn't think they needed to turn the
school into a Cameroonian village.

UCLA could definitely use more color, literally and
figuratively, that much Denise could not deny. Home to an
olympic-sized track stadium, sculpture garden, Nobel
Prize winners, stately brick buildings that reeked of erudi-
tion, the huge campus even gave birth to the first Black to
ever win the U.S. Open, Arthur Ashe. Despite its physical
attributes and reputation for producing winners, UCLA had

a long way to go in terms of meeting the needs of students of color.

Denise returned her attention to the handsome man, named Brother Jahid-Ali, who was advising the students that they must fully immerse themselves into African culture, and that included dressing and acting as though Black people were in Africa. He also spoke briefly of Maulana Imhotep's vision of a cultural revolution within the university. Black people needed to identify themselves as Africans. So by changing one's name, Maulana Imhotep felt that Black people would begin to feel Africa in their souls.

This was what Denise thought was ridiculous. There was no way she was changing her name. She could still feel Africa, even though she was an American. A Black American. Although Denise liked learning about Mali and Songhai, what she really wanted to know was whether Rosa Parks's reason for refusing her seat was that she was truly tired or if it was a planned act by the National Association for the Advancement of Colored People.

As Denise continued to listen to Brother Jahid-Ali speak, she took a couple of mental notes, beginning with the passion in his eyes. She still didn't buy the African village stuff or the rhetoric about dressing in African garb to look like her ancestors, but she was intrigued anyway. His smoldering intensity distanced him from some of the other militants on campus, including Kweli.

Brother Jahid-Ali made WEB's vision of cultural revolution come alive for her, while the other people were just talking to hear themselves. Too bad she didn't agree with the basic tenets of his organization. When the meeting ended, Denise would ask him a couple of questions concerning his views on Black nationalism and women.

African villages aside, Brother Jahid-Ali spoke with a

quiet determination and an eloquence that surpassed his years. Denise couldn't help but wonder if Brother Jahid-Ali spoke from his heart, or if was he just repeating what he was told.

Next Executive Vice Chancellor Brinkley gave his presentation. He said that the administration was prepared to add Black studies classes to the existing core curriculum. Sean, who had been quiet up until this point, interrupted the executive vice chancellor to ask him which classes he was talking about.

Brinkley drew in his breath. "We, the administration, suggest the Harlem Renaissance, Egypt and Africa, and a survey of Negro literature featuring Countee Cullen, Langston Hughes, and Gwendolyn Brooks."

Sean asked. "Mr. Brinkley, when you say Africa, which part of Africa do you mean?"

It appeared that without his notes, the vice chancellor was lost. "I . . . I must have left that page in my office."

Brother Jahid-Ali turned to Brinkley. "Are you suggesting that Egypt is not in Africa?" he asked with unbridled disgust.

"Yes. Egypt is in the Middle East." The students groaned in unison.

Brother Jahid-Ali's smooth voice became grave. "Executive Vice Chancellor, statements like that reiterate the reason why a Black Studies Department on this campus is crucial. You hold an important position at this institution and you don't even know where Egypt is located."

Brinkley stopped shuffling through his papers and responded, "Yes, Mr. Jahid-Ali, I do hold an important position here. I attended New York University, where I majored in philosophy. I then went on to Yale University where I received my master's and doctorate degrees in educational administration. As you can see, my academic training more than justifies my expertise."

"You're quite proud of those accomplishments." Brother Jahid-Ali was becoming subtly confrontational.

"Quite." Brinkley looked very satisfied with himself.

Denise smiled. The poor thing didn't see it coming. Denise liked Brother Jahid-Ali's plan of attack. He was giving the vice chancellor just enough rope to hang himself. If the other pseudo-revolutionaries in the room acted that way, Denise would have signed up a long time ago. Actually, she would not have joined the BSA, but she would not have capped on their nationalist agenda, either.

Denise was drawn to Brother Jahid-Ali's quiet strength. He was smart, but not arrogant about it. He seemed to be so easygoing, she couldn't wait to meet him.

"Mr. Brinkley, you have all of that knowledge and yet you don't even know where Egypt is located!" He was giving the vice chancellor one last opportunity to catch himself.

"Yes I do. I know exactly where it is. Is there a map in this room?" He looked around the room.

Beverly went to the chalk board and unrolled the world map. She handed the pointer to Vice Chancellor Brinkley.

"Why, it's right there." He pointed to the area near Syria and the Mediterranean Sea. "UCLA even offers two courses on African and Egypt history."

"May I have that please?" Brinkley handed the pointer to Brother Jahid-Ali. "Mr. Brinkley, Egypt is clearly in Africa. So the fact that the University offers one course on Africa and the other on Egypt is indicative of the Eurocentric practice of divide and conquer." Denise was impressed. Without grandstanding, Brother Jahid-Ali was able to make his point.

The students booed the flabbergasted Brinkley until Sean came back on stage. "Brothers and sisters, Brinkley deserves to be booed into never never land, but we have to keep the meeting going. Before we resume, I have one thing to say: Executive Vice Chancellor Brinkley, your offer has been unequivocally rejected!"

Shelly yelled out, "That's tellin' him Sean!" Denise was surprised by her outburst. She knew that Shelly, like the other students in the room, wanted a Black Studies program on campus; she just didn't know how much Shelly wanted one, until that moment. Shelly had become mesmerized by Kweli's speech and now Sean's comment. By the wide-eyed enthusiasm displayed by Shelly, Denise sensed that Shelly's life was about to change.

"Mr. Brinkley, widespread ignorance such as what you just exhibited is the precise reason for today's panel discussion. Egypt is in Africa—physically, mentally, spiritually, and emotionally!" Brother Jahid-Ali's beautiful tiger eyes sparkled. "I believe that with Maulana Imhotep at the helm, we can deliver the knowledge the Black students have been begging for."

Maulana's female entourage, who occupied the first two rows, sang, "Aluuaah!" in unison.

Brinkley tried to talk above the noise. "We will also hire qualified minority faculty, including members from the Black community."

"We don't need your handouts or your afterthoughts!" interjected Kweli, who had been quiet because his turn to speak had not yet come.

Denise found herself nodding in agreement. She began to question herself. Perhaps she was wrong. Maybe this Black power stuff was what she was looking for after all. There was an electric charge about the room. Denise liked it. It was like everything was happening in double-time. The rush of adrenaline in the room was exhilarating.

Just as she was getting used to the intensity, Kweli stood up and a hush fell over the room. Despite Kweli's height, Denise never thought of him as intimidating, but at that moment, he was a formidable figure. His revolutionary attire had taken on new meaning. Everyone's mouth was hanging open, except for Brother Jahid-Ali's. He looked unenthused. Denise wondered what Brother Jahid-Ali's look was all about.

"Brothers and sisters, it is imperative that action be taken immediately. My comrade Sean is correct in rejecting the crumbs offered by the University. I have spoken with some of you educated Negroes and I have come to the conclusion that a massive deprogramming is in order." He laced his fingers and cracked his knuckles. "It should be clear to you that the university is still out to control your minds. They have no intention of allowing you to explore your Blackness in a free manner!"

"That's precisely my point." Brother Jahid-Ali interjected, as he glowered at Kweli. "The students need knowledge. Brother Imhotep will be their mfalme . . ." He used the Swahili word for king.

"Brother Jahid-Ali, the Black Panther Party is the vanguard of the race. We want our forty acres and a mule, not some jive piece of concrete with an African mask decorating the front of it. When the time comes to play king of the hill, we will call you." Kweli hated Brother Imhotep and didn't care who knew it.

Brother Jahid-Ali was up on his feet. "You have insulted WEB and we will not tolerate your words, traitor!" His eyes flared. Brothers Bijou, Sphinx, and Ivory rushed to the dias.

Sean stepped between the two. A hush fell over the room. "Comrades, please. We cannot be divisive. Brother Jahid-Ali please sit down." Maulana Imhotep signaled to Brother Jahid-Ali to sit. "It is Kweli's turn to speak."

"Thank you, Maulana Imhotep," Sean said.

Kweli continued speaking, his words were heavy with venom that was quite obviously directed at Brother Jahid-Ali. Because the first part of his platform consisted of an impassioned political plea for the students to join together and help the poor overthrow the United States government, Denise faded in and out of his rhetorical speech. He was an activist through and through, and, as such, insisted that the university would only respond to armed revolution.

Denise found the first part of his platform almost laughable. How did he expect students to overthrow the government? That line of reasoning was ludicrous and went totally against her upbringing. Kweli's audacity was counterproductive. Blacks were still putting Watts back together from a few years before, and here he was trying to incite another riot. What Kweli should have proposed was that Black students, joined with other students on campus, flood the Chancellor's office with letters in support of a Black Studies Department. Then the university would feel the weight of the students' strength on campus, not just a wannabe coup d'etat from outside agitators.

The room was almost drop dead silent when Denise overheard a conversation between two girls sitting in front of her. Denise tuned Kweli out and began to stare at Brother Jahid-Ali, while she listened to the girls' conversation.

The girl on the left was whispering to her friend that Kweli and Brother Jahid-Ali had served as Lions together in the WEB organization a few years back. Denise found that hard to believe. Both men looked equally suited for their respective organizations.

First girl: "One night Kweli was on his way home from a meeting at the Black Congress, when Kweli was ambushed and beaten by the Los Angeles Police Department."

Second girl: "For real."

First girl: "Um hum. And, Kweli, who was taught by Maulana Imhotep not to retaliate, went to see the mfalme for back up. He was told by Brother Jahid-Ali that the mfalme was indisposed and could not be disturbed. With blood gushing from his head, Kweli said he had just been beaten. Brother Jahid-Ali said he had his orders and turned Kweli away. Kweli reminded Brother Jahid-Ali they were practically brothers, but Brother Jahid-Ali wasn't hearing it.

Second girl: "That sure was cold."

First girl: "Anyway, girl . . . Brother Jahid-Ali wanted to acknowledge their bond, but couldn't because of his allegiance to Maulana Imhotep. Kweli was pissed off and went directly to the Panther Headquarters on Vermont and Eighty-fifth street."

Second girl: "Who told you that?"

The second girl asked the exact question that was on Denise's mind.

First girl: "My cousin's sister's Uncle Vernon is the one who took Kweli in the night he was jumped. Kweli told him the whole story."

Second girl: "I guess you do know what you're talking about."

First girl: "Uncle Vernon also said that the police did not take Kweli to jail. They just jumped on him because they said that he was a recognized Black militant."

Second girl: "They sure mistreat the brothas."

That juicy tidbit, if true, explained the obvious animosity between the two men. The girls in front of Denise were finished gossiping about Kweli and Brother Jahid-Ali and started talking about the latest James Brown album. Denise returned her attention to Kweli.

The second part of his program intrigued her. Kweli had launched into a full explanation of The Black Panther Party's Survival Programs. "Brothers and sisters, we have the Free Breakfast for Children Program, Black Panther schools, sickle-cell anemia testing and a few other programs to suit the needs of Black people."

Since Denise was studying to be a social worker, she listened intently about the school program for children.

"Everybody is more than welcome to talk to me or any of the other Panthers in the room about our programs. You don't have to get permission from anybody to speak to us about the righteous work we do in the community." Kweli raised his fist in the air. "Power to the people." He smirked at Brother Jahid-Ali.

Sean finally adjourned the forum.

"Well, girl, what do you think?" Shelly and Denise were standing.

"I enjoyed the meeting," Denise said excitedly.

"See, Denise, I told you it was worth coming to." Shelly started dancing around. "I think I'm in love."

"With whom?" Denise asked though she knew the answer.

"Why, Kweli of course! He's so smart and so sexy." Shelly purred like a kitten. "Denise, I'm gonna join his organization."

"Just like that? You're going to join the Black Panther Party?" Denise was shocked.

"Yep. Look Denise, their ten-point plan sounded like a

good thing to me—housing, employment, freedom from harassment, I forget the others, but they sounded good too."

"He *was* making sense." Denise said. She only knew a little about the Black Panther Party. This was the first time she had ever heard a full explanation of the politics behind the party. "When and where did you learn all of that?"

Shelly winked at Denise. "I have my sources." Shelly turned and headed out of the classroom.

Denise walked along side of her. She couldn't help but shake her head in disbelief. Here she had come to the BSA meeting, the ultimate naysayer and was leaving considering joining the Black Panther Party.

Shelly continued. "I don't know about you, Niecie, but I want my forty acres and a mule. And, I want that man." She smiled slyly. "Will you join with me?"

Denise laughed. "Okay Shelly, you've made your point. But there is one catch." She stared at her hard. "I'm not cutting my hair!" Denise pointed to the other Panther women in the audience. Who were all dressed in black leather jackets, boots, and had afros.

While Shelly went looking for Kweli, Denise went to the bathroom. On her way out, Denise saw Kweli and Brother Jahid-Ali having a heated debate.

"The students don't appreciate you and the rest of the Lion cubs telling them how to run their Black Studies program." Kweli was practically breathing fire.

Brother Jahid-Ali responded, "Maulana Imhotep knows what's best for the chosen people of Africa. The seven principals of Nguzo Saba are: nia, umoja, ujaama, ujima, ku chichagila, imani. These principals represent the foundation of a value system for young sistas and brothas. They are also a means of restructuring our lives as African people. Nguzo Saba is Maulana Imhotep's way of not trying to control the young Africans, but a means of giving them a true sense of their African identity." He half raised his fist and added. "That is more than I can say for the big, bad Black pussycats!"

Kweli slammed his gloved fist into his palm. Denise heard the whack! of the leather bounce off his open palm, and the force of the noise caused her to jump. "I already know about Maulana's jive doctrine." The air became thick with tension. Kweli began to mumble viciously to Brother Jahid-Ali. She only caught snatches of their conversations and if her eyes and ears did not deceive her, the scene was about to turn ugly.

Afraid to stay, but afraid to move one inch, Denise held her breath. Kweli began to speak, his voice heavy with antagonism: "First of all, bro-tha, the Black Panthers are in tune with the needs of the students. We are on campus every single day providing knowledge, self-confidence and an understanding of what it means to be Black in America and not some fake village in Maulana Imhotep's imaginary kingdom!"

Denise agreed. She had briefly attended a couple of rallies during the previous Fall Quarter sponsored by the Black Panthers on campus. One rally was a call for foot-soldiers to run the breakfast program. This program was created to feed ghetto children before they went to school in the morning. Many of these children did not eat on a regular basis and thus were unable to concentrate in school. It was the goal of the breakfast program to ensure that each child went to school on a full stomach. Also, it was an opportunity to train children to be future revolutionaries. Many of the children's parents gave testimony at this particular meeting as to how grateful they were to the Panthers for their generosity. These parents also spoke of their child's increased attention span and improvement in their grades.

Brother Jahid-Ali's veins bulged in his neck and he spit his words out like fire. "You guys are nothing but a bunch of punks who have put the fear of God in these students, so much so that your way is the right way." From where Denise stood, he looked like a king cobra poised to strike. "Brother Imhotep is a *real* university professor who knows the ins and outs of the academic system, unlike that phony who calls himself the Supreme Servant. Your army of ragamuffins can't even read, let alone guide college students in their pursuit of knowledge about their Blackness." He paused to wipe the perspiration that was running down his brow. The size of his neck seemed to increase two sizes. "While you and the rest of the rag tag mob squad are running around toting rifles with your fist raised in the air, we are making cultural strides and raising the conscious of the masses."

"You son of a—" Kweli stopped in midsentence. He removed his sunglasses to reveal angry eyes. "If we were alone, I'd . . ."

"You'd do what?" Brother Jahid-Ali was calling his bluff. Kweli pulled back and stalked off into the crowd of students. He walked about five feet to the left of where Denise was standing.

As he watched Kweli walk off, their eyes met. Brother Jahid-Ali's eyes, hard as nails, turned to soft brown molasses, and the danger that surrounded him only minutes before was gone. Now that Denise had a close-up view of Brother Jahid-Ali, he was not what most women would call foxy, but his eloquence and intelligence more than made up for what he lacked aesthetically. His face was rugged and he was medium height for a man. The most significant thing Denise noticed about Brother Jahid-Ali were his sweet eyes, inviting air and sex appeal which radiated from his body like heat. Denise tried her best to stare back at him, but could only hold his gaze for a tenth of a second. Her cheeks grew warm and her insides turned to mush.

"Hi, my name is Brother Jahid-Ali." He walked toward Denise. His eyes danced when he spoke to her.

"Oh, hello, my name is Denise." She clutched her backpack tightly to her chest. Denise could hear her heartbeat in her ears. "I don't suppose that the Panthers and the WEB organization will be sitting down to dinner anytime soon."

Confusion passed over his face and then a gut-wrenching laugh filled the hallway. "You're funny. And how'd you guess that the last supper was postponed?"

Relieved that he had a good sense of humor, Denise asked him how education functioned within the WEB organization. He got started in the same rap he had given Kweli during their argument about the seven principles of Nguzo Saba. Denise stopped him midway through his spiel.

"You said those things a few minutes ago. What else can you tell me about your organization? What are the children taught in the village schools?"

"It is important that you thoroughly understand these principles, so that you will begin to understand the organization." He considered her request. "You should come to one of our meetings. We meet every Sunday at 2 P.M. on Normandie and Santa Barbara." Unlike other young women who approached Brother Jahid-Ali, Denise appeared to be sincerely interested in learning about the WEB organization. "Maulana Imhotep believes that through service, struggle and institution-building the diasporic African community can come together. Africans are communal people and as such we should live and learn together."

Denise was unmoved. "But why would anyone join an African village in the middle of the city?"

"You're missing the point. You would not be joining a village in the middle of the city, you would be bringing Africa to the city."

After finally getting to speak with Kweli, Shelly went looking for Denise. Kweli convinced her that revolution was inevitable and that this meeting was just a small taste of what Black students could do to make change at the University. She thought the Panthers were a legitimate organization and exactly what she was looking for in terms of making sure that Black people got their fair share of the American dream. He also told her not to even consider joining WEB.

When she asked him why she should join his organization and not the other, Kweli said, "The Southern California chapter of the Black Panther Party is righteous and could benefit from a committed sister like yourself."

"That's not a good enough answer," Shelly said flirtatiously. "For all I know you're just saying that to get close to me." She batted her eyelashes at him.

Kweli smiled. "I respect your uncertainty, but let me put it another way. A long time ago, the Panthers took me in, handed me a gun and made me a man. You will never experience that kind of growth with the WEB." With that last comment, he rushed away.

Shelly outwardly pretended to ponder his comments. On

the inside, she had made up her mind to join the Black Panther Party. First, in addition to being a vanguard for the revolution, there were an abundance of men for her and Denise to choose from. Second, she liked those cute little berets and; finally, she reasoned, she would look cute in an afro. Shelly wasn't wedded to her hair the way Denise was.

Shelly knew that Denise was going to be a hard sale. Denise was a bookworm and liked to play it safe. Her parents were very bourgeois and Denise was a bit of a snob, though she'd never admit it. The best virtue Denise possessed, despite her haughty tendencies, was her disdain for injustice of any kind.

Shelly remembered when they first met. They were both sophomores. Denise was working in the college library, and Shelly worked when she felt like it. It wasn't that she was wealthy; it was just that Shelly was a creative spirit and hated to be confined to any one thing for too long. In any event, Denise was in charge of library fines and Shelly owed the university at least twenty dollars. Shelly was in a panic, because the registrar's office would not release her transcripts until she paid the fine. She had been stalling her mother who had been demanding to see her grades. Shelly had the money for the fine, but spent it the week before on a Gladys Knight and The Pips album. When she couldn't stall her mother any longer, she went to Powell Library and climbed the gothic stairs to the second floor.

The inside of the library had cathedral ceilings, a dark blood-red interior and an unnecessary spookiness about it. Shelly thought the university was trying to scare people into learning. When she reached the top of the staircase, she saw two things. The first was her life as it flashed before her eyes. The stairs were murderously steep and Shelly was a little dizzy from the climb. The second, was Denise, who was standing behind the dark gray, marble counter. Denise's hair was pulled back into a ponytail and she was wearing a purple argyle sweater, with a matching purple skirt. In contrast, Shelly had on a brown velvet mini-skirt, white go-go boots and an orange short-sleeve shirt.

There was no one in line, so Shelly proceeded to lay her overdue notice on the counter before Denise. Out of nowhere, a girl pushed her out of the way. "Hi, my books are late." The girl was an Amazon compared to Shelly.

Shelly grabbed onto the counter to keep from falling. The blonde girl spread six books onto the counter. She proceeded to tell Denise which books were due when and why each one was late. Shelly was clearly outmatched, but was aiming to push her back, when Denise intervened.

Denise smiled at the strawberry blonde with the pixy face, and said, "I will be with you in one moment. I am helping that student over there."

Jody swung her hair in Shelly's face and asked, "Who?"

Shelly, who had just as much hair as Jody, shook her hair in Jody's face and responded, "Me."

Jody did not acknowledge Shelly's presence and continued talking. "I owe five cents on Dante's *Inferno,* ten cents on—"

"Wait a minute, I just told you that this student was in front of you." Denise's voice was constricted with disgust. The white students always acted like they owned the school. This type of behavior infuriated her.

Jody stopped talking. Without wasting any time, Shelly pushed Jody's books out of the way. "My name is Shelly Taylor, and you look just like my uncle's mother's cousin, Lucy." She winked at Denise.

"Taylor, hum . . . I think my mother's people are Taylors." She smiled, knowing what Shelly was up to. "My name is Denise Davis. Sorry about the delay."

They both looked in the direction of Jody, who was busy cleaning her stubby fingernails with her teeth.

"Girl, don't worry about it. It's not your fault that some people are rude."

Denise casually read Shelly's overdue notice and balled it up into a tight little ball. She rummaged through the card file and pretended to find nothing. "You know, the privilege is absolutely amazing."

"The privilege?"

Denise turned her amber colored eyes and stared hard at Jody. "Yeah, the privilege that white is right."

Shelly giggled. "Right on." Denise did not look like the type to crack on white people in front of them. Shelly was impressed.

Jody was growing impatient, but Denise didn't care. "There appears to be a mistake. You don't owe the library any money. I will call the registrar's office and ask them to remove the hold on your transcript."

That single gesture of kindness and solidarity against "the privilege" earned Denise Shelly's admiration. "Thank you."

Jody started tapping her foot and sighing heavily. "Are you finished yet?" she barked.

"As a matter of fact, we are not. I have to call the registrar's office and that may take a while." She took the phone off of the receiver and set it onto the marble counter that separated her from Jody. Then, Denise rolled her eyes at Jody.

"Shelly, where did you say you were from again?"

"Well, my great-great grandmother was, God rest her soul, from—" She continued until Jody got the hint and stormed off, leaving her books on the counter, mumbling something about finding the head librarian.

When she was out of their sight, both girls laughed hysterically. "Thanks, you didn't have to do that. I hope you don't get into trouble with your boss."

"If I do, it will be worth it," Denise laughed heartily.

The memory tickled Shelly and reminded her how such a small incident brought the two of them together and solidified their friendship.

Shelly began to work out the details of how she was going to convince Denise to join the Panthers with her, when she saw Denise in deep conversation with what looked like a member of the WEB organization. Upon first glance, their conversation looked like two lovers enmeshed in a deep exchange about how they would spend their evening together. Brother Jahid-Ali's body language was inviting, almost embracing Denise, and his expression was attentive. It was like he could see Denise's words before they left her mouth. Denise's head was cocked to the side and a smile danced flirtatiously across her lips.

Shelly didn't know what to do. She waited, but neither Denise nor Brother Jahid-Ali would look her direction.

Finally, Shelly began waving and called. "Yoo hoo, may I interrupt for a second?"

Brother Jahid-Ali was the first to react. "Oh, I'm sorry, I didn't see you standing there."

"That's okay. I'm Shelly."

"Habari Gani," he took her hand in his and kissed it. "My sista, my name is Brother Jahid-Ali."

Shelly grinned shyly at his formality.

"It was nice meeting you, Denise, and I hope to speak with you again." Brother Jahid-Ali took Denise's hand.

Not wanting to see him leave, but not knowing how to make him stay, Denise smiled. "Likewise."

Brother Jahid-Ali turned and walked away.

When he was out of earshot Shelly asked Denise, "How could you let him go like that?"

"What was I supposed to do?" Denise was distressed. She hoped that she did not miss out on an opportunity to have a new friend.

"Get his number, his address, something." Shelly was very animated. "Sometimes you are so slow."

"I'm sure that I will see him around somewhere." While Denise sounded sure of herself, she didn't think she'd ever see the intense Lion again. She changed the subject. "Where have you been?"

"I finally got to speak with that fox Kweli. He is the smartest, most intelligent and serious man I think I've ever met."

"Kweli and Brother Jahid-Ali had a big argument."

"Dang, I can't believe I missed it," Shelly said. "I must have talked to Kweli right afterward."

They exited the side entrance of Campbell Hall and took the long way to walk toward the front of the building. This exit placed them a short distance from the University Research Library. Denise made a mental note to go there after she and Charles met at the Coop. She needed an article for her psychology paper.

"He invited us to a meeting at the Panther office."

"Us?" Denise stopped walking. "Oh no you don't. I'm not getting involved with you and your rendezvous with Kweli."

"It's not a rendezvous, it is a party meeting. New members are welcome to join everyday of the week."

"So you're thinking about joining the Black Panther Party."

"Weren't you?" Shelly asked without looking at Denise.

"What makes you say that?" Denise gave Shelly a side long glance. She was feeling Shelly out to see how serious she was about joining the Panthers.

"I saw how you analyzed each speaker at the forum today. Since you are not the subservient type, I don't see you joining the WEB organization. Well, if you marry Brother Jahid-Ali, you might join, but otherwise, dressing up in African garb is not your kinda thing."

"Alright smarty, what is my type of thing?" Denise scoffed.

"You said that you want to be a social worker and be an advocate for children. I can't think of a better place for you to hone your skills than working with one of the survival programs offered by the Panther party."

Denise considered Shelly's idea. She thought she heard someone call her name so she turned around. Just as Denise turned to her left, she saw three men, dressed in dashikis, holding pistols. They were aiming for the front of the building. She jerked to her right and saw two men on the steps of Campbell Hall talking.

Denise opened her mouth to scream but nothing came out. Suddenly, gunfire blasted from her left. Shelly pulled her down onto the concrete. The next time she looked toward Campbell Hall, the two men who were standing in front of the building were now lying on the ground. At last Denise found her voice. She screamed and screamed from deep within.

Part 2:

What's Goin' On?

One

Kevin Ross and Carlton Wilson packed up and left Boyle, Mississippi together. Boyle was a sleepy little town with only two things to do—get married or leave. It was located between Jackson and the Tennessee state border. Kevin grew up on a cotton farm and remembered his mother and older siblings picking cotton, when he was young. His father was a country preacher and put the fear of God in each and every one of his eight children. Kevin was the youngest and the loudest. By the time Kevin reached the age of six, his father owned a church, God's Hands of Ministry. His father, the Reverend Satchel Ross believed that if problems, worries and fears were left in God's hands, then everything would be alright. As the youngest, Kevin was spared from picking cotton, but was expected to excel in school. Kevin graduated valedictorian of his eighth grade class and attended high school with equal success. By the time he was ready to attend college, his racial consciousness had awakened and he wanted desperately to join the Student Nonviolent Coordinating Committee.

It was the fall after the 1964 Freedom Summer. Kevin's religious upbringing gave way to the reality of racial hatred when he and the rest of the country learned about the senseless deaths of fellow Mississippian James Chaney. The others, Michael Schwerner and Andrew Goodman, were from the North. The year before, four young women had been killed in a church bombing in Birmingham, Alabama. What began as a low grade temperature turned into a full blown fever for Civil Rights. Though his father forbade him to join any organization that might get him lynched, Kevin was restless for social change. He had no choice but to leave Mississippi.

Kevin's partner in crime was Carlton. Both boys had a love for their families, church and their people. Growing up insulated by loving black hands is what saved both of them from the horror of lynchings that other youth their age faced all over Texas, Alabama, Mississippi and the rest of the Bible belt.

Carlton wanted to be a politician. A rich politician. He recognized at an early age that leadership in the Black communities was going to win opportunities for Black people. He used to listen to his uncles discuss Malcolm X. They said that Malcolm X did so much for Black people. He was able to convert and rehabilitate many thugs from off the street and turn them into clean, articulate, together men. Dr. King had a similar way of touching cords in people's lives and making them reach for the best they had to offer in themselves. Ella Baker was the back bone of SNCC and Fannie Lou Hamer led a grassroots campaign all the way to the Democratic National Convention in 1964. These people were leaders and Carlton's role models. Carlton also wanted to make a difference in the civil rights of Black people. In the words of Ms. Hamer, he was sick and tired of being sick and tired. He wanted some action, but his parents were in agreement with Kevin's parents and forbade him to join SNCC, CORE, the Nation of Islam, the NAACP and any other group remotely connected to political activity. Though Carlton acquiesced, he knew that as soon as he completed high school, he was leaving.

To Carlton, Boyle, Mississippi was just a stop on his journey to becoming mayor or a Los Angeles city councilman and then governor of California. He set his sights on California and headed west for college. There, he would fulfill his dreams by studying political science and business. He knew that in order to succeed, he would have to have business sense.

It was a sweltering hot August day in 1966 and everybody was standing around crying. Carlton hated to see his mother cry, but his mind was made up. Two houses over, Kevin kissed his mother goodbye and shook his father's hand. There was nothing left to say.

Who would have ever known that politically-minded Carlton, now Brother Jahid-Ali, second in command to the mfalme of WEB would reject the American Constitution in favor of Nguzo Saba. Or that God fearing Kevin would severe his friendship with Carlton to become Kweli, Captain of the Southern California Chapter?

One week later, Denise met Charles in the Coop. They were sitting face to face at a small table in the corner.

"Denise, where have you been?" Charles asked her.

"I've been around," she said evasively. Denise felt uneasy. She had a feeling that this would be the last time she spoke to Charles.

"Doing what?"

"Is this an interrogation?" Denise rolled her eyes. "Are you going to arrest me?"

"No." Charles said softly. "I'm sorry, I've just missed you."

Denise did not reciprocate the feeling. Ever since Denise witnessed the shooting at Campbell Hall, she had been avoiding Charles. He had left several messages with her mother, but she threw them in the trash. "Charles, things have got to change."

"Like what?"

"Things. Look around you, Charles." Denise gestered around the room. "This school, the people . . . everything is so different."

He followed her lead and looked around the room. "I haven't noticed anything new."

"That's just it. Nothing has changed and yet everything has." Denise shook her head in exasperation. "I shouldn't expect you to get it."

Beginning to get impatient with Denise's condescending tone, Charles snapped. "If this is about us not being engaged, I've already told you that you will get your ring for Christmas. And—"

Denise cut him off. "Charles, look at me. I was there the day those Panthers were killed. I was at Campbell Hall."

"You went to that meeting?" he asked increduously.

"Yes," she said defensively.

"Denise, I thought we agreed not to join any radical groups. Those people could get you kicked out of school. Do your parents know?"

Denise inhaled sharply. "Charles, I didn't plan on going, but I'm glad I did. We've been lied to by the system." She closed her eyes. "I wish you could have been there, then you'd understand."

"The only thing I understand is that you went to one meeting, behind my back no less, and now you think that you're Rosa Parks." Charles was mocking her.

"No, I don't." The inevitable was coming. Charles was

not going to be able to understand the changes that had taken place in Denise's soul.

"Yes you do," Charles said adamantly.

"You can say what you want, but the Black Panthers have a plan to obtain housing, land, employment,—"

Charles snatched his glasses off of his face. "I don't care what kind of plans they have. What about the plans we have? What about me becoming a doctor?"

"Oh Charles, you're so selfish. You see the whole world in relation to yourself. The Panthers have a school for children, where they feed and teach them. You can't tell me that that's not a good thing!" Denise surprised herself. She and Charles had never had a big fight before, and yet she felt that she was doing the right thing. In a way Denise was making up for not standing her ground in Professor Beale's class.

"I don't care."

The moment Denise had been avoiding was finally before her. "If you're not even willing to listen to what they're all about, then there's nothing left to say."

"Precisely. Let's talk about something more important." A look of relief passed over Charles' face.

"Charles, I got kicked out of Professor Beale's class and haven't been back since." Denise confessed.

"You didn't tell me that. When did that happened?" Charles took a sip of his orange soda.

"I also joined the Black Panther Party." Denise lied. She needed to see how he would respond when she actually joined.

"You did what?!"

"I joined the Black Panther Party." Denise said again.

"No girlfriend of mine is going to be affiliated with those hoodlums."

Denise stood up. "Then have it your way, I'm history." Denise began to walk toward the door.

"Denise, where are you going? Come back here."

"Come back to what? A life of ignorance? A life like my parents?"

"What's wrong with your parents' life? I thought that's what you wanted."

"I thought that's what I wanted, until I realized that I was part of the problem."

"What? Denise, what's going on?"

"If you can't see what's wrong with this world, then I can't help you." Denise turned and walked through the doorway. This time she didn't stop.

"This is for the people." Snip. "This is for the struggle." Snip. "This is for the revolution." Denise was talking to the mirror in front of her. What was left of her long hair was a short, lopsided afro that wasn't quite standing up.

"Denise, what are you doing?" Cornelia Davis, Denise's mother, demanded to know. She had just returned from the grocery store and to her horror, her daughter was standing before her cutting her hair. "Where is all your pretty hair?" Cornelia stared at the back of Denise's head.

"On the floor." Denise jestered to the fallen hair on the porcelain sink, tub and the toilet of the bathroom decorated in soft tones of pink, yellow, and white.

"What's the matter? Are you having trouble in school?" Cornelia was rooted in the doorway of the bathroom. She touched her own jet black hair that swung past her shoulders to the middle of her back. "Why? What happened to make you cut your hair? All of the Taylor women have long hair."

"No mother, I'm not having trouble in school. Hair is irrelevant and I don't need it anymore to prove that I'm pretty." Denise said matter-of-factly. Truth was she was terrified of losing her hair. But in order to prove that she was down with the revolution, Shelly told her that they were going to have to cut their hair.

"Denise pretty girls have long hair. You know that." Cornelia started to cry. "You'll never get a husband looking like a little boy. Grandma is going to be mad. And your father, he's just going to die."

It hurt Denise to see her mother cry, but she had to remain strong. "I don't care what Grandma or Daddy says, they're just Negroes like yourself who like looking like white people."

"What are you saying? Where is this language coming from?" Cornelia was stunned. "Did Charles put you up to this?"

"No." Denise did not bother to tell her mother that she broke up with Charles. "Charles is a Negro, too."

"Then it was that Shelly. You just can't trust a girl with one parent. I warned you about that girl. I just knew that one day she'd get you in trouble." Cornelia was looking for answers. There was no way her straight-laced little princess would ever do something like this on her own.

"No mother, it wasn't Shelly. I was speaking in the language of the people." Denise continued cutting her hair. "The language of the disenfranchised."

"You're not disenfranchised, Denise. You're middle class. I don't understand what you're talking about. We belong to Jack and Jill, Links, the Urban League . . ."

"Mother, I'm talking about revolution." Denise slammed the scissors onto the bathroom counter.

"Revolution!" Cornelia clutched her heart. "You must have hit your head or something."

"Mother, I didn't hit my head, but I wish that I did a long time ago, then I would've known the evils of capitalism way before now. The white man is pulling a fast one over you and you don't even see it." Denise admired her short hair in the bathroom mirror. She patted her 'fro. Denise was going to have to wash it to make it stand up like a real afro. "Mother, I gotta go." She'd wash her hair when she got back.

Two

"Denise, you cut your hair." Kweli was smiling at the top of Denise's head. She and Shelly were at a new members meeting for the Black Panther Party. They were dressed in jeans and T-shirts. Denise felt self-conscious about having no hair, but was trying real hard not to show it.

"When I saw you the other day, you know, last week at UCLA, I saw you point to my hair." She was making a reference to the awful scene she witnessed the day John Huggins and Bunchy Carter were killed. Denise was having trouble sleeping at night. Shelly recovered much faster than she did.

In the melee, Kweli really did not remember too much about that day. Those men who died were his comrades, his brothers, his friends—his leaders. One week had passed and he still felt the sting of their lost. Thinking back, he recalled seeing Denise and Shelly. Denise was screaming, but he could not get to her. There were too many people around. For his own safety, he was escorted by other members of the BPP away from Campbell Hall.

"Ahh, I do remember now." He laughed easily. "Denise, I wasn't pointing to your hair, I was pointing to your mind. I was trying to tell you to open your mind." Kweli chuckled again and placed his hand on her shoulder. "You still look beautiful."

Denise felt silly; she thought for certain that Kweli was commenting on her hair. After Shelly pulled her away from the chaos, they ran into Kweli. He pulled them both close to him and whispered in Denise's ear, *"What's it going to be, them or us?"* Kweli was challenging her. She looked over at Shelly who returned her stare with a tear-streaked face. Kweli's bodyguards pulled him away. As he walked away, he pointed to her head and mouthed, *"Think about it."*

Sitting in the room in the office, Denise looked around the room and noticed that the walls were decorated from top to bottom with posters, advertisements, manifestos, and pictures. "Power to the People" jumped out at her, as did scenes of Panthers holding their fists raised high in the air. There were several posters highlighting the Survival Programs and one in particular caught Denise's eye. It was a poster of a woman serving children breakfast. She learned at the meeting that program's name had been changed to the John Huggins Free Breakfast for Children Program. Denise made a mental note to ask if she could volunteer to work with the children.

There were other pictures of Huey Newton, Eldridge Cleaver, Bobby Seale, and Kathleen Cleaver. Some of the photographs were so intense that they frightened her. Maybe she wasn't revolutionary material after all. Everyone in the Southern California headquarters looked so serious. Denise knew that it was going to take more than an afro to turn her into a revolutionary.

"Sista, you have a perplexed look on your face?" Maxine could recognize a new recruit a mile away. They all had the same look, dazed and confused. "I bet you're thinking, 'What have I gotten myself into'?"

Startled, Denise did not even realize that the meeting was over and everyone was mingling. Shelly was in the corner talking to Kweli and Denise was sitting by herself. *When had Shelly gotten up?*

"You're right. I was trying to remember why I'm here."

"Let me refresh your memory. Black and poor people in this country and around the world are under siege. We are the wretched of the earth and will remain this way until something is done about it. My sista, it is up to us and our men to make a difference in our lives and the lives of our children." Maxine let her words sink in. "Come with me, I want you to meet someone."

Denise joined Maxine and they went and stood outside the front of the office. "By the way, my name is Maxine. You are?"

"I am Denise Davis."

"Comrade Denise, I want you to meet Comrade Pauletta." The women shook hands. "Pauletta is in charge of the P.E. classes."

"P.E.?" Denise hoped she wasn't going to have to exercise.

"P. E. stands for Political Education classes. Huey and Bobby require all new members to take these classes to get a firm understanding of the political situation in the United States and elsewhere. Many of the new members are not up to speed on current events and they feel that the P. E. classes are the best way to give new and old members a clear understanding of the party's platform. Let's go back inside, so that I can give you the books you need to learn, internalize and be ready to die for in the event the revolution takes place tomorrow."

Pauletta's words were heavy and spoken with conviction. "And in case you're wondering, the revolution will not be televised. This is the only announcement you will get."

A few weeks later, Denise was dressed in her Panther uniform: A black leather jacket, black miniskirt, black beret, chambray shirt, and boots.

"Young lady, where are you going dressed like that?" An authoritative voice boomed behind her and made Denise jump.

"I'm just trying on my uniform, Daddy."

"Uniform, did you join the army or something?" Percy Davis said sarcastically. "Or did UCLA issue a requirement that all students wear uniforms?"

"Today Shelly and I officially joined the Black Panther Party." Denise had never been afraid of her father. Percy was a gentle man who had spoiled his only child rotten. As far back as she could remember, Denise had never seen him angry. He was a distinguished looking gentleman with gray eyes, smooth skin the color of baked apples. Denise inherited her hazel colored eyes from her daddy. Today she saw a side to him that she did not know existed.

"You joined, did you?" Percy sucked his teeth. Cornelia had already filled him in on the details. "I don't want you runnin' around with those rifle-totin' hoodlums. They're all a bunch of lowlifes and I want you to stay away from them."

"At least you know who they are," Denise smirked.

"Of course, I know who they are. I read *The Sentinel.*" *The Los Angeles Sentinel* was a local Black newspaper that had been in existence for twenty-four years. Percy swore by *The Sentinel.*

"Anyway, Daddy, they are not hoodlums. They are conscious brothas and sistas who want to see Black people attain freedom in America." Denise stood tall in front of her father. "And by the way, don't worry about sending tuition to that capitalist institution in Westwood. I don't go there anymore."

"So on top of becoming a hoodlum, you quit school?" Percy shouted. "I've heard it all now."

"Yes."

Percy rubbed his beard. "There is something that I am not understanding. What do these people have to do with you?"

"Everything." Denise maintained her composure. "I am fighting against the racist powers that control Blacks and other poor peoples. It is my duty to help my people, something you obviously don't know nothing about."

"Let me tell you something, young lady. I was a soldier in the Second World War and my father was a soldier in the First World War. We fought to save this country so that you wouldn't have to. In the 1950s, the South was a terrible place to be. I begged, borrowed and stole to get to California to have a better life. You have no idea how difficult life was for a Negro back then."

"Black, Daddy, we are Black people." Denise said with irritation. "Daddy, you act like Black people don't have it hard now. We've made virtually no progress since the '50s."

"That's not true! We can sit wherever we like on the bus, we can eat at any restaurant, we can go into any store we want . . ."

"Daddy, you are speaking about creature comforts. What about the poor people? They can't do anything except hope that the mailman isn't late with their welfare checks.

Or they slave all day at a dead end job trying to make ends meet."

"Denise, their struggle has nothing to do with you." Percy tried to reason with Denise.

"They can't do it by themselves, I have to help them struggle." Denise had not wavered.

"Black, Negro or otherwise, you don't know a damn thing about struggle. Your mother and I have given you everything you could possibly want. And how do you repay us? You go and align yourself with an asinine group of young people who think that wearing a leather jacket and a dungaree shirt is going to make the difference." Percy was seething with anger.

"As long as we have this," Denise thrust her clenched fist into the air. ". . . we will survive."

"Not in this house. Denise, your mother and I have talked it over." Percy paused for effect. "Either you go back to school and quit that organization or you leave. You will not disgrace this house with some melodramatic nonsense about revolution."

Unprepared to be put out of the house, Denise fell silent. *Where would she go?* Since she quit school, she could no longer stay in Heisman Hall.

"What's it going to be, them or us?" There wasn't any room in her father's tone for negotiation. This was it.

From somewhere deep inside of her, Denise's voice came through. "That's cool that you don't want me here. I'll get my things and be out of your house as soon as possible." Denise went into her bedroom.

Cornelia followed her. "Denise, please don't leave. Daddy's just mad, he'll calm down in a couple of hours."

"Forget it, mother. He doesn't want me here." Denise

unzipped her suitcase. "I knew you guys wouldn't understand."

"Baby, this new stuff is hard for us to understand." Cornelia pleaded with Denise to understand their point of view.

"Mother, it's only hard to understand because your life is easy. You have a roof over your head, a car and extra money to vacation every year. Poor people don't live excessively like you and Daddy." Denise looked around her room at her white eye-let bedspread with matching curtains. The posters of the Jackson 5, Smokey Robinson, and, The Supremes on one wall, and a mile high stack of stuffed animals against the other wall. Denise owned her own desk and a typewriter. The sight of so much opulence made her sick to her stomach. "This is disgraceful."

Cornelia winced at her daughter's words. She and Percy were losing Denise to some unknown force, right before their very eyes. "Denise, can't we talk about this?"

"No." Denise grabbed her car keys and headed for the front door. "My mind is made up. I am a Black Panther."

"I bought that car, it belongs to me." Percy said.

Denise tightened her grip on the keys. "Mother." She hoped her mother would come to her rescue.

Cornelia sighed deeply. "Take the car, Denise."

"Cornelia!" Percy looked at his wife.

"Percy, Denise is taking the car. The streets are too dangerous for a young lady to be walking around in." Cornelia turned to Denise. "Honey, where will you go?"

"I don't know." Denise saw the pain in her mother's eyes and she longed to reach out to her. "Don't worry, the people will protect me."

Denise backed out of the doorway quickly before she broke down and cried. She didn't stop walking until she reached her white convertible Mustang.

"I love you, Denise."

"I love you too, Mother." Denise waved. "Goodbye Daddy."

Percy stood in the doorway, angry as hell and not saying a word. "Cornelia, you're just going to let her go."

As Denise was pulling off, Cornelia said, "You're the one who put her out, Percy. Not me."

"I didn't mean for her to leave." Percy said softly.

"It doesn't matter, honey. Our baby's gone."

Percy reached into his pocket and pulled out his car keys. "I'm going to follow her!"

"No you're not." Cornelia blocked the door.

"Yes I am. I'm not letting her go." Percy tried to step around his wife.

"Percy, when your daddy told you that there was only one man in the house and that was him, you made up your mind to leave Arkansas, didn't you?" Cornelia asked.

"That was different."

"No it wasn't." Cornelia took the keys away from him. "You decided that you were grown and no matter what your mama, grandmama, uncle, aunts or cousins said, you were leaving. And you left. Darling, it's Denise's turn to become a woman."

"So you agree with this Panther stuff?" Percy was outraged.

"Not in the least. I only know that there is a stubborn streak in our daughter that stretches a mile long. If you follow her, you'll only make things worse. All we can do is pray."

Percy considered his wife's words. She was right but it didn't stop him from feeling helpless. "What am I going to do without my baby?"

Cornelia rocked him gently.

Three

1971. Two years had passed and the war in Vietnam was still going strong. There were people everywhere. "U.S. Out of Cambodia!" and "Make Love Not War!" were a couple of the sentiments expressed by the anti-Vietnam protestors. Hippies, parents, the young, the old, Black and white alike demonstrated in support of forcing Nixon to withdraw troops from Vietnam.

Denise had done a lot of growing in a very short period of time. She was proud of herself for surviving without her parents or Charles. The Black Panther Party had empowered her mentally, spiritually and emotionally. Denise had finally learned to think for herself, and it felt good.

Denise, comrades DeeDee and Leonard were picketing the federal building in Westwood. This intimidating building reached high into the sky and was located less than half a mile from UCLA. Its tenants included the F.B.I., C.I.A., as well as armed services recruitment offices. Denise had been to this building once before. Her family was planning a trip to Europe and needed to get a passport. The irony was poetic. Then, she was a naive Negro wanting to see people in a different country. Today, she was a conscious Black woman, who wanted an end to imperialism around the world. In fact, the only travelling she wanted to do was to Africa or China. That's where the real revolutionaries lived.

The rally was in full swing, and included members from the Black Panthers, SDS, SAS and other student organizations. It was the anniversary of the May 4, 1970 murder of four young protestors at Kent State University in Ohio. The people were out in mass protest to let the government know that their deaths were not in vain.

"Denise?" Brother Jahid-Ali couldn't believe his eyes. It had been over three years since he had last seen her. Before she lowered her picket sign from in front of her face, he thought he had made a mistake. The last time he'd seen her, Denise's hair was down her back, and she was dressed like a sorority girl. This woman who stood before him with luscious, unpainted lips seemed so powerful, so rigid, he wasn't certain that she had ever been a girl-child.

Denise was a demonstrator against the Vietnam War, and a representative of the Anti-War movement on behalf of the Panthers. Among her many duties, she believed that it was important to stop the war before more lives were lost. Not to mention her personal interest in seeing that her cousin, Leon, came home alive from 'Nam.

"Oh my God! It is you! How are you?" She gave him a big hug with a smile to match. As they embraced she begged her memory to offer up his name. He looked so familiar, but she couldn't quite place him. He was definitely a Lion and clearly outnumbered, not to mention out of place at the rally. *Who was he?* The years seemed to pass through her soul like sand through an hourglass. Sometimes, Denise didn't know whether she was going or coming.

Sensing that she did not remember who he was, Brother

Jahid-Ali answered the unasked question on her lips. "Brother Jahid-Ali."

Denise's brow furrowed. He could see her mind working and hoped that when she arrived at January 17, 1969 that she would not push him away. Brother Jahid-Ali had nothing to do with the deaths of Huggins or Carter, but he was being fingered as one of the trigger men.

Denise took a deep breath. She remembered the sexy stranger. Her allegiance to the Black Panthers made her remove herself from his embrace. "Oh yeah. I do know you." Her voice changed. "What are you doing here?" her voice was strangely crisp, even for a cool spring day in May.

"I am here to support the cause," said Brother Jahid-Ali. They were standing in the middle of the picket line.

Brother Jahid-Ali was clearly not welcome by the other Black protestors. He knew that the WEB organization was taking the rap for murders of the Panther men, but there was nothing he could do about that. The F.B.I.'s ability to create a rift between the WEB organization and the Black Panthers was much bigger than him.

Brother Jahid-Ali's green and gold dashiki reflected the bright sunlight and danced all over Wilshire Boulevard. He wore white pants and brown leather sandals. Though he normally wore prescription glasses, he did not need them to see Denise. She was as beautiful to him that day as she was the first time he laid eyes on her.

Denise was wearing a brown suede miniskirt, a powder-blue button-down shirt, and high-heeled leather boots that zipped up the front. Her jet black beret sat askew on her short afro. She found herself looking into the eyes of the man who argued so vehemently with Kweli three years before. It was coming back to her in waves—her attraction to his mind; the shooting; and the day her life changed forever.

Brother Jahid-Ali gently led her completely out of the picket line, and walked her over to a low park bench. "I am out here to help bring our soldiers home. Black men should not be fighting their brothers." His sparkling brown eyes were so sincere.

"I agree." Denise couldn't help but smile. She knew that she was sitting face to face with the enemy, but something inside of her wanted to hear what he had to say. "I'm surprised that Maulana Imhotep allows his people to demonstrate." She looked down at her poster. "I'm not too familiar with his politics, but I assumed that anything that doesn't affect Africa, doesn't affect him."

"That's where you're wrong. It is his philosophy, as well as my own, that the real war is not overseas, it is right here at home. His goal is that of a cultural revolution, after that happens, the political revolution is sure to follow."

"How old are you?" she was curious.

"I'm twenty-five."

"Weren't you drafted?"

"Yes, but I am a conscientious objector." Brother Jahid-Ali's day at the selective services office was memorable to say the very least. He told the jar-head recruitment officer that he was not an American, but an African, and as such, he was not eligible for the draft. He further informed the uniformed officer, who was trying his best to stare him down, that if a weapon was placed in his hand, he would throw it to the ground.

"Really?" Denise was impressed. "I will support any brotha who has the heart to say no to the man."

He smiled. "Thank you. My father wasn't too pleased about my decision, but he got over it . . . I think."

Thinking of parents, Denise knew the underlying anguish in his words. Going against the status quo made Denise an embarrassment to her family. She thought about his words for a moment. She was about to respond, when she noticed that some of the other Panthers were giving her the evil eye.

She stood up abruptly. "I've got to go." Denise began walking in the direction of her comrades.

Brother Jahid-Ali was flabbergasted. "Wait, I want to talk to you!"

"I can't. Goodbye." Denise slammed him with her words. She walked away.

Away from Brother Jahid-Ali, Denise resumed her position in the picket line. Amid chants of "Hell No! We Won't Go!," she felt the weight of a woman's hand on her shoulder.

"Comrade, who was that you were speaking to?" DeeDee saw Denise talking to the Lion.

"Oh, some brotha who wanted to rap about the war." Denise wasn't telling a complete lie, though something told her not to tell anyone that she recognized Brother Jahid-Ali.

"Are you sure that you don't know him?" DeeDee was suspicious. Panthers could not associate with members of the WEB organization.

"I don't even know his name." Denise said dismissively, without looking at DeeDee.

"If you don't know him, why did you embrace him? Don't you know that he could be the man who killed Comrades Huggins and Carter?" DeeDee was indignant. She hated the new johnny-come-lately's, like Denise. The new Panthers had no idea how close they were to the revolution. No matter how educated or affluent their backgrounds, they had no clue as to politics and where they fit in destroying the fascist, racist U.S. government.

"I embraced him because he is out here in support of ending the war."

"But he is a member of WEB!" DeeDee nearly shouted.

"I know that. I recognized his dashiki." Denise defended Brother Jahid-Ali, even though she knew that this might get her into trouble. "He is also against sending Black people off to war to kill yellow people."

"This is not a game Denise! We are at war."

"Don't you think I know that, DeeDee?" Denise was insulted. Her commitment to the struggle was being questioned and all behind an innocent conversation with Brother Jahid-Ali. "Everyday, I am up at 5 A.M. preparing lessons for the young revolutionaries at the Freedom School! As soon as they leave for school, I modify my lessons for the adult P. E. courses, sell the *Black Panther* newspaper and, go to bed each night holding on to my gun. I ditch unmarked police cars; teach ignorant, bourgeois Negroes who live in the hills of Los Angeles that they are part of the problem; and still manage to walk with my head held high! So don't tell me we are at war, because I already know." Denise was seething with rage.

"Well, seeing as you are willing to negate all of your positive activity by flirting with the enemy, I had no choice but to ask." DeeDee snapped back. "We'll see what the captain has to say about this!" DeeDee stalked off to the car. Though they rode together, she left Denise at the Federal Building.

Denise felt so frustrated. The early morning euphoria had worn off and all that was left was a bad taste in her mouth. DeeDee had a thing for Kweli and probably couldn't wait to tell him what had happened out here.

Maybe it was time for Shelly to know that DeeDee was after her man. For the past year, Shelly and Kweli had been dating seriously. Denise knew that Shelly would not take too kindly to DeeDee pushing up on Kweli.

Denise looked around for someone to bum a ride home from. Not seeing any people, Black or otherwise, whom she could hitchhike home with, she slowly walked to the bus stop.

Brother Jahid-Ali watched Denise from a distance. He wanted to call out to her, but was afraid of getting her in more trouble. He knew that it was dangerous for them to meet, but he had to find a way to talk to her.

He lingered at the Federal building until Denise was safely on the bus. There was a ton of work waiting to be done at the WEB office, but he was in no hurry to get there. Some of his sistas and brothas acted like they couldn't do anything without him. He was beginning to feel ambivalent and slightly regretful.

While Brother Jahid-Ali believed that he made the right decision to stay with WEB, after all of the stuff went down with Kweli, he often missed his friend. They were more than friends, they were family. If their parents knew that they hated one another, they would both get a whuppin', just like when they were kids.

From a distance, Brother Jahid-Ali watched Kweli's rise through the Panther ranks. There were spies in each organization and it wasn't hard to get info on practically anybody. He knew that Kweli worked hard and believed in the Panther ten-point platform. He saw the virtues of the plan. Hell, who didn't want a job and a house? Brother Jahid-Ali sure did.

Brother Jahid-Ali knew in his heart that WEB was not the end all be all for him. He was beginning to hear the voice call out to him in the middle of the night. lt was telling him that in a little while, he was going to have to be true to himself. He sighed. Their friendship died four years before. Such were the casualties of war, he kept telling himself.

Four

"Comrade Kweli, do you think that I could assist you and brothas Leonard and Darnell with planning strategies?" Denise had been waiting a whole week to speak to Kweli alone. As president of the Southern California Chapter of the Black Panthers, he was up and down the coast and even travelled throughout the country to help establish Black Panther Headquarters in other states.

"Do you think you're ready? You know the man is not going to relinquish power just because we ask, ya dig?" He was sizing her up. Denise was definitely leadership material. She was a true revolutionary, but he didn't know how tough she was.

"I know." They were standing in the entryway of the living room of Denise's apartment. This room was scarcely decorated, because it was used for planning meetings. There were six fold-a-way chairs and a brown card table. Shelly and the other women had not returned from their respective jobs. The only other people in the house were Leonard and Darnell.

"Let me lay it on you like this. Denise, you are a foxy mama and many brothas ain't gonna be too cool on you tellin' em what to do."

"I didn't join the party to win a beauty contest. I joined to save the people." She raised a clenched fist into the air.

"You don't have to prove yourself to me. I already know what a righteous sista you are. What I'm trying to tell you is that you're too new. You've only been here a few years."

"That's jive and you know it. I've been here three years and I can do everything any man can do, and in some instances, better," Denise continued, "And anyway, I don't remember the bylaws requiring a member to have served a certain length of time to become part of the planning committee."

Denise definitely had spunk. Kweli handed his jacket to Leonard. Comrade Leonard put Kweli's leather jacket in the closet and came back to where she and Kweli were. This annoyed Denise, but there was nothing she could say. She even tried giving Comrade Darnell the evil eye so he would let them speak in private. No use, Comrade Darnell settled himself into a chair. Kweli sat down in a brown overstuffed chair and stretched his long legs out, while she stood. "I got a couple of questions for you: When and where was the party founded?"

"The BPP was founded in Oakland in 1966."

"Who are the founders?"

"Are you serious?" Denise never heard of any of the men being quizzed on the history of the party. "I bet the brothas are never asked these questions."

He didn't flinch. Denise had trouble reading him and answered his question. "Huey Newton and Bobby Seale."

"Who came up with the name of the party?"

"It was borrowed from the Lowndes County Black Panther Party in Alabama."

"Who was our first casualty of war?"

"Lil' Bobby Hutton."

"Who killed him?"

"The Oakland pigs," she scoffed. Everybody knew that.

"What date did all of this go down?" Kweli doubted that Leonard or Darnell knew the answer to this question, but he asked Denise anyway.

Denise scratched her head. "I don't know."

"Baby girl, how do you think that you can help plan, when you don't even know the date of our first slain brotha?"

"But—"

He didn't allow her to speak. "The brothas would remove me from office, if I let you in." Kweli turned to Leonard. "Man, gimme five!"

"Denise, you are not ready. Perhaps when you learn a little bit more, we'll talk again." He did not sound like he meant what he said.

"Brotha Kweli, I think that you are being unfair. Lil' Bobby Hutton's death has nothing to do with what is going on now. Huey's in prison and the party needs help. Why won't you let me help?"

"Comrade, revolution is not fair! Death is not fair! You work at the school, you see those kids, so don't act like you don't know what I'm talking about."

"I thought that the fight for liberation was for everybody, including women." Denise whined.

"It is. The brothas are taking care of you." Kweli lit a cigarette to signify that their discussion was over. "How much do you know about the revolution in Algeria? Have you ever been to a communist country?"

Tears welled up in her eyes.

"You don't know the answers do you? Sista, if this discussion has made you cry, you won't stand a chance with the others."

She wiped her face quickly. "I'm not crying. Smoke makes my eyes water."

"We'll rap another time. I gotta split." Kweli wasn't trying to hurt her feelings, he was just trying to toughen her up. His spirit was divided. On the one hand, Denise would probably be a good asset to the leadership of the Southern California Chapter. On the other, a woman with power could be very dangerous.

Kweli left without looking back. Denise reminded him of himself when he was one of the footsoldiers. Though only four years had passed since he left WEB, Kweli had grown and changed so much that it felt like a lifetime. It was also a lifetime ago that he and Carlton, alias, Brother Jahid-Ali loaded up the car and headed West. Too bad that brotha chose his dashiki over his family.

"I'm not going away Kweli, we will talk again." Denise yelled this after him. If Kweli heard her, he kept on walking.

Five

Marvin Gaye was standing in the cold rain, staring down at her. His black slicker was wet from the element and his mustache was decorated with raindrops. Though his eyes were cast off, Denise detected the pain in his heart. She was lying on her bed listening to a duet by him and Tammy Terrell.

She shared this room with Shelly. Their room was covered from floor to ceiling with posters of Che' Guevara, Mao Tse Tung, Huey Newton and of course, Marvin Gaye. Shelly was in love with Gil Scott Heron and Kweli. Gil was the ghetto poet from New York whom everyone thought was so cool. Kweli was the man who had stolen Shelly's heart.

Denise liked Gil, though his songs were so urgently dismal. Talk of revolution was all around them and some days that frightened Denise. *Would she be willing to die for the movement? Would she be able to live with herself if she didn't?* As for Kweli, Denise had her reservations about that brotha. He was righteous and all, but Denise felt that he was a bit too intense.

A six-drawer, oak chest held their personal belongings. Before moving here, her room was decorated with a white chest and dresser with matching vanity. The party taught her that she could exist on very little and what a slave she had been to material things. Gone were her platforms, multicolored hair barrette, Diana Ross false eyelashes, and her UCLA identification card. Who needed that fascist institution! Her real education would be found in the street, among the people. Denise reached up and rubbed the tight coils on top of her head. She also left her hair on the floor of the bathroom, much to her mother's anguish.

Hair. The Black women's overseer and master. Denise suspected that brunettes, redheads, and brown-eyed Susies also suffered from never achieving true Nordic beauty. She didn't think that she could be a real revolutionary thinker and go around frying her hair up. Pressing, permanent, conking and all the other artificial efforts to make one's hair flow was the epitome of contradiction to Denise. She also believed that hair made a statement about a person's personality. For too many years, she was cautioned not to play in the water when she was young, or told that she could not go swimming, because she'd mess her hair up. What a con! With her new look, she could go to the beach, take a hot shower, and walk in the rain without fear of her hair "going back," wherever "back" was.

There was no mirror in their bedroom, no perfume, no lipstick or any other cosmetic that would cover Denise or Shelly's natural beauty. Her one vice was forty-fives. Denise tried but knew that she could never part with her music.

Though she adjusted to her new lifestyle, Denise sometimes wanted to sneak out to see a movie. She loved *007* and *Shaft*. Richard Rountree was so fine, with his porkchop sideburns, sexy voice and cool indifference. Revolutionaries could not relate to blaxploitation films, no matter how fine Shaft was. She knew that if she even breathed a word of her affection for Shaft, she would be labeled a traitor to the people for giving her money and time to the establishment. Hollywood, while good for donating money to the Black Panther party, was nothing but a tool, used by capitalists to lull Black people to sleep. In any event, being called an Uncle Tom was ten times worse than being called bourgeois.

In the midst of a hectic schedule, Shelly found time to fall in love. Her job was to write articles for the *Black Panther* newspaper. On occasion, she also submitted entries to *Ramparts* and *The Black Scholar*. Shelly was a budding journalist and was currently on the trail of discovering who shot John Huggins and Bunchy Carter. Maulana Imhotep, head of the WEB organization, insisted that the FBI was trying to sabotage his organization. He said that the informants dressed up like Lions and shot the two men. Maulana Imhotep argued that it was a government ploy to stymie the Black Power Movement. Shelly was not buying it.

Shelly was also lying across her bed, lost in thought.

"Shelly, what are you thinking about?" Denise raised herself up on her elbows.

"Oh nothing, girl, I'm just tired." Shelly let out a loud sigh and then closed her eyes.

"Guess who I saw today?" Denise was nervous about telling Shelly that she saw Brother Jahid-Ali.

"Who?" she mumbled.

"If I tell you, you have to promise not to tell a soul—not even your boyfriend Kweli!" Denise sat up.

"I promise."

"Girl, you've got to do better than just promise. I mean, I could get in a lot of trouble if anyone finds out."

Awakened by the secrecy in Denise's voice, Shelly traced

an imaginary cross over her heart. "Who?" Shelly urged. "Tell me."

Denise tiptoed to the door. She opened it. No one was standing behind it. She turned around and faced Shelly. "Do you remember a Lion by the name of Brother Jahid-Ali?"

Shelly shook her head no.

"We met him three years ago at UCLA. He spoke at the BSU meeting, because Maulana Imhotep had laryngitis."

It took Shelly a minute to place him. "Oh yeah, I remember him."

"I saw him today at the Anti-Vietnam rally." Denise found herself becoming giddy at the memory. "He's looking well," she added offhandedly.

"No you don't!" Shelly sat bolt upright.

"What? I haven't done anything. I saw him, he came up to me and we talked."

"For how long?"

"About five minutes. We sat down on a park bench at the Federal Building—"

"Together?"

"Well, yes. It was only for a minute, I don't see what the big deal is."

"Denise, stop being so naive, you know what the big deal is! He and the rest of the so called "cultural nationalists" are trying to ruin the strides made by Huey. Not to mention, he is under suspicion for being one of the trigger men. Is his last name Steiner?"

Panicked, Denise asked her. "I don't know what his last name is. Who told you that? You don't know if he did it. For all we know, the FBI did it."

"Denise, I'm surprised at you. You are defending a murderer." Shelly was ticked off. She remembered the chemistry between Brother Jahid-Ali and Denise, but that took place over three years ago. Denise was crazy if she thought that she was going to pursue a relationship with the enemy. "You know, Black police are generally harsher on the community than the white."

"We are not talking about the police."

"Yeah, but my point is the same. Pigs in uniform and pigs in dashikis with bald heads and African names are sometimes worse than card carrying members of the NAACP." Shelly flopped back on her bed. "He is not to be trusted, dig what I'm sayin'?"

Crushed, Denise instantly regretted her mistake. "I shouldn't have told you, Shelly." She knew that she had taken a risk talking to Brother Jahid-Ali, but Denise really did not see the harm in their brief conversation. It wasn't like she told him Panther secrets.

"Did anyone see you talking to him?"

"Comrade DeeDee and the others saw us. DeeDee is such a little busybody. She already told me that she was going to report me. I guess I'll just wait for my reprimand."

"Don't make jokes, Denise. You could be kicked out of the party for talking to him." Shelly's voice was hard. "The people might think that you are an informant."

"Shelly," Denise said seriously. "You know I'm not an informant. I resent your insinuation."

Shelly did not respond. Denise returned to her bed and buried her face in her pillow. She felt dejected and hurt. Above all, she felt alone. She didn't have an answer for why she defended Brother Jahid-Ali. He was nothing to her, and yet, there was a place inside of her, which extended beyond logic and reason, that told her that he would be the only one who understood her. Denise decided against telling Shelly about DeeDee wanting her man, because she didn't want Shelly to think she was simply trying to get back at DeeDee. As far as she knew, Shelly and DeeDee were friendly, though DeeDee kept her chilly distance from the Panthers who were not there from jump.

Shelly and Denise, like most of the Panthers, lived communally. Their other housemates were Retha, Faye, Tyrone, and Kweli occasionally. The household chores were divided along gender lines. The women did the cooking and cleaning and the men strategized. Both men and women cleaned guns, sold panther newspapers and worked at the Freedom Schools. It was an egalitarian setup, though Denise wished that she could partake in the political strategies developed by the men.

Whenever Kweli came over, which seemed to be pretty often lately, Shelly would mysteriously disappear. Tonight was no exception and Denise resigned herself to turn in early, when she heard Shelly and Kweli whispering in the hallway. After her conversation with Shelly earlier, Denise had pretty much kept to herself. She could not make out what they were talking about, but then the door flew open.

"Comrade, I hear that you were talking to a Lion today." Kweli paced back and forth in front of Denise. "Were you so mad at me for not letting you join the planning meetings that you went to the enemy?"

Denise jumped out of bed and struck a military style pose. Her back was stiff, her chest was thrust forward, and her heart was racing. She was wearing a "Free Huey" T-shirt and panties, and felt self-conscious about being barely dressed in front of the Captain of the Southern California branch of the Black Panthers.

"No, comrade I'm not mad at you." Denise was afraid. Her reprimand was in full effect. "I-I was just talking to another protestor at the rally."

"I heard that you were talking to a Lion. You know how the party feels about the WEB organization." He was pounding his fist in his hand. Kweli was flanked by Shelly, DeeDee and Darnell. "I can't believe you, comrade! Who was he?"

"Brother Jahid-Ali." Denise was stricken with panic. "I'm sorry. We—we only talked for a minute." Sweat was beginning to gather on her brow.

The sound of heavy boots and leather echoed on the hard wood floors. "Tell the truth, comrade!" DeeDee's voice was full of venom. "You were carrying on with him, like you two were out on a picnic. And if it hadn't been for me, you probably would have continued talking to your lover."

"My lover?" Denise was stunned.

"Did you plan to meet him there?" The question was rhetorical, but the voice was unmistakable. Shelly. "You can tell me."

"No! I haven't seen him in several years . . . since before I became a Black Panther. I don't even know him." Denise pleaded with her. "Shelly, you know that."

"Dig it, all I know is that you were talking to the enemy. They are the reason that two of our leaders are no longer alive. What did he say to you?" Kweli said.

Denise was wracking her brain. All of her sudden her mind went blank. Everyone was staring at her with hatred in their eyes. The room was getting hotter and hotter, and she couldn't stop shaking.

"Stop stalling, comrade, and answer Kweli's question!" DeeDee was standing in front of Denise breathing in her face.

Denise took a deep breath and tried to compose herself. "I think he asked me if I remembered him."

"You think?" DeeDee took her place behind Kweli. "She's lying."

Denise felt like she was stuck in the middle of a bad "B" movie. She couldn't believe her ears. All of a sudden her hearing faded. She could see their mouths moving, but could not hear a sound. It was like she fainted, but she had not fallen. When her hearing returned, she heard something about being suspended.

"What?" her voice was a whisper. Adrenaline was pumping in her ears.

"Comrade, you have been suspended for violating executive order number five. No fraternizing with the enemy—white or black."

"Suspended? For how long?" her mind was a blur.

DeeDee answered this question for her. "You are suspended for thirty days, during which time you are not to go near the Freedom School, sell a newspaper or even associate with the other Panthers. You bourgeois niggas are all alike. You think that you can just talk to anybody you feel like talking to! Well, as far as we are concerned, you are incommunicado."

"Where will I go?" Denise looked to Shelly for support. None was forthcoming.

"That's not our problem. In fact, why don't you call your Lion boyfriend and tell him to come and get you?" DeeDee laughed.

Denise stood stock still. She couldn't believe what had just happened. The next time she saw Brother Jahid-Ali, she was going to cuss him up and down Central Avenue. When she got through with him, he'd wish he had gone to Vietnam.

* * *

Kweli made a mental note to have Denise watched. If she was cool with the WEB organization, there was no way she could be trusted, let alone have rank within the Black Panther Party. By now Denise would be on to DeeDee, so he needed to find some other comrade to tail Denise. Shelly. The thought made him smile. Without Shelly or Denise knowing it, he would have Shelly spy on her best friend.

Of all of people in WEB, why did Denise have to be friends with Carlton? Why not some brotha he didn't know? Actually, Maulana Imhotep named both of them. After Kweli left the WEB organization, he had changed his name back to Kevin. But, Kevin no longer sounded right, so he stuck with Kweli. In spite of this one good thing, he, however, still kicked himself for ever believing in that fake revolutionary. The thought of Maulana Imhotep made him want to spit.

While DeeDee went to get the car, Kweli blinked his eyes. It was just yesterday that he and Brother Jahid-Ali headed West from Mississippi, in the little VW bug. Oh, the plans they had for California! They were going to enroll in college, join the Black Power Movement and then Carlton was going into politics. Kweli didn't know what he was going to do with himself, all he knew was that Black people needed help, badly.

Though they came to California together, neither of them saw the fork in the road that would eventually divide them. That was the real reason he suspended Denise. He knew that she was telling the truth. She was just a kid. Kweli also knew that he overreacted and was sure that he would get some lip from Shelly about it. But he didn't care. It was his job to protect the party.

Six

Denise's heart had been heavy for the last few days and she needed relief. She was depressed and felt alone. The only good that came out of the last seventy-two hours was that she was able to stay with another panther, Pauletta, who thought that Kweli was showing off by suspending her.

Pauletta was a few years older than Denise and understood that people, even a bad brotha like Kweli, was prone to let his title go to his head. Another reason Pauletta let Denise stay with her was because Pauletta was on her way out of the party. She joined because the Panthers gave her her first taste of Blackness, but lately her rainbow was enough. Four years later, Pauletta was ready to take her revolutionary spirit underground.

If Pauletta had not have taken her in, Denise feared that she was going to have to go home. There was no way she could go crawling back. Her Dad was still mad at her. Even if they allowed her to come home, Cornelia and Percy would still be reactionary and unable to relate to the movement. Pauletta, however, told her not to worry, because she had seen comrades treated worse than Denise, and had some extra money stashed away that she saved for such occasions.

Shelly's mother was very supportive of Shelly. They

talked all the time and their closeness made Denise wish that her parents would try to understand her decision to join the Black Panther Party.

On Pauletta's suggestion, Denise decided to go to the Watts Coffee House on One Hundred and Third Street. On Friday and Saturday nights, jazz was played and poets blew their heavy poetry. Pauletta had to teach a political education class and could not accompany Denise to the Watts Coffee House. She, however, insisted that Denise get out of the apartment and have a good time.

Denise dressed as counterrevolutionary as possible. She did not want to further her humiliation by dressing in her Panther uniform, only to be snubbed by the other comrades. The news had travelled faster than the speed of light and before she could even leave her pad, five comrades had called to see if she was really suspended. All of the phone calls weren't bad. In fact, Pauletta was one of the callers. She, however, was the only caller who offered help.

Denise wore a red, green and black liberation jumpsuit. At least, the tag said "liberation" on it. Being liberated from the Panthers was not quite the liberation she planned to participate in. The shiny polyester clashed with her dusty combat boots, but that was the least of her worries. Her jumpsuit screamed that she was a bourgeois, reactionary Negro pimping the revolution.

Denise adjusted her eyes to the duskiness of the coffee house. Housed in a large building, the inside of the coffee house had a piano, ten cocktail tables, and chairs. Its decor was African with masks, zebra skins, bongo drums, and a giant size poster of a sista with a humongous afro. The caption underneath the woman in the poster read BLACK IS BEAUTIFUL. "Solid." Denise said to the poster. She had unconsciously raised her fist, but then remembered that she no longer had that right. If she had known that she was going to blend in with the color scheme of the coffee house, she would have left her polyester number in the bottom of her suitcase.

Denise found a table near the front of the area that faced the stage. In the old days, before joining the Black Panther Party, Elaine Brown used to sing there, and jazz pianist Horace Tapscott tickled the ivories. That must have been outta sight, Denise thought. A cocktail waiter came and took her order of sangria. Slowly the room filled to near capacity. The crowd was predominantly members or hopeful members of the WEB organization. Ordinarily she would have felt out of place. Somehow the sangria made her forget that she was in the heart of enemy territory. Wait a minute! She was now a friend of the friendless and an enemy to her beloved Panthers to boot. As she continued to berate herself for being so stupid for talking to Brother Jahid-Ali, a tap on her left shoulder made her jump.

"I'm sorry. I didn't mean to startle you."

Denise could not believe her eyes! Brother Jahid-Ali was standing right in front of her. She threw the remaining contents of her glass onto his milky white dashiki. "How dare you talk to me!"

Brother Jahid-Ali tried to dodge the wine, but was too slow. His crisp white dashiki was ruined. "What's wrong with you?"

Denise was immediately surrounded by five men. She dared any one of them to touch her.

"Sista, are you crazy?" Brother Bijou's big voice boomed inside her ear.

More mad than scared of the men, Denise responded. "You got me in a whole lot of trouble."

Realizing that his men were still at attention, Brother

Jahid-Ali waved them away. "Denise?" he blinked. The cigarette smoke in the room was thick and he didn't recognize her immediately. "What are you doing here? Do you know where you are?"

Somebody put on a John Coltrane album and a poet was making his way to the stage. "Come with me." And he took her by her elbow.

"I'm not going anywhere with you. That's how I got into trouble in the first place!"

Brother Jahid-Ali gripped her elbow tighter and practically lifted her out of her chair. "It's not safe for you to be here. Let's go somewhere so we can talk."

He was returning from Fremont High school, where Swahili classes were taught on Tuesdays and Thursdays. Though it was a Friday night, he had a special tutorial for some of the WEB members who could not attend the Thursday Swahili class. The whole night he was distracted. He had the strangest feeling that he would see Denise again. Here she was! This time he would not let go of her.

Denise tried to struggle against him, but he was too strong and the crowd was too thick. She relaxed and leaned her body into his. As soon as they got outside, she jerked her arm away from him. "Just when I thought things couldn't get any worse . . ." Denise was so mad the words got stuck in her throat. Seeing him made her tremble the way she had three days before. Then the shakes were in fear; this time they were the result of rage and disgust.

Brother Jahid-Ali could visibly see her anger and knew that she wanted him to leave her alone. He thought he also detected a longing underneath her mask of fury.

Denise stared hard at him. When he returned her stare, she averted her gaze by looking at the coffee house. She refused to look at him for fear of giving herself away. She started to speak, but decided against it. She let out a huge sigh.

Trying to diffuse the charged air, Brother Jahid-Ali finally broke the silence. "Sista, I just wanted to talk to you."

"Do you know how much trouble you have caused me?" Denise screamed at him.

"I know that I've only seen you twice in my life, but you've left footprints on my soul." Brother Jahid-Ali began to admire the red, black, and green jumpsuit Denise was wearing. The color enhanced the green in her amber colored eyes. She was more beautiful at this moment than any woman he had ever seen in his life.

What was wrong with him? Couldn't he see that her world has come to a screeching halt! "Puh-leeze! I may have left footprints on your soul, but your big mouth got me kicked out of my party."

"I see that you are upset with me . . ." He spoke to her in soothing tones.

"Upset! That's not even the half of it. I've been suspended, called a "traitor," and "reactionary." You even made my best friend turn against me. Do you dig what I'm saying?" She walked away and then turned back sharply, "And another thing, don't patronize me!"

"Sista', I'm sorry."

"Sorry, my butt." Denise began walking toward the bus stop.

"Where are you going?" Desperation laced Brother Jahid-Ali's voice.

"Away from you."

"Please, let me drive you," he begged.

Denise just shined him on and kept walking. Brother Jahid-Ali ran to his beige Volkswagon bus and followed along side of her. He was driving on the wrong side of the street, while trying to keep a watchful eye out for the police. He called out to her, "It's dangerous for a beautiful woman to walk alone at night."

"The people will protect me." Her Panther fire had returned.

Brother Jahid-Ali stopped his car, but Denise kept walking. "I know that you already know this, but this is the heart of WEB territory and if a Panther member sees you, well, your temporary suspension will become indefinite."

Denise stopped in midstride, sighed heavily, then walked over to his car. "This does not mean that I forgive you."

Inwardly, he smiled. As she rounded the front end of the car, he ran over to the passenger side to open the door for her. Her shoulder brushed past his chest.

"Let me move those papers out of your way." Brother Jahid-Ali grabbed a handful of newspapers and tossed the papers in the backseat.

Fingering his once immaculate dashiki, he admonished Denise. "By the way, just because I'm giving you a ride, doesn't mean that I have forgiven you."

She smiled as she got into the car. By the time he closed the door, Denise managed to give him a straight face.

Brother Jahid-Ali drove very slowly. He didn't know where to go. If they stayed in the neighborhood, they ran the risk of being spotted by WEB organization and Panther members alike. The only alternative was to drive as far away from the Watts Coffee House as possible.

"This is a bad ride you've got." Denise was teasing him. Brother Jahid-Ali's VW bus definitely left something to be desired. It was a dusty beige color with rusted chrome accents, and it also backfired a lot. "I bet they hear you coming a mile away."

Brother Jahid-Ali laughed because it was true. If he was

going to rendezvous with a Panther woman, he especially needed a new car so as not to be recognized. The WEB organization needed at least two more buses to accommodate the membership. That decision, however, was up to Maulana.

"Ms. Smarty, where is your car? Or, should I say your bus pass?"

"For your information, brotha, I've got a convertible white Mustang."

Not believing her. "If this is so, why were you sitting on the bus stop last week after the rally?"

"My comrade left—" Denise shut her mouth quickly. It was none of his business. She cleared her throat. "I dedicated my car to the struggle."

"Um. Hmm. What you really mean is that you gave your car to the men of your party and they gave you ladies that bucket your comrade was driving." He said referring to DeeDee's old station wagon. Denise never even asked where she got that car. She just assumed it was hers. And now that he mentioned it, she didn't know where her car was either.

"You don't know what you're talking about." She shrugged her shoulders. "The Panthers are not a materialistic group. What would I need a car for, when I can walk to the Freedom School?"

"You mean the Free Breakfast for Children School."

Surprised by his knowledge, Denise responded. "I nicknamed it the Freedom School."

"Why?"

"Never mind. Dig this, where are we going?" It now occurred to Denise that she really did not know Brother Jahid-Ali and he could be taking her anywhere.

He looked over at her. "Are you hungry?"

Brother Jahid-Ali's soft eyes allayed her fears. "Actually, I'm starved."

"Good, so am I." The tension was beginning to ease between them. "I think Norm's is still open." Norm's was a twenty-four hour diner. The menu contained everything from Norm's famous milk shakes to meat loaf and mashed potatoes to spaghetti and meatballs. It was also reasonably priced, and they would be able to eat in privacy.

"So, Denise, where are you from?"

"I was born and raised in the Negro section of Los Angeles."

"Is the Negro section of Los Angeles as racist and evil as the Negro sections all over the South?"

She bit her lower lip. "I doubt it. In Los Angeles, the bourgeois Negro is the Black communities' worst enemy."

"Why do you say that?"

"I know that Maulana Imhotep has already given you the low down on L.A."

"He has. I just wanted to know what Huey and the rest of the pussy ca—, I mean Panthers told you guys."

"Guys?"

"Yeah, guys, ladies, comrades, you know, y'all." Brother Jahid-Ali realized he felt very comfortable with Denise.

Denise rolled her eyes. She didn't know what to make of him. "Anyway, where are you from?"

"I'm from Mississippi."

Denise slapped her thigh. "I knew it! I knew it! That *y'all* was something straight out of the South!" She began to chant. "M-I-Crooked letter-Crooked letter, I-Crooked letter-Crooked letter-I-Hump back-Hump back-I." She laughed at the nursery rhyme from her childhood.

"I'm shocked you know that out here." Brother Jahid-Ali was amused. "I thought only we sang that chant."

"There are a lot of people who live in Los Angeles, who migrated from Mississippi after the war," Denise explained.

"How right you are. By the way, how old are you?" He tried to sound nonchalant.

"Does it matter?" He was beginning to get too personal. Denise turned her body to face him. "Look, we are not friends. The only reason I got in this hoopty was so that I didn't run into any of my comrades on the street. I am going with you to Norm's, not because I like you, but because I am starving." Denise turned away from him. "Damn, you don't even have a radio in this bus. How do you stand the silence?"

Without answering her, Brother Jahid-Ali reached into the glove compartment and handed Denise a transistor radio. "You might have to tilt it to get a clear sound."

He drove a piece in silence and then said. "Last week, I told you my age."

Denise pretended not to hear him.

Finally they reached their destination. Norm's was a short distance from the corner of La Brea and Manchester in Inglewood, near the city council, senate office and other legislative offices. Pulling into the driveway of Norm's resurrected Brother Jahid-Ali's secret desire to hold office. He averted his eyes quickly from the majesty of the formidable cement building that hovered against the black sky. Since joining the WEB organization, he had traded in his old dreams for the vision of a cultural revolution. He wondered for the first time in four years if he had made the right decision.

Noticing his heavy silence, Denise touched his shoulder lightly. "Are you okay?"

He nodded affirmatively.

When the menus arrived, Brother Jahid-Ali set his aside. He was concentrating on Denise.

Feeling his eyes on her, she asked. "May I help you?"

"Yes. You can start by not being so defensive. I've already apologized for getting you into trouble with your comrades. I just really need to talk to you."

"Then say what's on your mind, brotha." Denise set her menu on the table. "I'm all ears." She folded her arms across her chest.

He was on the spot and feeling nervous. "I really dig you."

"You don't even know me." She grabbed her menu again. "And if this is just a line to get me into bed, you can forget about it." Denise motioned to the waitress to come and take her order.

"That's not what I want from you. I just think that you're cool and I've just been diggin' your vibe for years now."

"Wait a minute. Do you expect me to believe that? That is the tiredest, jivest thing I've ever heard. You haven't seen me and you know nothing about me. So that there is no confusion, I am not puttin'-out for the cause. You and your brothas are all the same." She dropped her voice and leaned across the table. *"Ah, my sista, you are so fine and so in tune with the movement. I just know that we could find destiny in each other's arms. You know, the revolution appreciates strong sistas like yourself."* She winked at him. *"If ya dig what I mean."*

"Denise, you have me confused with your comrades."

"Brother Jahid-Ali, don't act like that doesn't go on in the WEB organization!" Her tongue was sharp. "Your organization is no less immune to the sexist treatment of women." She returned to character. *"Baby, can you do this? Sista, can you cook a soldier a meal? And after the dishes are done, can you come lay with me so that we can get down tonight."*

"Okay, okay, you've got a point." He threw his hands up. "Those are some of the pitfalls of being a revolutionary. But, back to what I was saying. I know you."

"No you don't. Brotha this is the first conversation we've had in three years. Like I said before, you don't know anything about me."

"Then tell me all about yourself," Brother Jahid-Ali said patiently.

The waitress, who was keeping a polite distance, finally came to the table. "What can I get you two?" The waitress's name tag read Thelma. She had one more hour left before she got to go home, and wished the two people in front of her would hurry up. While Denise gave her order, Thelma looked her over. Her rainbow jumpsuit was missing the color purple and the man needed to wash his shirt or dress or whatever he was wearing. She shook her head. Hippies were all the same—dirty and high. She figured that they must have been high, because only somebody high would walk out of the house in those clothes.

Thelma took their orders and proceeded to walk away. She took three steps and turned around. "In my day, young Negro men and women dressed up to go to dinner."

"Yes ma'am." Brother Jahid-Ali nodded his head.

"I am not a Negro. I am Black. It's people like you—"

Brother Jahid-Ali cut her off. "You better pay some respect to your elders. That woman is old enough to be your grandmother!"

"But she's not my grandmother, and we are not down South. I don't have to call her ma'am and I don't have to pay her a damn thing, but the check when it comes."

"I am going to believe that is the party talking and not you. I know that you were raised better than that."

"I am a part of the party and it is a part of me." She shined the insinuation about her upbringing on. "I am not disrespecting that lady, I just want her to know that Black people need to shed their slave mentalities and stop allowing the man to give them a name. Black people did not call themselves Negro. White people did that to us."

"Cool. Cool. When ole girl spits in your food, we'll see what you have to say then."

Denise shut up immediately. She didn't want Brother Jahid-Ali to think that she didn't have any couth. She changed the subject. "Where do you get your clothes? I mean, your dashiki is boss."

"Why thank you." He patted his dashiki. "I bet your hair would look bad in a wrap."

"I doubt it." She took a sip of water. "Anyway. I couldn't fit my beret over a wrap."

"Denise, I want to get to know you better."

"I don't think that's possible." She attempted to sound serious. "In case you forgot, you are the enemy. I shouldn't even be here with you."

His eyes twinkled. "Ah, but you are."

Brother Jahid-Ali was right. She was sitting in Norm's with him. In fact, this was the best she'd felt in three days. Denise wondered what it was about him that made her feel so good.

They ate the remainder of their meals in silence. Denise looked at her watch. "It's one o'clock, I really need to get home." She reached for the check.

His hands were quicker than hers. "This one's on me."

"Thank you. I'm impressed."

"Why? The bill is only five dollars."

"I am pleased that Maulana has taught his Lions to be chivalrous."

Brother Jahid-Ali grimaced. What would Maulana Imhotep say if he saw him right now? It didn't matter and he didn't care. "Denise, you know that I'm from the South." He paid the bill and they left Norm's.

At that time of night, there was too much static on the transistor radio to hear any music. "Denise, do you go to the Watts Coffee House a lot?"

"No, tonight was my first time."

"I try to stop by there every Tuesday and Thursday." Brother Jahid-Ali hoped that this was not the last time that they would see one another.

"What made you come on a Friday night?" Denise was trying to get a feel for him, without asking him outright about his routine.

"I was hoping to see you."

"Yeah right." Denise smacked her teeth.

"Actually, I went to meet one of the other Lions, but he wasn't there." He winked at her. "Lucky for me."

He pulled up in front of what appeared to be an abandoned building. "You live here?"

"Yes." Denise did not want him to know where she really lived. He seemed like a cool cat, but he was still a member of WEB. She couldn't be too careful.

"Thanks for the lift and dinner."

"Hakuna furaha bila upendo. That's swahili for 'there's no joy in this world without love'," Brother Jahid-Ali said seductively.

Denise blushed. "Thanks again."

"Anytime. Maybe I'll see you on Tuesday."

"Maybe you will—may be you won't." She smiled coyly. Denise watched Brother Jahid-Ali drive off. She turned and walked in the opposite direction to Pauletta's apartment.

Seven

With twenty-five days of suspension left, Denise had lots of time on her hands. She survived the weekend by sleeping in, but after two days of almost non-stop sleep, Denise couldn't take it anymore. She had to get out. Pauletta suggested that she go to the beach and relax, but Denise was tired of relaxing.

On Monday morning, she got dressed and went to UCLA. It had been well over a year since she was on Bruin soil. The last time she was there, Ralph Abernathy was speaking. Denise had vowed never to return to this capitalist institution. As fate would have it, she was not only back, but in a funny kind of way, Denise was happy to be back.

It was early and she didn't expect to see any of her comrades recruiting for the party. To avoid any accidental encounters, Denise decided against going to Powell Library. That place was not only her former place of employment, but the place where the undergrads met to socialize. No real studying was ever done there. For this reason, Charles always studied in the Bio-Medical library, on the side of the campus reserved for the eggheads.

Denise hadn't thought about Charles since the day they broke up. When she quit school, she left everything behind, including him. She did not contact him to tell him where

she was or why she left. By now he was in his third year
of medical school. Denise often thought of contacting him,
but what would she say? He was a member of the NAACP
and could not relate to the Black Power Movement. He
once told her that the Panthers and other paramilitants were
hoodlums. He also said that the fact they carried arms with
them proved that they were a Black gestapo. In the old
days, she agreed with Charles. They were both so ignorant.
Neither of them knew more than the lies told by the evening
news. Denise would probably still feel this way had she
not been thrown out of Beale's class. That was a turning
point in her life. How could she make Charles understand
that?

If only Charles had seen those men gunned down, she
thought, *then he could have joined her in her search for
revolution.* Thinking of Charles made her feel guilty. *"If
only I wasn't so caught up in my visions of our perfect life
together, maybe I could have saved him."* She stopped herself. *Charles was just like she used to be, part of the problem.*

Denise made it to the University Research Library without incident. Once she got inside, she buried herself in a
corner and took out her list of books. Since joining the
Black Panther Party, she received a whirlwind political
education. Now that she had time, she wanted to delve
deeper into the philosophies that were so near and dear to
Huey.

She returned to Fanon and Mao, but found herself getting
too bogged down in the rhetoric. However, Denise was determined to learn these and other political theories, so that
when she returned to the party, she would be able to help
implement strategy for revolution. Comrades Leonard,
Kweli and Bobby told her that if she studied real hard that

she would be able to join the other women in leadership positions. Though she didn't think Comrade Leonard meant to uphold his end of the bargain, Denise remained on track. Now that she had time on her hands, she planned to learn all she could to prove to Kweli that she was serious about revolution.

On Tuesday evening, Denise put on a pair of worn Levi jeans, a polyester burgundy shirt and her boots. She reached into the bottom of her duffle bag and pulled out a long cream colored scarf. She tied the scarf around her neck and twisted the knot to the right. The butterfly collar on her shirt was large enough so as not to hide her scarf. Denise admired herself in Pauletta's bathroom mirror. She kept some of her civilian clothes, because Pauletta told the new members that the police recognized their uniforms, and that in some instances they would need to wear their street clothes. This was the first time in two years that she had given any thought to her appearance. Denise told herself that she was checking herself out in the mirror because she had not worn civilian clothes in so long that she didn't want to look too out of touch.

"You look nice. Where are you going?" Pauletta was passing by the bathroom and noticed Denise.

"Oh, nowhere." Denise quickly looked away from the mirror. "Well, I kinda dug the Watts Coffee House the other night. I thought that I'd go back."

"That sounds like fun. Are you going alone?"

"Since I don't have any friends anymore, I guess so," snapped Denise. "I'm sorry, you didn't deserve that."

"That's okay. I know that you are under a lot of pressure." Pauletta hoped that Denise did not grow embittered by her suspension. The movement, though a bit misguided, was a good one.

"Do you want to go with me?" Denise hoped that she would say no. Though Denise would not say it out loud, she was hoping that Brother Jahid-Ali would be there.

"No, I have some pamphlets to put together for the rally at UCLA tomorrow. You should check it out."

"What time?" Denise had not been to a rally on campus in a very long time.

"Noon at Meyerhuff Park."

"Hmm. I'll have to think about that. You know that a lot of the comrades will be there. I'm not ready to face any of the others, just yet. Who *is* speaking tomorrow?"

"H. Rap Brown."

"Damn." Denise shook her head. Her voice grew soft. "I can't believe this. I'm gonna miss him."

Pauletta patted Denise on her back. "Don't worry, your suspension will be up in no time and then you will be able to dig all of the revolutionary brothas and sistas who speak at UCLA and any other place." Her supportive words made Denise smile. "You have fun tonight. I gotta split."

Pauletta left and Denise grabbed her purse. It was a little chilly and she reached into Pauletta's closet and took out a plaid cape. It was a gold and brown patchwork poncho with buttons down the front.

She arrived at the Watts Coffee House thirty minutes later and sat at the same table where she sat on Friday night. It just so happened that some of the ghetto children were putting on a play. One of the older children had written it and was trying to get the younger children to stand still. The young writer's name was Cynthia. Her play was entitled *The Ghetto—Life in the Big City.*

Denise ordered a glass of sangria and quietly surveyed

the room. So far, Brother Jahid-Ali was nowhere to be seen.
Eight o'clock. It was still early she told herself. He'd probably be there later. At nine, Denise decided that she was
crazy. *What was she doing there?* The play was almost over
and her third glass of red fruit wine had washed over her
like a soft kiss. Denise tilted her head slightly backward
and closed her eyes. The gentle kiss from the wine washed
over her again.

"Habari gani."

Her eyes flew open and she saw Brother Jahid-Ali's full
lips inches from her own. "Don't you know better than to
sneak up on a person like that?" Denise tried to sound stern,
but couldn't. His breath was intoxicating.

Ignoring her, he said, "Habari gani." He slowly moved
away from her. "Your eyes are so beautiful."

"What?" Denise tried hard to be unaffected by his com-
pliment. "You're wolfin' and you know it. My eyes are red
and tired."

"You have the sad but alert eyes of a soldier. Whoever
suspended you needs to borrow my glasses. In fact, he
needs bifocals if he can't see the commitment in your eyes."
He gently stroked her left cheek. "Yes, Denise, eyes are
the window to the soul."

Denise felt her body grow warm from his touch. One
more sangria and she would be his.

"Habari gani is Swahili for 'hello.' Whenever someone
says 'habari gani', you say habari gani or njema, which
means 'very well, thanks'." He took the seat in front of her
and sat down. "Let's try it again. Habari gani, sista."

"Gani bari yourself." She purposely destroyed the greet-
ing, but he didn't seem to mind, because he kept talking.

"What brings you here?"

Denise shook herself free from his invisible embrace. "It's a free country, I can go where I want."

"I can dig that. I was hoping that you were here to see me." Brother Jahid-Ali looked hopeful.

Denise looked away and mumbled. "I didn't know that you would be here tonight."

"I told you on Friday that I come here every Tuesday and Thursday." What he didn't tell her was that he usually met Maulana Imhotep here on those nights. They usually discussed Maulana Imhotep's agenda and plans for the up-coming meetings held every Sunday. He had never missed a meeting, but was willing to risk the wrath of the mfalme. Brother Jahid-Ali knew that if he did not take advantage of this opportunity, he might not get to see Denise again. "Never mind, let's get out of here."

This time Denise did not resist. She wanted to be with him and secretly hoped that when they were away from the crowd that he would kiss her again.

Once in his VW bus, Brother Jahid-Ali began speaking. "I thought about you all weekend." He paused. "Did you think about me?"

She missed him too, but wasn't going to tell him so. Instead she lied. "I was so busy this weekend, I didn't have a chance to."

"What did you do?"

"I did so much, I don't know where to begin." She was about to go into a long spiel about all of the imaginary things she did, but decided against it. If he had asked her about the weekend before last, she would have given him a laundry list of events beginning with Freedom School for the children to arts and crafts to helping best (now ex-best) friend Shelly write an article for *Black Panther* newspaper, ending with target practice in the desert. "What is your position in the WEB organization?"

"I am first Lion to Maulana Imhotep."

"And what does that mean?" Denise was fascinated and wanted to know why he joined.

"I provide first line of security for him, and I am his chief advisor. I train the other Lions, teach Swahili, and assist in the planning and implementation of the cultural revolution that will be upon us at any time." Brother Jahid-Ali held back on his other duties. If he told her that he was in charge of surveillance of the Black Panther Party, she would surely hate him.

"What else do you do?"

"I preside as second in command at the Kwanza celebration."

"What is that?" Denise was amazed. There were so many levels to WEB.

"It is an Afro-American celebration. It is a seven-day period of joy, beginning the day after Christmas. Each day a different candle is lit and a gift is exchanged with a loved one." He winked at her. "I will celebrate Kwanza with you this year."

"We'll see about that."

"What are your duties in the Panthers?" It was his turn to inquire into Denise's life.

Denise was intentionally vague. "I work at the John Huggins Free Breakfast for Children school and ditch the F.B.I, but I told you that last time I saw you. You know, typical revolutionary work. Back to you, how did you get your name—Jahid-Ali?"

"Maulana Imhotep gave it to me," he said with pride.

"Are you married?"

He hesitated and then answered. "Yes."

"In that case, you need to take me home." Denise had heard about brothas in the WEB organization having more than one wife.

"I am married to WEB," Brother Jahid-Ali answered seriously.

"You say that like you mean it." Denise gave him a beguiling smile.

"I do. Maulana Imhotep says that WEB is the future for all Black people."

"I'm tired of hearing what Maulana Imhotep says. What do *you* say? Do you ever think for yourself?"

"Yes, Foxy Brown, I have dreams and plans of my own." Her outfit was definitely foxy and he couldn't wait to wrap his arms around her waist.

"If you are dreaming that everybody is going to drink Coca Cola and wear dashikis, you might as well wake up right now," Denise lightened her antagonism with a smile.

They pulled into a deserted parking lot that was adjacent to Dockweiler State Beach. Denise had come here once for her cousin Kelly's birthday party and bonfire.

"I've never told anyone this before, but there is life after WEB. Don't you agree?" Brother Jahid-Ali said nonchalantly. He was baiting her to see just how strong was her commitment to the movement.

"No. There might be life after WEB, but for the rest of us, the struggle continues. I will continue to work for the revolution for as long as it takes. You know that the revolution will not be televised," Denise said with conviction.

"Now who's quoting someone else?" Brother Jahid-Ali cocked his head to the side and looked intensely into her eyes.

"Dig it brotha. You know as well as I do that revolution is imminent." Denise's conviction was strong.

"It might and might not be. Denise, look at what's happening in the world."

"Like what?"

"Let's take the Vietnam war. Nixon is going to have to bring the troops home soon. As long as Black people were dying in rallies no one cared. Now that white students are being killed by the police, he's got to do something. Also, Black people have gained rights through those government programs, like Kedren and the Watts Health Foundation."

"Those programs are all run by poverty pimps. The bourgeois don't care about the people. All they care about is getting their chump change from the fascists who run this decadent country." Denise was indignant. "As for the war in Vietnam, Nixon has to bring the troops back home if he plans to win another term in the White House."

Brother Jahid-Ali stared ahead at the darkness. Denise was exactly what the Black Power Movement needed. She was young, smart, and naive. He had watched many young students like her get set up for a disappointment. He hoped that she got out before it consumed her and made her into a bitter woman. "You have so much to learn."

"And I guess you know everything, huh Priest?" Denise giggled.

He ignored her comparison to Ron O'Neil. "No, I just don't want to see you get hurt." Brother Jahid-Ali embraced her. "You look so much prettier in the moonlight." He kissed her.

"So do you." Denise removed his glasses and returned his kiss.

"Denise—"

"Sh. Just hold me."

Brother Jahid-Ali was so easy to talk to. She reminded

herself not to get too caught up. "This is a fantasy. You know that we can't get involved with each other."

He sucked her bottom lip. "Who says we can't?"

Eight

Two weeks later, Brother Jahid-Ali was gathering material for Maulana Imhotep. He was sitting at a metal desk at the office on Vermont. Normally, he worked at home, but he was behind getting this speech written. There was going to be a rally at UCLA in a couple of days, and Brother Jahid-Ali was in a hurry to complete the speech that Maulana Imhotep would deliver. The substance of the speech was Negro History and why it was only focused on one week out of the year. Maulana Imhotep wanted to challenge the students at UCLA to demand that Negro History week be expanded to every month of the year.

It was after 10 P.M. and the office was still buzzing. Sistas were cleaning the office and the brothas were trying their hardest to rap with them. It saddened Brother Jahid-Ali that in the midst of fighting for cultural revolution and conscious raising, brothas treated sistas with little or no respect. Denise was right, his organization was not immune to jive treatment of its women.

Ordinarily, speech writing was easy for Brother Jahid-Ali. He just researched the topic and put pen to paper. Tonight his brain and his hand would not agree on what to say. He told himself it was a form of campaign writing, a skill he would need later on when he left WEB. That was his problem. He was ready to leave WEB, but did not want to admit that to himself. There wasn't even anyone he could tell. His fellow Lions would say that he was a punk revolutionary and deem him irrevelant. And Maulana Imhotep might not let him live if he left. He saw the pain that came with being a revolutionary. And to get suspended wasn't nothin' nice. He didn't think that he was strong enough to take the ostracism. Denise was strong. In a couple of weeks, she would go back to the Black Panthers. If the situation were reversed and he had been suspended, he didn't think he'd ever be able to return to WEB.

Maulana Imhotep would go through the roof if found out about his plans to leave. Brother Jahid-Ali was divided over the issue himself. While he liked the WEB organization and what it stood for, he was beginning to feel out of touch. He felt himself growing and moving past some of the rhetoric.

Each day had become more and more challenging and it was becoming easier to lie to Maulana Imhotep about his whereabouts the last two Tuesday nights. He knew that their secret rendezvous were dangerous, but Denise was worth it. She had captured his spirit and was always on his mind.

Standing and stretching, Brother Jahid-Ali dropped the pen onto the yellow notepad. Maulana Imhotep would be arriving any minute, and the speech was still only half-written.

As if on cue, Maulana Imhotep came through the door. "Habari gani, Brother Jahid-Ali." Maulana Imhotep's entourage had grown over the years. It went from four Lions to eight and his wife travelled with him.

"Habari gani, Maulana Imhotep." He lowered his eyes to the floor. "That's a cold buba you are wearing." Maulana Imhotep's dashiki was bright orange with silver thread intricately sewn into swirls. There were polished silver buttons the size of silver dollars glued onto the bottom of the buba. His light gray turtleneck, which was underneath the V-neck dashiki, matched the silver thread. Maulana Imhotep's black pants complemented the black African traditional dress worn by his wife, Tasha.

"Thank you brotha. We are going to a play at the Watts Coffee house tonight. We're going and so are you."

Caught off guard, Brother Jahid-Ali's eyes widened. "Mfalme, please forgive me, I forgot all about it." The whole office came to a screeching halt. It was a fairly large office with six metal desks, four typewriters and a mimeograph machine.

"I guess that young sista that you've been seen with at the Watts Coffee House has clouded your mind."

Brother Jahid-Ali knew not to interrupt Maulana Imhotep. The silence was growing thicker.

"It appears that the sistas here are not good enough for you," Maulana Imhotep said circumspectly.

"The sistas in the WEB organization are as beautiful as mother Africa herself."

Maulana Imhotep jabbed his silver capped staff into the floor. "If that's the case, why are you looking elsewhere?" His high pitched voice was screeching in Brother Jahid-Ali's ears.

"I'm not looking Maulana Imhotep," mumbled Brother Jahid-Ali.

Maulana Imhotep walked right up to him and said, "Look at me."

The brotha obeyed. He willed himself not to blink. One long minute passed and the muscles in Brother Jahid-Ali's eyes were beginning to twitch. Maulana Imhotep finally left and continued his tour up and down the main aisle of the office and wordlessly inspected everything and everyone. Brother Jahid-Ali hadn't even realized that he had stopped breathing until his head began to feel light.

Lion Ivory rushed and cleared a seat for Maulana Imhotep to sit. Everyone lowered their eyes when he stood near them. This form of deference was beginning to get old to Brother Jahid-Ali and was another reason why he was ready to leave WEB. Once Maulana was seated he focused his attention on Brother Jahid-Ali. "Is the speech finished?"

"Almost." He cleared his throat.

Maulana Imhotep sighed heavily. "Read me what you have."

Brother Jahid-Ali adjusted his glasses and began to read aloud. "Habari gani, brothas and sistas. Negro History week is just that one week, yet we've been in this country for three hundred and fifty years. Known as the white man's burden, Negro people in this country have received nothing but disrespect . . ."

Maulana Imhotep listened with his eyes closed. He liked the way the young brotha's voice dipped and swayed to the rhythm of his words. Brother Jahid-Ali had been a good choice for head of the Lions. Lately, however, things didn't lay right. Maulana Imhotep had a hunch that his star pupil had other things on his mind. "Right on, brotha. That was a righteous speech."

Brother Jahid-Ali nodded and set the tablet back on the table. "Right on. I'll have the rest of it completed tonight."

"The speech will have to wait until tomorrow, you are coming with us tonight."

He removed his glasses. "Maulana Imhotep, I can't make it tonight. I have some things to complete for tomorrow and tonight is the only time I can finish them." Brother Jahid-Ali said respectfully.

"If the speech had've been written when it was supposed to, then we wouldn't be having this conversation," Maulana said sarcastically.

"You're right Maulana Imhotep." He chose his words carefully. "I fell behind and in order to ensure that it doesn't happen again, I think that Bijou and Ivory should go with you tonight."

Maulana Imhotep gripped his staff until his brown knuckles turned white. "We will speak tomorrow."

With Maulana Imhotep out of the way, Brother Jahid-Ali completed the speech in peace. He lied when he told him that he had work to finish. Truth was he did not want to be bothered with Maulana Imhotep.

Denise was riding the bus to campus. She was looking out of the window and thought she saw Shelly. When she looked again, she realized that she was wrong. Denise had not thought about Shelly in two weeks. She had gotten caught up in her research in the library and her budding relationship with Brother Jahid-Ali.

Denise closed her eyes and thought of the day she was suspended. *How could Shelly be so cold to her?* she thought to herself. She replayed the days leading up to her suspension and could not pinpoint the exact moment she lost Shelly to the Panthers. Denise admitted their shared loyalty to the party, and recognized that she stopped speaking to her family, but she would never in a million years have guessed that she would do her like that.

No use having a pity party. It was useless to look for answers. Shelly was in love with Kweli and anything he said was gospel. Denise felt sorry for Shelly and hoped that her love for Kweli did not inspire her to have a baby for the revolution. Pauletta had told her about the women who had children for the revolution. While the concept was a good one, the women usually cared for the children alone. Pauletta warned Denise not to fall into that trap. Denise promised that she wouldn't, although she didn't know if Shelly would be as strong.

When Kweli and Shelly first got together, Denise was excited. For the first time, Shelly was faithful and seemed to be fulfilled. She was comfortable with herself and Kweli brought out the best in her. Under Kweli's guidance, Shelly's writing flourished and level of commitment deepened. Initially, he challenged her and made her think. Later, their relationship changed. Shelly began to echo everything Kweli said. Her whole spirit was consumed by him and Shelly's interest in struggling for the people became dependent upon what Kweli thought, said or did.

Denise never thought that a man would get the best of her friend. Whatever, she was through thinking about Shelly. Kweli was Shelly's problem and if she let her man control her, then that's what she got for choosing a man over friendship. Denise was getting mad all over again. There was one good thing that came out of her suspension, she learned who her friends were. She had Brother Jahid-Ali to thank for that.

Thinking of him, her body quivered. It was almost June and yet she felt cool just thinking about him. She could still feel his breath on her face from several days before. His caress was so gentle. Brother Jahid-Ali did not make her feel guilty for being a revolutionary princess. He made her want to hug herself right there on the bus.

Denise tried to return to reality. Brother Jahid-Ali was

tampering with her soul. On the one hand, she felt connected to him, on the other hand, he was ruining her authenticity. There was no way she could fall in love with the enemy. It just couldn't happen; unfortunately there was no denying the fact that he had touched something inside of her. She needed to clear her mind. If it wasn't for her daily trips to the library at UCLA, Denise would go crazy thinking about Shelly, Kweli, being suspended, and her new love, Brother Jahid-Ali.

Denise reached up and pulled the cord that ran the length of the bus. The ting ting sound alerted the bus driver that she had arrived at her stop. The noise also jolted her attention back to why she was in Westwood. Denise needed information. She did not want Kweli to think that she had ceased studying revolutionary thought. Denise was serious about climbing the ranks in the party.

After getting off of the bus, Denise pulled the collar up on her shirt. She did not want anyone to recognize her as she walked to the library. There were only two weeks left of her suspension.

Nine

"Habari gani, handsome." Denise greeted Brother Jahid-Ali with a smile.

"I'm impressed." He joined her at what had become 'their' table at the Watts Coffee House.

It had been an excruciating week for Brother Jahid-Ali. All he did was work and think of her. He didn't realize how much he missed her until he was staring at her smooth skin. "Is there any place we can go?" He began to look around the room furtively.

"Where's the fire?" Denise followed his gaze, but did not see anything out of the ordinary. Brother Jahid-Ali's paranoia was catching and Denise found herself in a mild state of panic. "What's shakin'?"

He saw the worried look on her face and laughed. "Oh nothing, sweetheart. I just wanted to pick up where we left off." He blew a kiss to her from across the table.

"Oh." Denise pouted because she wanted to be alone with him, too, but didn't know where to take him. There was no way she could take him to Pauletta's. Well, maybe she could. Pauletta was cool and since she was on her way out of the party, she might not mind. But then again, WEB was the enemy and Brother Jahid-Ali wasn't exactly easy to overlook. "I don't know about all that."

"I'd take you to my pad, but one of the Lions is teaching the women how to sew bubas there."

"In other words, a bunch of chicks are at your pad learning to beautify themselves for the men, while the brothas are out socializing."

"Denise, I don't feel like being revolutionary tonight. For once, can we have an evening without contemplating the fate of the people?" His voice was heavy with disgust. "I fight the man everyday, and the last thing I want to do is fight with you."

"See, that's the difference between me and you. The revolution doesn't stop because I'm tired or hungry or disgusted with the way brothas treat sistas. The revolution is with me at all times. That's why I take the long route to the library every single day to learn more about struggle and commitment." Her voice deepened. "Brotha, as long as children go to bed hungry at night and black, brown, yellow, and red people are massacred by capitalism, I will continue to contemplate the fate of the people. This is not a game."

Brother Jahid-Ali slammed his fist down on the table and leaned in Denise's face. "I know that, Denise." She did not flinch. This was the type of challenging Denise needed to prep her for her next conversation with Kweli. The room fell silent.

Two Lions ran to Brother Jahid-Ali's aide. Realizing their discussion had turned combative, he attempted to relax. "Look, I'm not trying to down the movement . . . I just don't believe that it needs to consume my every waking moment. There will be life after the revolution." He waved his men away, but they did not move. "That's all I'm sayin', Denise."

"Brother Bijou, you and Brother Ivory can go."

"Brother Jahid-Ali, who is this woman?" Brother Bijou asked defiantly.

"She's a friend of mine," Brother Jahid-Ali said dismissively.

"Isn't this the same woman who threw her drink on you at the Coffee House?"

"Yes and it's not a problem." Brother Jahid-Ali had to think quickly. "Denise, I'd like you to meet Brothers Bijou and Ivory."

"Habari gani, sister."

"Habari gani, brothers." Denise winked at Brother Jahid-Ali. Fortunately, Denise was wearing civilian clothes, so the Lions did not suspect her true identity.

Sensing that the situation was under control, Brothers Bijou and Ivory left Brother Jahid-Ali's side.

"Denise, I need to talk to those Brothers for a moment, so that they won't come back over here."

"Okay."

Brother Jahid-Ali and his men stepped outside for about five minutes. Denise hoped that he was able to throw them off.

"I told them that you were my old lady from way back and that's why you threw the wine on me the last time they saw you."

"Did they believe you?"

"Of course, they believed me. I'm their superior."

"Right on." Denise also relaxed. At that moment, the passion in his voice caused her to lean forward and kiss him playfully on the lips. "I just thought of someplace we could go."

When they got outside of the coffee house, Denise took his thick hand in hers.

"Where are we going?" he asked. Brother Jahid-Ali

wasn't worried, he would put his life in her hands any day of the week.

She was silent for a few seconds. Denise cleared her throat. She was taking a risk and did not want to appear unsure about her decision. "I'm taking you to my pad." Her certainty was returning. "Well, it's not really mine, I'm just crashing there until my suspension is up."

"Cool."

Pauletta's apartment was four blocks from the Watts Coffee House. Denise took Brother Jahid-Ali on the scenic route, so that he would not know how to get there. It was a silly gesture on her part. They were in the middle of WEB territory and she was sure that he knew every street within a five mile radius. Denise watched him anyway, though he never asked her what street they were going to or appear to recognize Pauletta's street.

Once they arrived at Pauletta's apartment, Denise rapped softly on the door. Pauletta lived on the ground floor of a two-story apartment building. It was an unassuming structure, just the kind of place that a real revolutionary would live in. The neighborhood was lively. This was due to the fact that a middle school was located across the street.

"Don't you have a key?" he asked.

"Yeah, but she might be in there and I don't want to surprise her, especially since I have company."

Brother Jahid-Ali was relieved to learn that Denise did not live with a man.

As luck would have it, Pauletta was not home, nor did it appear that she had been home at all that day. That wasn't unusual. In the last couple of weeks, Pauletta would disappear or go out of town on a mission. Although the apartment was only big enough for one person, Pauletta and Denise managed to stay out of one another's way. Pauletta worked all day and night, and Denise spent most of her time at the library or at the Watts Coffee House.

Denise walked over to the card table, which doubled as the kitchen table, and set her purse down. There was a kitchenette, mini refrigerator and incense all over the place. Pauletta said that the incense released her spirit and opened her mind, so she could work late into the night. Pauletta also smoked weed, listened to John Coltrane and rapped with someone on the telephone for hours. Denise suspected that she was speaking to a man, who lived in another state, because she never saw Pauletta with anyone. All in all, their living arrangement worked and Denise was eternally grateful to Pauletta.

Denise led Brother Jahid-Ali over to the huge brown, blue, black, and gold patchwork pillow that took up most of the floor in the front room. The pillow had an Indian design on it. Denise thought that Pauletta bought it at a reservation near Palm Springs. Each color represented something, but Denise didn't know what. "Have a seat."

"I want to show you something," she said over her shoulder as she disappeared into the room she shared with Pauletta. Their bedroom was really more of an office than a place to sleep. If Pauletta was home and working, Denise slept on the pillow in the front room. Otherwise, she slept in an army green sleeping bag on the floor.

Brother Jahid-Ali stretched his legs out in front of him and leaned back on the pillow. His brown dashiki matched the pillow he was lying on. He traced the thread on the pillow and looked around the small but neat apartment. There were poster boards stacked in one corner, a typewriter in another corner, leaflets everywhere and a beaded curtain that separated the front room from the bedroom and bathroom. The multicolored beads caught his attention.

Denise had just passed through them, and the clack clack of the beads was almost melodic.

Denise reentered the room with a stack of books in her arms.

"You weren't jivin'! You have been studying." He jumped up from his seat and took the books from her arms. "Let's see what you've got here." Brother Jahid-Ali followed Denise over to the pillow and sat cross-legged in front of her. *The Autobiography of Malcolm X* by Alex Haley, *Long Shadow of Little Rock* by Daisy Bates, *Things Fall Apart* by Chinua Achebe and I see that you sneaked in some poetry by Nikki Giovanni. I can understand the first three, but how does Nikki figure into this?" He was impressed by her collection.

"I love Nikki. She's a bad sista, who isn't afraid to say what's on her mind." Denise enjoyed sharing with him. He made her feel confident. "I also have a sociology book."

"You are serious, aren't you?" Brother Jahid-Ali stroked Denise's neck. "I love the fact that you have your own mind. So many brothers and sisters just repeat what they've heard. You're doing your own investigating and are not afraid to say what it is and what it ain't."

She nodded in agreement. "Brotha, you'd be amazed at how many sistas could run circles around the leadership of the Panthers, WEB, NAACP and all of the other reactionary organizations!" Denise was getting excited. She finally had someone to release her thoughts to without fear of reprimand. "Women's voices get drowned out by all that macho bull. We need a bigger voice and we need to be heard, but instead we are silenced." She picked up Nikki's book. "That's why I dig her so much. Men and women respect her fire."

"So do you want to be like her?" He was still stroking her neck.

If his touch didn't feel so good, Denise would have laughed out loud. Oh, he was wearin' her down. "No. Nikki's too much of an individualist for me. She has her own thang goin' on. I enjoy workin' with the people too much."

Denise made sense. Nikki had been criticized for having her own agenda. Maybe Nikki knew something the others didn't. Brother Jahid-Ali uncrossed his legs and gently laid her head down in his lap. "I want to read to you."

No one had ever read to her before. "I can dig that." Denise closed her eyes.

Brother Jahid-Ali fumbled with Nikki's book. "Ah ha, here it is." He removed his glasses. "Are you comfortable?"

She closed her eyes. "Yes." Her voice was breathy and deep.

He spoke. "Introducing Me"—

From out of the depths/of my soul I'm calling/hoping that you will/respond to the lonely/lover's plea./And come to hear more of my story/and if you can dig it, talk to me./My name is Jahid-Ali, and/I'm a revolutionary./A lifestyle so hard/and so cold that love/I had all but forgotten/how to let flow/I felt that I didn't have time/nor could I afford to let anyone get close/And my pent up emotion/and my need to feel/tenderness I expressed/in my anger and I raged/against the oppressor and/I screamed to be free!

He paused. "Baby, are you still with me?" Brother Jahid-Ali hoped that he wasn't getting too deep.

"Every step of the way." Denise was enjoying the song in his voice.

"Till one day I looked/around and I was alone/with my comrades jailed/scattered or dead, and/my people afraid of me./Against a racist, exploitive/bloody system so treacherous/How did the people expect me to be?/With deep contempt and/confusion I searched/for the answer to why/the people I loved turned their backs on me./I went on existing/as a writer, gang counselor, teacher, hustler, dopefiend, pimp/ But all these activities/were only masks to hide this/Broken heart./I felt guilt ridden and/pain for those who/over the years had/got hurt and I ran/and I ran 'till my/little game played/out./And I wound/up in jail, where/I ran deep into me . . . /"

The rhythm of his voice gripped Denise deep within. "I hear you brotha, keep blowin'." He penetrated her soul. For the first time, she realized the divisions between men and women. For the second time in her life, she was forbidden to be who she wanted to be, because of some letters. This time, WEB, last time BSA. In an instant, she promised herself that she would not let rhetoric come between her and Brother Jahid-Ali.

For I yearn for love/but I've been so cruel/to love, that now my/love is gone from me./And in this void I linger/And, for now, all that I/seek are some mellow/words, a tender thought/an open mind and an/open heart.

He stopped again. "Denise open your eyes." She sensed the urgency in his voice and the pain in his heart.

" 'Sista, these are the beginning phrases to a new song,

and if you can catch the rhythm, Hey! come swing along.' "[1]

Denise turned to face him completely. "Brotha, Nikki didn't write that poem."

He smiled. "I know. Did you dig it?"

"Dig it? I loved it!" She threw her arms around his neck and kissed him hungrily. "I didn't know that you were a poet. What else have you written?"

He squeezed her tightly. "I didn't write that, my best friend did."

"Where is he?"

He almost told her the truth. "Even though I didn't write that poem, it expresses how lonely I feel sometimes."

"Who wrote it?"

"Someone you don't know, and I can't say so please don't ask me again," he said evasively.

Denise was too caught up in the euphoria of the moment to notice the bittersweet shadow that crossed his face.

"Do you have anything to drink?' he said changing the subject.

"Oh yeah. I should have offered you something earlier. What would you like?"

"Water's fine."

While Denise was in the kitchen, Brother Jahid-Ali went over to the stereo and flipped through the records.

From the kitchen, Denise yelled out. "That really was a bad poem. You should blow down at the Coffee House. You're just as good as the regular poets who go there."

"Niecie, I don't have time to be a poet. I've got work to do." He caught himself. "Is it cool that I call you, Niecie?"

---

[1]Austin, Harold, *En Route To Saoud*, c. 1996

She handed him a blue glass with ice water filled to the brim. "Baby, after that poem, you can call me anything you want." Denise revelled in the passion of his poem and felt close to him for the very first time.

Together they flipped through Pauletta's albums: John Coltrane, Gil Scott Heron, Miles and the prophet from San Francisco, Sly and the Family Stone. Denise and Brother Jahid-Ali had retreated into their own private worlds. He was thinking about how the revolution was a jealous task master and once again returned to the place that asked what's goin' on? In contrast, Denise was more excited than she'd ever been. Brother Jahid-Ali was a mystery to her. There was so much inside of him. Denise could see why he was so tired. It was hard being a soldier for the people, especially one who was so lonely.

She broke the spell of silence. "Kweli wrote that poem, didn't he?" Denise placed her hand over his.

Brother Jahid-Ali winced when she said Kweli's name. "What makes you say that?"

"You used the word 'comrade' in the poem. 'Lions' don't use words like that."

He rubbed his knitted brow. If his loneliness was to end, he had to tell her the truth. "Yes."

"I heard that you two used to be friends."

Brother Jahid-Ali searched for his glasses. When he finally found them, he mumbled, "Yeah, that was a long time ago."

Denise did not press the issue. "Can I ask you something else?"

He started to say no, but saw the twinkle in her amber-colored eyes. "Yes, Denise."

"Are you okay? I mean, you walk around with your chest puffed out, bald head glistening in the moonlight, dashiki blowin' in the breeze, and I just never would have guessed that you were so lonely. I felt it in the words of the poem. And even though you did not write it, the loneliness is there with you. I want to know how I can make it go away." Her eyes changed to the color of honey.

For the second time that night, Brother Jahid-Ali took his glasses off. "It might take a long time."

Denise felt the longing in his eyes. "I'm not going anywhere."

He removed the gold love beads from around her neck. "Is Pauletta coming home anytime soon?"

"I don't think so."

Brother Jahid-Ali slowly undressed her. He unbuttoned her green polyester blouse and kissed the base of her throat. She felt hot chills spread all over her body. The last time she made love, it was with Charles. He was definitely a boy compared to the man who was caressing her and whispering sweetly in her ear. Tonight, Brother Jahid-Ali would make her a woman.

His touch was so gentle she forgot where she was. Denise closed her eyes and gasped when his mouth brushed past her exposed nipple. She found the bottom of his brown buba and lifted it over his head.

She was seeking destiny in his arms. Brother Jahid-Ali kissed the soft spot between her collarbone and shoulder. Her body began to respond and a smile as big as Mississippi spread across his face. Tonight, he would be lonely no more.

Ten

Denise was getting nervous. There was only one week left to the end of her suspension, and she felt torn. On the one hand, she was ecstatic about returning to the Black Panthers. She missed her students at the Freedom school and the adults she taught political education courses to. With all of her studying, Denise would be able to confront Kweli and prove to him that she was worthy of moving up the ranks within the party. She would also be able to move back to her old apartment. Her mind paused at that thought. Moving back would mean having Shelly in her life again. Denise did not know if she was ready for that.

Her one big reservation about rejoining her comrades was Brother Jahid-Ali. Denise had fallen in love with him and didn't know how she could give her one hundred percent to the party and still be with him. Her heart ached with panic. So far, they had not discussed how they would continue their relationship once her suspension was up.

In the three weeks that she had been suspended, Denise had grown. She believed that she was stronger, smarter and most importantly, seeing the revolution through open eyes. Her studies taught her that Mao was bad, but he also preached that the identity of political wisdom was a man. Women were not part of his teaching. This infuriated her, especially since she taught P.E. to men and women. Her favorite mantra was "We Have Nothing To Lose But Our Chains." Upon first hearing those words, Denise lighted up. She wholeheartedly agreed that black, brown, yellow, red, and poor people had nothing to lose but the chains of oppression and capitalism. If only she had known the real meaning behind Mao's words, Denise never would have uttered them. Freedom was the ultimate goal of a people poised on the brink of revolution. Now, she learned that Mao, like other chauvinistic leaders, was perpetuating patriarchy. By exhorting the venerable wisdom of men, women were once again silenced. *"Hell,"* she said out loud to herself, *"Women carry the legacy of civil rights in their blood and in their wombs!"* It was hard to conceal her rage. When would brothas and sistas learn that paternalism within liberation movements was a carbon copy of the way white men treated black men?

Denise reached for her leather jacket. She hated to lug a jacket all the way to the library, but June weather in Los Angeles was often cool. This year was no exception. Fortunately for Denise, the library was warm inside. Funny, she had not spent this much time in the library since she worked in the College Library a few years before.

It was five o'clock and the library was closing early for the Fourth of July holiday weekend. *Independence Day,* she scoffed, *for whom?* She knew that she would not spend her weekend eating pork ribs, pork n' beans, potato salad and drinking lemonade like the rest of the reactionary Negroes. Denise was going to boycott the fireworks and irrelevant celebrating that went on.

The year before the Fourth of July fell on a Thursday, not like the day of the week mattered. Denise worked at the school and assisted the sistas and brotha who taught the political education classes, as well. She did not teach by herself until October 1969. She had been in the party about ten months by that time, but Denise felt like she'd been in the Black Panther Party her whole life. Sometimes, it was easy for Denise to forget what her life was like before her consciousness was raised.

This year, she planned to spend her Friday evening with Brother Jahid-Ali. Denise smiled at the thought of his strong arms holding her after they made love. Without Pauletta or Brother Jahid-Ali, she didn't think that she would have made it through her suspension. Then, she had an idea! Denise would plan a celebration of her own. To-night she would introduce Pauletta to Brother Jahid-Ali. This would be Denise's second expression of her new self. The first was sharing her love for the revolution and her body with Brother Jahid-Ali.

Denise picked up her pace. She had to hurry, so as not to miss the last bus to Pauletta's apartment. Denise hoped Pauletta was home because she wanted to tell Pauletta about meeting Brother Jahid-Ali, before she brought him home.

Pauletta was sitting at the card table, typing away when Denise got home. Her afro was so big that Denise could only hear the typewriter and not see it.

"Hi Pauletta." Denise sat in the fold-a-way chair across from her.

"Hey, girl." Pauletta glanced up from the typewriter with a pencil in her mouth. "How are your studies going?"

"Cool." Denise tried to sound nonchalant, but her in-sides were jumping. "What'cha workin' on?" She reached across the table and picked up three typed sheets. Denise concentrated on the pages in her hand, but was unable to hide the smile that must have been a mile wide on her face.

Pauletta stopped typing and looked at Denise. "That's the first time since you moved in that I've seen you smile. Looks like someone's excited about something."

"Oh, well, my suspension is up in a week and I'm ready to get back to my life. I really appreciate you taking me in. You could have gotten into a lot of trouble."

The tap-tapping noise of the typewriter keys resumed. "No one said that revolution was gonna be easy," Pauletta said sincerely. "How do you feel about returning to the party?"

"I guess about the same as you do about leaving it."

"What makes you say that?" Pauletta got up and grabbed a box of Kool cigarettes.

"When I first moved in, you said that it was time for you to go. Almost thirty days later, it is time for me to return. I've learned a lot and I need an opportunity to prove myself to Kweli." Denise moved to the mini fridge and pulled out last night's bottle of red wine. She found two plastic cups in the cupboard and poured a cup of wine for herself and Pauletta.

"So, you're not nervous." Pauletta sipped her wine slowly, as she handed Denise a cigarette.

"Yes and no." Denise inhaled deeply. "I don't know how my comrades are going to treat me, you dig? And—" She took a swig of wine. "I don't know what I'm going to do about Shelly."

"That's your best friend, right?"

Denise scowled. "Ex-best friend." She drained her cup. "I can't believe that she turned on me like that!"

"That's some bull," Pauletta said with conviction. She stamped out her cigarette in the glass ashtray that was next to the typewriter. "Shelly probably thinks she is in love with Kweli, and that's why she did what she did." She had a far away look in her eyes.

Denise was shocked. "You're not defending her are you?"

The far away look in Pauletta's eyes turned soft. "No, not at all. I'm just saying that when a woman is in love, she'll do a lot of things against her better judgment."

"Whatever." Denise rolled her eyes. "If Shelly calls that love, she's got another thing coming!"

"I can dig that. Kweli isn't capable of truly loving anyone but himself and the party."

Denise sensed a shift in the spirit of their conversation. When she first sat down, Denise was terrified of telling Pauletta about Brother Jahid-Ali. Now, it seemed that Pauletta was the one with the secret. Denise hesitated, but asked anyway, "Pauletta, are you speaking from personal experience?"

Pauletta did not answer right away. Then, "Like you and Shelly, Kweli brought me into the party. He had just joined so we were on more or less equal footing. We sold the *Black Panther* together, smoked weed together, listened to Coltrane, and recruited people to join the party. I dug him and he dug me, and so one thing led to another, and before we knew it, I was in love." Pauletta's voice was wistful.

"Did he love you back?" Denise asked in a small voice.

"I thought he did, but I learned the hard way." Pauletta patted her 'fro. "Men like Kweli are lonely beyond repair. I hope your girl, Shelly, knows that she's in for heartbreak." Pauletta's voice rose in a clear and confident manner.

"I don't know what to say. I'm sorry, I didn't know." Denise thought about the poem Brother Jahid-Ali recited to her and had to blink, to hold back the tears that had formed in her eyes. Denise knew that Pauletta was not lying about Comrade Kweli.

"Don't worry about it, that was a long time ago." She collected her material from the table and spread everything out on the floor.

For an instant, Denise felt sorry for Shelly. Shelly had no clue what was in store for her. "I have something to tell you." Pauletta nodded and waited for Denise to speak. "I want you to meet someone. His name is Brother Jahid-Ali."

"He's with WEB, right?" Pauletta separated the paper into three piles.

"Yeah." Denise put her hands in her lap.

"That brotha's also a Lion." It was more of a statement and less of a question.

Denise's voice went up an octave. "Yeah."

"Isn't he Maulana Imhotep's right hand man?" Pauletta turned and looked at Denise.

"I—I think so." Denise's head was bowed. She was beginning to feel like a fool.

Pauletta looked Denise square in the face. "Denise," she said firmly. "Look at me."

Denise slowly raised her eyes, which had turned a dark brown. "Okay, yes, yes that's the one."

"Damn girl! What is wrong with you? Are you a glutton for punishment or what?"

"I know that it's stupid and I tried not to fall in love with him. It just happened."

"Denise, isn't he the reason you were suspended in the first place?" Pauletta threw her hands in the air. "What's wrong with the child?" Pauletta asked the ceiling.

"Yeah. I didn't know him then." Denise defended herself.

"When did you two start seeing each other?" Pauletta

raised her hand. "Never mind, I really don't want to know.—"

Denise cut her off. "Listen, listen. I saw the brotha the first night I went to the Watts Coffee House. I didn't know he would be there. It was your idea that I go there," Denise said defensively. The night she was suspended fell upon her like bricks.

"So this is my fault?" Pauletta pretended to be mad.

"Sort of—" Denise shrugged.

"Oh, hell no."

"Pauletta, when I realized it was him, I threw my sangria on him." Denise laughed at the memory of that night. "Then we went to eat and talked. That's it."

"That's it! Don't you know that that's all it takes?" Pauletta fell onto the floor laughing. "What am I going to do with you?"

"Can I bring him by to meet you?"

Pauletta was still laughing. "Sure. You know what?"

"No, what?"

"You crazy. But I guess if a brotha that bad was after me, I'd have trouble surrendering to him." Pauletta grew serious for a moment, "Are you sure that this isn't a set up?"

"Yes." Denise said confidently.

"How do you know that he's not a plant? Maybe this is a test and Kweli is trying to see if you are going to fail." Pauletta was playing devil's advocate.

A shadow of doubt clouded Denise's face. "That's a good question." Denise shook her head. "No, Pauletta, he's not like that. Brother Jahid-Ali isn't like that at all."

"How do you know?"

"I just do. I can feel it." Denise said a silent prayer. She was placing a lot of faith in someone she just met.

"I hope you're right." Pauletta winked at her. "I can't wait to meet him."

"Good, I knew you would understand." Denise ran over to Pauletta and hugged her. "Thanks."

This was the last Friday that Denise would be going to the Watts Coffee House. She knew that once she rejoined her comrades and put on her Panther uniform, she would no longer be welcome in that place. It saddened her to think that Black people could divide themselves so easily.

As expected, Brother Jahid-Ali was sitting at *their* table.

"Hi baby." Denise kissed the top of his bald head.

He grabbed Denise around her waist and pulled her down onto his lap. "How was your day?"

"It was good."

A woman was playing the piano and singing a smooth ballad. "I missed you."

Denise kissed the tip of his broad nose. "I missed you too."

"Do you want to stay here or go elsewhere?" He was nibbling on her ear.

"Let's listen to the music for awhile." Denise closed her eyes and listened to the woman's throaty rendition of Aretha Franklin's "Natural Woman."

Brother Jahid-Ali squeezed her tightly. "Anything you want, baby." He offered his cup to her. "Do you want me to buy you a drink?"

"Maybe later." Denise whispered. After her talk with Pauletta, she felt brand new. She mused to herself that her mother was right about one thing, you can pick your friends, you can't necessarily choose who to fall in love with.

After the woman finished singing, a young brotha from the back of the room walked up to the stage and sat down on the stool. He cocked his big red and green apple hat to the side and pulled a sheet of paper from out of his back pocket. He wore denim window pane pants and a red velour pullover, V-neck shirt. His poem was entitled "Rebirth of a Revolutionary." It was short, militant and to the point.

When the brotha was finished blowin', several people in the audience said, "Right on." Denise was so wrapped up in her thoughts, she didn't even realize that he was finished.

There was a pause in the program. The couple at the next table lit an incense and somebody dimmed the lights. The mood of the room had changed from revolutionary to romantic.

Brother Jahid-Ali tapped Denise on her thigh. "I need to speak to that brotha over there." He pointed to a man, who appeared to be a waiter. "I'll be right back."

Denise stood up and let Brother Jahid-Ali pass. He seemed to be taking an excessive amount of time to return. Just as she was about to go looking for him, he walked out onto the middle of the stage.

His voice was strong, so he did not use the microphone. "I want to dedicate this poem to my old lady, Niecie." Brother Jahid-Ali winked at her.

Denise returned his wink by blowing him a kiss.

He sat on the stool, cleared his throat and closed his eyes.

Beautiful Black Woman, there is no revolution without you/the sun may set/the guns may pop/but you stand at the center in plain view/I've often wondered where you've been/Afraid that if I blink/I'll

miss the soft subtle contour of your chin/Beautiful
Black Woman, there is no revolution without
you/Your proud words and regal back/send me fallin'
for a love coup/Beautiful Black Woman, there is no
battle too strong/No river too wide to keep me away
from you/I hear that the hand that rocks the cradle
rules the world/Oh how I desire to always be your
man/Together our love will unfurl/ Beautiful Black
Woman, Denise, you precious dove/Remember there
is no joy in my world without your love.

Brother Jahid-Ali opened his eyes and smiled at Denise.
Denise ran to the stage when he was finished. He hugged
her to him tightly, knowing that somewhere in his heart,
this was possibly their last free night together. "I think I'm
falling in love with you," he said in a husky voice.

"Me, too." Denise blushed.

"Let's get out of here." Brother Jahid-Ali was eager to
have Denise all to himself. Five people must have given
him five between the stage and the front door.

"That poem was bad! I can't believe that you wrote that
just for me." Denise was thrilled.

"Well dig it, 'cause I sat up all night writing it."

Denise pulled away and smiled up at Brother Jahid-Ali.
"I have someone I want you to meet."

"Who?" He asked her once they got outside.

"Pauletta."

"Who's that?" They walked to his VW bus.

"She's the sista I stay with," Denise said excitedly. "Why
are we driving? You know, I only live a few blocks from
here."

He opened the passenger side door and waited for her
to get in. "I know, but when we leave your place, I want

to take you to my pad." Brother Jahid-Ali grinned mischie-vously.

"You're a bad bad boy." Denise's voice was heavy with lust. She leaned over and kissed his right cheek.

"Badder than Leroy Brown?" Brother Jahid-Ali sang as he turned his head so that she could kiss his left cheek.

"Baddest man in this whole damn town." Denise purred like the cool, black Panther that she was.

They laughed simultaneously.

"Umm, it smells good in here," Denise said as she en-tered Pauletta's apartment.

Pauletta was cooking spaghetti in the little kitchenette. "I hope you guys like wheat spaghetti," Pauletta called out.

"That sounds cool." Brother Jahid-Ali responded. He walked into the small kitchen space. "So, you're the sista saint who took Niecie in when no one else wanted her." He laughed good naturedly.

Pauletta extended her hand. "Sista Saint Pauletta in the flesh."

Brother Jahid-Ali kissed her hand. "Habari gani, sista, my name is Brother Jahid-Ali."

"I know, Denise told me." Pauletta looked over at Denise. "A gentleman. You might want to keep this one."

Denise was happy that Pauletta approved of Brother Jahid-Ali.

"Dinner will be ready in a minute." Pauletta returned to stirring spaghetti sauce in the pot on the stove. "Brotha, can I get you something to drink?"

"I had something to drink at the coffee house." He turned to Denise. "Niecie, are you thirsty?"

"I'd like some water." Denise headed toward the kitchen. Brother Jahid-Ali blocked her way. "I'll get it." He squeezed into the kitchenette with Pauletta. "Excuse me sista." He said to Pauletta.

"No problem." Pauletta appreciated the brotha's diligence. She handed him a cup.

"Is that all you want to drink?" He filled her cup with water from the faucet.

"Yeah, I'll have a glass of wine when dinner is ready." Denise sat down on the pillow.

Brother Jahid-Ali joined her on the pillow. While she sipped her water, he rubbed her back. "Why are you so quiet?"

"I was just thinking how lonely I'm going to be when you go back to the party," Brother Jahid-Ali said tenderly.

Denise did not respond right away. She knew that they were going to have to talk about their relationship at some point. "I feel the same way."

Pauletta came into the front room where they were with a bowl of spaghetti noodles. "Hey, no long faces. Denise hasn't left yet." She tried to sound cheery, but Pauletta was also going to miss her new roommate.

Denise stood up. "You're right. I'll get the sauce."

Brother Jahid-Ali was right on her heels. "And I'll grab the wine."

In the meantime, Pauletta pulled out her Kente cloth bought on her trip to Africa several years before and spread it on the rug. It was purple, gold, orange, and green with black stripes running the length of the fabric. The cloth was symbolic for many reasons. First, it was directly from Africa and one of her most prized possessions. Second, she bought it before Eldridge Cleaver and Huey Newton fell out and the Black Panther Party split into two factions. While she chose to remain with Huey's faction, the party hadn't been the same since. Third, it was on this cloth that she and Kweli made love for the last time.

"Oh, Pauletta this cloth is boss!" Denise exclaimed. "Where did you get it?"

"The motherland," responded Brother Jahid-Ali. "Only Mother Africa could produce a cloth that intricate in design and brilliant in color."

"I pulled it out, because tonight we are going to party." Pauletta grinned. She directed them as to where to put the spaghetti sauce and the wine. When everything was in place and Denise and Brother Jahid-Ali were seated, Pauletta said. "We're missing one thing."

"What?" Denise and Brother Jahid-Ali said in unison.

"The bread." Pauletta headed for the kitchen. "We need something to sop the sauce up with."

"Right on." Denise and Brother Jahid-Ali slapped palms.

They finally ate and by the end of the meal, Pauletta, Denise and Brother Jahid-Ali had polished off two bottles of wine and were a bit drunk. Alcohol made Denise talkative and she decided to recite a poem.

On wobbly legs, she stood up. "Paulet-ta and brotha baby, I got somethin' to say." Denise held on to Brother Jahid-Ali's shoulder for support.

"Go head, girl." Pauletta clapped her hands.

"Preach, Niecie," Brother Jahid-Ali said.

Denise cleared her throat and tried to make her tongue straighten out. There was no use, until the wine wore off, she was bound to slur her words. "Paulet-ta, even 'dough this is yo' house, I'm gonna tell you 'bout ma house." She pointed to herself when she said "my" house. "Ya dig?"

"I can dig it." Pauletta answered.

"Okay." Denise cleared her throat again. " 'My House' by Denise Davis, alias Nikki Giovanni."

Pauletta and Brother Jahid-Ali both clapped.

"I only want to/be there to kiss you/as you want to be kissed/" Denise kissed the top of Brother Jahid-Ali's shiny bald head. "When you need to be kissed/where I want to kiss you/cause it's my house/and I plan to live in it."

Denise's voice got louder. "I really need to hug you/when I want to hug you/as you like to hug me/does this sound like a silly poem?"

"No sista, not at all!" Pauletta screamed out.

"I mean it's my house."

"Yo' house!" Brother Jahid-Ali added.

"Who's house?" Denise cupped her ears with her hands.

"Yo' house!" Brother Jahid-Ali and Pauletta responded to Denise's call.

Denise resumed her recitation of Nikki's poem. "And I want to fry pork chops/and bake sweet potatoes/and call them yams/cause I run the kitchen/and I can stand the heat/I spent all winter in/carpet stores gathering/patches so I could make/a quilt/does this really sound/like a silly poem?"

Denise's voice was as clear as a bell. She patted her 'fro and rapidly said the fifth and sixth stanzas. "I'm saying it's my house/and I'll make fudge and call/it love and touch my lips/to the chocolate warmth/and smile at old men and call/it revolution." She thrust her right fist high in the air. This was the first Black Power salute she had given in almost thirty days. "Damn, that felt good," Denise said to the ceiling.

". . . cause what's real/is really real/and I still like men in tight/pants cause everybody has some/thing to give and more."

"Niecie, what about brothas in tight dashikis?" Brother Jahid-Ali asked.

"I like them too." Denise winked at him. "Let me finish, brotha baby."

"Where was I?" Denise paused for a minute. "Oh yeah, "important need something to take/and this is my house and you make me/happy/so this is your poem."

Denise bowed and sat down.

"Right on, sista." Pauletta hugged her and so did Brother Jahid-Ali.

"Pauletta, I saw your collection of Trane. Do you have "A Love Supreme?" Though he was speaking to Pauletta, Brother Jahid-Ali was staring at Denise. "Niecie, you are my love supreme."

"And you are my fox in shining armor," Denise said as she smiled slyly. She moved closer to him so that she could nestle herself in Brother Jahid-Ali's arms.

"Got it? Brotha, that's like askin' me if I've got a pick for my afro." Pauletta asked sarcastically. She reached behind her and pulled a black pick, with a green and red handle, which was in the shape of a fist, from her 'fro. Pauletta went over to her records and grabbed Trane. In an instant, the room was filled with the deep sounds of Coltrane's horn.

Pauletta grabbed her pack of Kool's from off the speaker. She offered Brother Jahid-Ali a cigarette. He declined, but Denise accepted. In the smoky haze of the two cigarettes, a serenity descended upon the room. Denise wished life could always feel this free and peaceful.

After "A Love Supreme" played, Pauletta spoke. "Just sitting here reminds me that I am doing the right thing."

When neither Denise nor Brother Jahid-Ali did not interrupt her, Pauletta kept talking. "I have finally realized that Black people need to move past labels. Just looking at the two of you proves that Panthers and the sistas and brothas of WEB can trust one another. And, as long as there's trust, then in theory, we should all be able to work together."

"In theory is right," answered Brother Jahid-Ali. "I dig what you sayin', but some many brothas and sistas ain't ready to hear that."

"That's too bad." Pauletta did not want to divulge her plans to leave the party to Brother Jahid-Ali, so she changed the subject. "I really dig "A Love Supreme." Do you want to hear it again?"

He nodded affirmatively.

After a couple of minutes, the music carried each one of them high above their bodies. And for a time, Brother Jahid-Ali was able to forget that in a few short days, Denise would be leaving him. Meanwhile, Denise gave herself over to the moment, and Pauletta imagined that Coltrane was standing in the corner of her apartment, playing his horn just for her.

Part 3:

Living for the People

Eleven

On Denise's first day back at the party headquarters, she marvelled at how many changes had been made. Huey was exiled in Cuba; an international Panther headquarters had been established by Eldridge in New York; Elaine had taken over Eldridge's place as Minister of Information; and word on the street was that the troops would finally be removed from Vietnam, sometime in '73.

Also, many of the old faces at the headquarters had been replaced by new ones. Denise stayed at the headquarters long enough to be resworn in. *Funny,* she thought to herself, *the last time she was sworn in, she was a nervous wreck. Her mind had gone blank.* This time, Denise had plans for the Black Panthers. She stood at the front of the room pronouncing each syllable of the Black Panther Ten Point Plan loud and clear. She could be heard over everyone, including the men.

Kweli arrived later to meet the new recruits. When he spotted Denise, he sauntered over to her. "Well, Comrade Denise. I almost didn't think you'd return." He said with a smile. In spite of himself, he was glad to see her.

"It's going to take more than thirty days to keep me from freeing the people," she said with conviction.

"That's the attitude we need around this camp." Kweli

hugged her. "Gimme five!" Denise slapped his gloved right hand.

"Is Shelly here?" Kweli asked Denise.

Denise looked around the room. That was one person who was definitely missing. Denise was so caught up in the Panther oath that she forgot all about Shelly. "No, I haven't seen her."

"I'm sure she'll be here later." Kweli took a step back and stared at Denise. There was something about her that was different . . . stronger, he thought to himself.

Denise left the headquarters and went to her apartment. She originally thought that she would stay with Pauletta. Well, she'd stay with Pauletta until Pauletta went underground. Pauletta was against the idea, not because she didn't want Denise to stay with her, but for practical reasons. Pauletta told Denise that once she reentered the Party, Denise would probably be watched. If Denise voluntarily moved back to her old apartment, then it would lessen any suspicions about her being a traitor or informant. Pauletta also reminded Denise that if she was sincere about moving up in the party ranks, Denise would have to prove that there were no skeletons in her closet. Denise reluctantly agreed that Pauletta was right.

When Denise opened the door to her old apartment, Shelly was waiting for her.

"Hey, girl, what's up?" Shelly jumped off the couch and embraced Denise.

Denise returned the hug, but it was a half-hearted gesture.

"I really missed you and I'm sorry for everything that happened," Shelly said.

Even though Denise believed that Shelly was sincere,

Denise still felt angry, but she smiled anyway, and set her duffle bag on the floor. "Where is everybody?"

"Retha and Tyrone are on a mission. And Faye is at HQ. working on the newspaper." Shelly picked up Denise's bag. "You travel lightly." Shelly was attempting to keep the conversation cool.

"Well, true weapons of revolution lie in the heart, not in the material world," Denise said poetically.

"Right on." Shelly raised her right fist in the air.

The silence was growing between them, and Denise could see the tension growing in Shelly's face. Denise saw that Shelly was sinking, but did not bother to bail Shelly out.

When Denise did not return Shelly's Black Power salute, Shelly cut to the chase. "Niecie, I feel partly responsible for you being suspended."

Denise suppressed her anger. Instead, she responded, "Let's just drop it, okay? Today's a new day." Denise took her bag from Shelly and headed toward the room they shared.

"Whatever you say, Niecie," Shelly said petulantly.

Denise began to unpack her bag, when she noticed that Shelly was standing next to her. "Yes?"

"Oh nothing, I just wanted to help you." Shelly sat down on Denise's bed.

"I'm cool, thanks." Denise was getting annoyed.

"I left your side of the room, just like it was before, you . . . well, from the last time."

"Thanks." Denise rolled her eyes, though her tone remained mellow.

"Niecie!" Shelly whined. "I'm sorry. Are you ever going to forgive me?"

"Should I?" Denise felt amazingly calm.

"Yeah. Nobody told you to talk to him. You know the rules and you broke them. What was I supposed to do?" Shelly's voice had turned shrill.

"Don't worry about it, Shelly. It's over. I survived and I'm back." Denise was able to smile genuinely. She had such a good time while she was suspended, that Denise didn't have time to be mad at Shelly, DeeDee, Kweli or anyone else for that matter. Denise had found love and a little bit more of herself during her time away from her comrades. As far as Denise was concerned, her suspension was a blessing in disguise.

Shelly sighed. She didn't know if Denise was mad at her or not. Denise's collectedness made Shelly all the more nervous. "Your 'fro is bad. I think I'll let mine grow out." Shelly's hair was still cut low.

"I bet that would be cute on you." Denise patted her hair.

"Yeah, Kweli would probably dig me with long hair." Shelly smiled at the thought. "It's been so long since I had hair, I probably wouldn't know what to do with it." Shelly tried to picture herself with a large afro.

"Shelly, I have a feeling that you would get used to it." Denise knew that Shelly, nicknamed 'Hour glass' in college, wasn't about to pass up an opportunity to look boss. Even though she wore the Panther uniform, preached Panther rhetoric and dated the captain of the Los Angeles Chapter of the BPP, Shelly was the baddest dressed Panther in all of Southern California.

Denise finished putting her clothes into the drawers.

"Do you want to go to The Kyte later on tonight?"

"What's that?" Denise had never heard of it.

"It's this cool little after hours spot that Kweli and some of the other comrades go to. It's off of Crenshaw and Washington. I've been a couple of times." Shelly thought hard about how to describe The Kyte. "It's kinda the party after the party. I think that you'd dig it." Shelly was getting excited and hoped that Denise would say yes.

It seemed to Denise that her affirmative answer meant a lot to Shelly. Denise turned to face Shelly. This was the first time she really looked at Shelly in a month. Shelly looked the same. A little frayed around the edges, but otherwise, everything seemed to be in place. "That sounds cool."

Finally unpacked, Denise sat down on her old bed for the first time in thirty days.

"What are you about to do?" Shelly said anxiously.

"I'm a little tired. I've been at the headquarters all day," Denise yawned.

"You should probably take a nap."

"That's a good idea." Denise stretched out on the bed and closed her eyes.

As soon as Shelly left the room, Denise opened her eyes. She looked around the room and was grateful for Marvin's watchful eyes above her head. "Oh Marvin," she said aloud to the poster. "I've really missed you." Denise looked over at the picture of Gil and blew him a kiss. At last, Denise was home.

It was about one o'clock in the morning when Shelly and Denise arrived. Well, the 'party after the party' had gotten started on time. Apparently, no one must have been wearing a watch, because that place was jumpin' like it was nine thirty, and no one had to be anywhere the next day.

They found a table and ordered a glass of wine. Denise was still a little groggy from her nap. Shelly was upbeat.

Denise compared her new hangout to her beloved Watts Coffee House. The vibe was the same, but her man wasn't there, so The Kyte came up short in Denise's eyes. One good thing about The Kyte was that there were brothas and sistas from the Black Panther Party, WEB, the Black Congress, and other organizations. *At last,* she said to herself, *a place where we can all come together and just be cool.*

"Niecie, what did you do while you were suspended? Shelly asked shyly. I was worried and nobody knew where you were."

"I mostly hung out at the library." Denise wasn't completely lying. It was only Denise's first day back and she still didn't trust Shelly.

Shelly studied her friend from across the table. "There's something you're not telling me, Denise Marie Davis."

Denise feigned innocence. "What are you talking about?" She pulled out a pack of Kool cigarettes. To avoid Shelly's penetrating stare, Denise surveyed the room. She didn't recognize anybody in the room. Finally, her eyes settled on a man sitting across the room. He was about the same complexion and build of Brother Jahid-Ali, but his back was to her, so she could not see his face. His bald head and ornate dashiki indicated that he was one of the Lions from WEB. *Could that be Brother baby?* the question echoed inside her head. *Oh my god, what am I going to do?* Just as she was about to panic, the Lion turned around. It wasn't Brother Jahid-Ali. This dude wasn't even close to being her love.

Noticing the change in Denise's demeanor, Shelly's head whipped around to where Denise was staring so intensely. "What's the matter? You look like you just saw a ghost."

"Oh girl, nothin'. I think I've been listening to too many Marvin Gaye and Diana Ross songs." Denise hummed the tune out loud. "You know that song, 'You Are Every-thing' "?

Shelly sang a line from the song. *"Today I saw some-body/who looked just like you . . .* What about it?"

"I thought I heard someone singing it," Denise lied.

A little tone deaf and a half note off, they sang the chorus of "You Are Everything" together. The other brothas and sistas in The Kyte turned to stare at them, but that didn't make them stop.

Shelly forgot the last verse and so they made up the rest of the song. When they finished singing, they fell into a fit of laughter. "Stop jiving Denise. You look, um," Shelly cocked her head to the side to stare at Denise. "It is like you're glowing or somethin'."

Denise took a drag on her cigarette and blew a ringlet of smoke to the ceiling. Laughter aside, Denise leveled her most serious gaze at Shelly. "I look the same as I did before. The only difference is that my hair is longer." Now, that was a bold faced lie and Denise knew it. She didn't care, though. There was no way Denise was about to tell Shelly about Brother Jahid-Ali. As long as Shelly's nose was open about Kweli, there was no way that Shelly would keep that information to herself.

"Whatever. I don't know what you're tryin' to lay on me, but somethin' has changed about you." Shelly wasn't going to let Denise off the hook.

Rather than answer and accidentally give herself away, Denise blew another ring of smoke into the air.

Denise was excited about returning to the Freedom School. Though it was the summertime, the children were still in school almost the whole day. The long hours with the children meant that Denise crashed every night when she went to bed, but the fatigue was worth it. Denise was ready to put her all into the party.

On Denise's second day back in the party, the inevitable happened. Denise ran into DeeDee.

"Comrade Denise," said DeeDee, as she inspected Denise from head to toe. "Who do you think you are, Foxy Brown?" DeeDee said with disapproval. DeeDee and Denise were standing in the doorway, watching the children at the Freedom School. It was recreation time, and some of the children were drawing, while others were playing with one another.

"Excuse me?" Denise didn't know what DeeDee was talking about.

DeeDee pointed to Denise's afro. "Your beret won't fit over that 'fro." DeeDee said with disgust.

Denise hadn't had a haircut in a month and a half. She had always worn her afro short, but, while she was suspended, Denise decided to let it grow. Now it was about four inches around, almost as big as Pauletta's.

"I decided to let it grow," said Denise without looking at DeeDee. Self-consciously, Denise touched her hair. She didn't think anything was wrong with it. Denise was getting sick of DeeDee, and was having trouble hiding it. This was the best time of the day for Denise. The children were waiting for their parents to pick them up. While they waited, the children learned revolution songs, played games and ate. Every now and then, Denise would sit down and have a one on one with the children. She enjoyed answering their many questions and marvelling at their keen children's logic. DeeDee was spoiling this moment for Denise. Ever since Denise's return to the party, DeeDee had been hawkin' her every move. DeeDee's constant presence in Denise's life made her transition back bittersweet.

"Some people might question your loyalty, you dig what I'm sayin'?" DeeDee added nastily.

Denise dug her boots into the asphalt. "No I don't. Kathleen doesn't wear a beret, and no one questions her commitment to the Party," Denise responded cooly.

Before DeeDee could say anything else, one of the children ran outside. "Niecie, Daric fell and hit his head," Miesha said, as she pulled on Denise's skirt. Miesha was seven years old and one of the brightest students at the Freedom School.

"Oh no. Take me to him," Denise said.

Before Denise could open the door completely, DeeDee said. "Denise,—"

"What, now?" Instead of turning around, Denise stopped where she stood. Denise scowled, but smiled when she realized that Miesha was watching her and DeeDee.

"I'll deal with you later."

Denise let the door slam behind her.

The weeks flew by. Kweli gave Denise double the amount of work she was doing before she was suspended. Denise rose to the challenge, much to Kweli's surprise and DeeDee's dismay. With her added responsibilities, Denise needed a car. More specifically, she needed her car back. To test how sorry Shelly really was, Denise told Shelly to get her car back. In less than a day, Shelly handed Denise the keys to her white Mustang. It had been washed and waxed. Shelly never did say who had Denise's car or how she got it back. Denise didn't care to know the particulars, she was glad to have her ride.

Denise decided to let bygones be bygones and tacitly forgave Shelly. They started hanging out on a regular basis. It was like old times, except this time Denise was smarter. She learned a hard lesson: nothing in life is guaranteed, not even ties between best girlfriends.

Denise thought about Brother Jahid-Ali everyday. She couldn't call him and knew that he couldn't call her. Her best bet was to hope that she bumped into him somewhere. Denise found herself looking around the crowd for bald heads or dashikis. Her comrades thought she was assessing the vibe of the crowd. They often commended her for her thoroughness and dedication to the struggle. If they only knew that she was on the lookout for a Lion, whose sweet eyes sparkled in the moonlight, they would have lynched her for real. Denise even dropped by Pauletta's to see if she had seen him.

Denise knocked on the door of Pauletta's apartment. It seemed like years, instead of a few weeks, had passed, since she left this place.

"Who is it?" Pauletta asked.

"It's me, Denise."

Pauletta threw the door open and pulled Denise inside. "Girl, it's good to see you! How are Kweli and the rest of the comrades treating you?" Pauletta stood back to get a better look at Denise.

"They're as jive as ever, but I can't complain." Denise went to sit on Pauletta's big brown pillow in the living room. "I'm happy to be back."

"Right on. That's positive news." Paulette saluted Denise.

Denise looked around the room. Most of Pauletta's things were packed. "So, you're getting ready to make your move."

"Yeah, it's about that time." Pauletta joined her on the pillow.

Denise was at a loss for words. "I don't know what I'd have done without you."

"You would have survived," Pauletta touched Denise lightly on her shoulder.

They talked a little while longer about the party and what Denise had been doing. At last, Denise couldn't take it any longer. "Pauletta, have you seen or heard anything from Brother Jahid-Ali?"

Pauletta looked down at her hands. "No, I haven't." She felt sorry for Denise. "The revolution, unfortunately, does not have any rules regarding love."

"I'm beginning to see that," Denise said sadly. "I don't know what to do or where to look."

"Let your heart guide you to him." Pauletta said wistfully. "If it's meant to be, you will find him."

Brother Jahid-Ali was missing Denise something terrible. There was no way he could call her, and meeting at the Watts Coffee House was out of the question. Now that Denise was restored to full Panther status, she was required to wear her uniform and Panther attitude everywhere she went.

If he was slacking off before, Brother Jahid-Ali was slacking off big time now. Maulana Imhotep was getting suspicious, and Brother Jahid-Ali noticed that some of the other Lions kept their distance from him. He wasn't too worried about the Lions. They couldn't go too far, he was still number two in command. And he wasn't nearly as worried about Maulana Imhotep as much as he should have been.

In their short time together, Denise had changed him. She had single-handedly replaced his tunnel vision with a kaleidoscope pattern of love, trust, tenderness and companionship. Brother Jahid-Ali selfishly wished that her suspension had been indefinite. Then, she would still be with him.

He was so desperate with longing for Denise that one night he went to Pauletta's to see if Denise was there. He knocked and knocked on Pauletta's door, until his knuckles were red. Finally, an upstairs neighbor came downstairs and told him that Pauletta had moved and no one knew where she moved to. Brother Jahid-Ali was devastated. That old feeling of loneliness washed over his entire body. *"Denise,"* he prayed to himself, *"Come back to me."*

Twelve

"Comrade Denise, I have a question?" A little brown hand waved in the air.

Denise was writing the Declaration of Independence on the board so the children could dissect it and fully understand its meaning, when she heard someone call her name. "Yes lil' brotha, what is it?" Denise nodded in the direction of Jamal.

"What is revolution?" Jamal's face was twisted in consternation.

Forty pairs of eyes focused on Denise. The last time she received this much attention, she had been invited to leave her history class at UCLA. This time the eyes belonged to her little charges at the Freedom School. And since she was the teacher, there would be no patronizing or belittling in her classroom.

"Revolution is change."

"Oh yeah." He seemed to be satisfied with Denise's answer.

"Do you understand what change is?" Denise wanted to allow the discussion to flow wherever the children had questions. She found that to be an effective mechanism for teaching. If they did not get to a discussion about The Declaration of Independence that day, the next day would be soon enough. Denise did not follow a timed curriculum.

She believed that it was important to make sure the children understood the important concepts, rather than fill their heads with a bunch of insignificant details that had nothing to do with the liberation of her people.

"Change occurs when things need to get better." Jamal was a bright seven year old. "Is that what we're learning in school?"

"Yes. We are trying to teach you young soldiers how to wage change in unjust, racist America."

Other hands shot up into the air. "Comrade, comrade, what does liberation mean?"

"Sista Jamila, liberation is freedom from oppression and other evils." Jamila was Jamal's younger sister. She was five and sharp as a tack.

"I have a question . . ."

"I have a question . . ."

The kids fired questions at Denise in a rapid fire succession. By the time she went home, she was tired and didn't want to speak to a soul. Yet the children rejuvenated her spirit. It was simply their inquisitiveness that left her feeling exhausted but fulfilled at the end of each day.

Later in the week, Denise's prayers were answered. It was Thursday evening and she was purchasing much needed supplies for the Freedom School. Crayons, markers, writing pads, chalk, glue, pencils, and dictionaries for the older children. Denise had just paid the cashier and was walking out of the Kmart on Imperial and Crenshaw, when she walked right into Brother Jahid-Ali.

Without speaking, she rushed into his arms. He embraced her quickly and escorted her out of the store.

"Niecie, someone might see us." Brother Jahid-Ali whispered in her ear. His arms ached with joy.

"I don't care." Denise's voice was full of emotion. She didn't want to let go of him.

"You say that now, but you'll be singin' a different tune if we blow our cover."

Denise let go of him. "You're right." She knew that she would die right then and there if they couldn't be together. "What are we going to do?" Unexpected tears had risen in her eyes.

"Go to your car and follow me. Make sure that you drive two cars behind me." Brother Jahid-Ali was speaking rapidly. He didn't want anyone to accidentally see them speaking again. If they were busted by the Panthers, Denise would surely get expelled from the Black Panther Party. If they were caught by WEB, Malauna Imhotep would see to it that he too was expelled, or worse. In Africa, treason was punished by death.

"I'm right behind you." Denise's adrenaline was pumping. She was so excited, she was beginning to shake. Denise ran/walked to her car.

Brother Jahid-Ali drove carefully in a westerly direction down Imperial Highway. He didn't know where he was going, he just knew that one of the beach communities would be safe for them, except for the Santa Monica Pier. After all-that stuff went down with Geronimo Pratt, that area was swarming with cops looking for black militants. Also, it was going to be a sultry night in Los Angeles and that beach would probably be crowded.

They needed to go somewhere secluded. When he reached the San Diego freeway, he made a right and headed north. He checked his rear view mirror every two seconds to make sure that he could see Denise. After fifteen minutes, he switched to the Santa Monica freeway, and drove west. When the freeway ran out, he made another right and continued to drive up the coast. In thirty more minutes, they would be out of the Los Angeles city limits.

Brother Jahid-Ali finally pulled his VW bus into a lookout point at Point Dume. The cliff was near the edge of Malibu and overlooked a small beach that sat between the Santa Monica mountains and Pacific Coast Highway. With the ocean below them and the mountains surrounding them, seclusion was possible.

"Where are we?" Denise asked Brother Jahid-Ali as soon as she got out of her car.

"Somewhere where no can find us." He wanted her so bad that he could barely speak. He picked her up and kissed her deeply.

Overwhelmed by his passion, Denise started to cry.

"Baby, what's wrong?" He wiped her tears.

"Oh nothing, I'm just so happy to see you." She smiled through her tears. "I thought you forgot about me."

"Never. I'd never forget about you." Brother Jahid-Ali said reassuringly. "I didn't know what to do. I looked everywhere I could, even Pauletta's."

"So did I!" Her face brightened; he really did care about her. "She's gone."

"That's what her neighbor said. Where did she move, do you know?" Brother Jahid-Ali dusted off a place for her to sit on the rocks.

"Nope." Denise could not betray Pauletta's trust.

"Talk to me, how is everything going? Is Kweli treating you all right? What about Shelly?" He wanted to know all that she had done in the time that they'd been apart.

Denise kissed him. "Slow down. One question at a time."

"The sun is setting." Brother Jahid-Ali pointed because he couldn't take his eyes off of her.

She followed his finger. "How beautiful." The bright orange sun hovered just above the water. From its periphery, powerful rays emanated like paint brush strokes across the sky. The shades were variations of the color orange. One stroke was so light that it was almost yellow, the other was the essence of orange and, the last and most powerful ray was burnt-orange. Slivers of blue and turquoise wove their way through the orange. The scene was breathtaking and for a split second Denise saw the sun dance across the ocean's surface. Even the white foam that smashed against the rocks seemed to crash in tune with the sun's dance.

The fading sun warmed Denise's face. She was so caught up in the majesty of the moment that she thought she was imagining wet droplets on her face. Actually, Brother Jahid-Ali was planting little kisses all over her face and neck. He unbuttoned the top three buttons on her chambray shirt.

She turned to face him. "I just want to look at you."

Brother Jahid-Ali paused and inhaled her essence. "You are so beautiful." He kissed her excitedly.

They were too caught up to speak, so the two lovers stood, held each other and watched the setting sun disappear into the ocean.

They agreed to make this their secret meeting place. Brother Jahid-Ali said that he could meet her after his Swahili classes on Tuesdays and Thursdays. The weekends would be trickier to maneuver, however. He sat perplexed and stared out into the semidarkness. Denise came up behind him and hugged him, "Baby, don't worry. Let's just start with Tuesdays and Thursdays. We'll be able to figure something out."

"I hate this, Niecie. Why is it that when I finally find a

woman I love, I can't be with her? Isn't that what the movement is all about? Freedom for Black people to live and
love just like the rest of the world?" Brother Jahid-Ali said
angrily.

Denise didn't say anything. She pressed her head into
his back and continued to rub his stomach.

He turned around and kissed both her hands. "I love you
so much. I don't want to be apart from you . . . not for a
minute, an hour, let alone days." Brother Jahid-Ali's voice
was tight with emotion. He was so passionate that it took
Denise's breath away. "It's not fair, Niecie." He dropped
his head onto her shoulder.

Thirteen

"Comrade Denise." Kweli was pacing in front of Denise. "I hear that you're practically running the Freedom School single handedly." DeeDee came running to him that Denise wouldn't let anyone make any decisions regarding the school.

"It's more of a collective effort that runs the school, not just me." Denise was standing stock still and staring up at Comrade Kweli. It was late in the evening and Denise had received a message that Kweli wanted her to meet him at the headquarters. Denise was tired. She had been on her feet all day and the last thing she wanted to do was stand at attention. "DeeDee, Pamela, Diane and Carolyn work there."

"I know who's there. But, I hear that you've made some important improvements in the curriculum." Kweli laced his fingers together and cracked his knuckles.

Denise's shoulders were beginning to ache for holding them so still. She wished that he would get to his point. "I changed some of the literature they are reading to include a feminist perspective on race relations."

"Who authorized that?" Kweli barked.

"No one," Denise snapped back. "I just think that the children need to know that men are not the only ones involved in the struggle for liberation for our people."

"You think I don't know that? Fannie Lou Hamer is the reason I joined the Black Power Movement in the first place," Kweli said with conviction. "I followed her and other women into civil rights. I thought that the tactics of the Civil Rights Movement were a little square, but I believed in what they were doing."

"Well, that's a news flash to me. The only people I ever hear you rappin' about are Huey, Mao, Malcolm and a few others." Denise let her leather bag fall onto Kweli's desk with a slam. "I have never heard you even breathe Fannie Lou's name, let alone Anna Julia Cooper or Daisy Bates," Denise said disgustedly. The pain in her shoulders ceased and she was poised for battle.

"Denise, I dig where you're coming from, but you can't just upset the balance in the school, 'cause you feel like it." Kweli's tone had softened. He cracked his knuckles again.

"I also can't be true to the revolution if I don't teach future leaders the whole story about change and solutions. What's so wrong with little boys and girls learning the whole story? Hell, many of them don't even know that Elaine is chair of the Black Panther party."

Kweli looked around the office before he answered her. He didn't want the other comrades to hear what he was about to say. "We're working on changing the attitudes of the men in the party. You have to admit that there are even women in the party who don't want a woman to lead them."

"Those comrades are ignorant. Maybe if they knew the truth then they would embrace our new leader." Denise had to admit that she overheard some of her female cohorts complaining about having a woman as the head of the entire party. While Denise didn't think it would take a woman, specifically, to rally the party to its original stature, she did, however, recognize that Elaine had a lot to contribute and couldn't do any worse than Huey had.

Kweli ignored her comment and finished speaking. "All I'm sayin' is that it is going to take time. You don't know how many people have told me about the new curriculum. If you were going to change things, you should have come to me."

For the first time, Denise detected a weakness in Kweli, or maybe it was a strength in herself. Whatever it was, Denise was not backing down. "Kweli, if we were in battle and I saw the enemy coming from the left and you didn't because you were facing right, would you want me to ask your permission to shoot him?"

"I'd expect you to blow his head off." Kweli moved Denise's bag out of the way and sat down on the edge of his desk.

"Damn right. So, what's so different about this situation? I see the enemy of sexism and patriarchal domination rampant coming from within and without the party. Comrade, I'm trying to stop it before it becomes a cancer and destroys all of us."

Kweli put his hands on either of Denise's shoulders. "Don't get me wrong. I dig what you're sayin'. You just should have come to me first."

"So the real reason you called me to your office isn't about the new curriculum." She removed his hands from her shoulders and stood her full height. "You're angry that I did not follow protocol."

Kweli didn't respond.

Denise pointed to her bag and he handed it to her. "I thought so." She turned on her heels and left the office.

* * *

Seated in a corner booth at The Kyte, Denise took a slow drag on her cigarette. It had been a long day and she was looking forward to shooting the breeze with some of her comrades. While she waited, Denise thought about Brother Jahid-Ali. Two weeks had passed since she had seen him. *Oh, how she missed him!* In their haste to catch up, they forgot to determine which Tuesday or Thursday they would meet at Point Dume. When they left Point Dume, at close to midnight, Brother Jahid-All trailed her back into the Los Angeles city limits. They both drove slow, so as to make the moment last. Denise had been so excited that she didn't even realize that she did not know when she would see him again until she was almost home. She was so upset by this, that she went to bed in tears. She later thought of going to Point Dume on Tuesday and Thursday, but Kweli was at her apartment visiting Shelly. Denise knew that if she tried to leave, he would ask her where she was going. And the last thing she wanted to do was arouse Kweli's suspicions.

Shelly's presence startled her.

"I didn't see you standing there." Denise smiled and flicked an ash into the green ashtray in front of her.

"I don't guess that you could see too much with sparkles in your eyes."

Denise blushed.

"Niecie, I invited Russell to meet us here tonight. I told Kweli to come, but he probably won't be able to make it."

"Who's Russell?"

"He's a comrade from Frisco."

Denise knew that Shelly had not been to the Bay Area in the last few months. "When did you meet him?"

"In June."

Denise thought back. June. "Oh yeah, while I was suspended," she said matter-of-factly. Her suspension was no longer a source of pain.

"Yeah, Kweli let me go with him to the national head-quarters. I met Elaine while I was there."

"Really?"

"She was real cool."

"I can dig it." Denise said sincerely. She hoped to one day get to meet the party's new chairperson.

"Niecie, I think that you will like Russell."

"What makes you say that?"

"He's your type." Shelly paused. "Russell is real militant and believes that women should have a larger voice in the party."

Though she knew that Brother Jahid-Ali was the love of her life, she pretended to be interested. "Hmm. I look forward to meeting him." Denise made up her mind that no matter how handsome or progressive he was, she would not let anything happen between her and Russell.

"He flew down this afternoon. One of the comrades is going to drop him off. They should be here any minute."

Just as the words left Shelly's mouth, a handsome man walked toward their table.

Shelly jumped up from her seat. "Comrade! I'm so glad that you were able to make it."

Russell kissed Shelly on her cheek. "What's happenin'?"

"I'm cool. This is my sista in the struggle, Denise Davis."

Russell whistled. "Hey, foxy mama." He had a booming voice and several people at the next booth turned to look at them.

"Hello, Comrade," Denise said dryly. So much for respecting women, she thought to herself.

Russell stood in front of Denise and grinned. Denise looked from him to Shelly and then at the ashtray in front of her.

"Sit down, Russell." Shelly gave him a slight nudge. Russell bypassed her and slid into the booth next to Denise.

"So, Denise, I hear that you are runnin' stuff down here." Russell dropped his voice to a baritone whisper. His voice was very low and Denise had to lean close to him to hear him.

Denise looked around the restaurant trying to ignore Russell's attempts at getting her attention. She finally gave in when he started talking about the direction of the party.

"Like I was sayin' Shelly, I think that Elaine really is doing a great job," Russell said.

Denise leaned in closer. "I dig what you're sayin'." She put her cigarette out in the ashtray. "What is the attitude of the brothas and sistas in the Bay?"

"Well, you know how some comrades are."

"No, what do you mean?"

"Let's just say that some of our less enlightened comrades are slow to change."

"What are you doing about it?" Denise quizzed him.

Russell seemed caught off guard. "I-I do what our Sista-chairwoman says. She's a bad sista, but I'm sure being a bad sista yourself, Comrade Denise, that I don't have to tell you what that's all about." Russell winked at her.

Denise smiled in spite of herself. "Right on."

The conversation continued and Denise found herself enjoying Russell's company. She settled back into the booth, which placed her right in the crock of Russell's arm. Denise thought to move his arm, but decided that he was harmless and remained where she was.

* * *

Brother Jahid-Ali spotted a woman who looked just like Denise sitting in the back of The Kyte. He did not immediately go over to the table, because he told himself that there was no way that she would be there. And besides, Denise would not be hugged up with a man. *Unless she forgot about you,* his conscience whispered in his ear.

He took his seat with the group he came with, but was unable to concentrate on what they were talking about. They were seated near the entrance of The Kyte. Brother Jahid-Ali could see Denise, if that was Denise, but she could not see him. He kept looking over his shoulder. *Could that be Denise?*

"Hey, is somethin' goin' down tonight?" asked Brother Ivory.

No response.

"Hel-lo. I said, is somethin' goin' down tonight, Brother Jahid-Ali?" Brother Ivory began looking around the restaurant.

Finally, hearing the serious note in Brother Ivory's voice, Brother Jahid-Ali looked up. "No, what makes you say that?"

"You keep lookin' over your shoulder."

"Oh, just thought that I saw someone I knew," he said. "Who?"

"Nobody." He took a sip of the glass of water in front of him. Brother Ivory looked unconvinced. To avoid being asked any more questions Brother Jahid-Ali put the conversation back on Brother Ivory. "Say brotha, did you dig Maulana's rap tonight at the meeting?"

Brother Sphinx was looking directly at Brother Jahid-Ali, and Brother Jahid-Ali focused his attention on Brother Ivory, hoping that Brother Sphinx would really believe that he was looking for a friend.

"Yeah, it was pretty righteous." The three men exchanged five.

"Did you write his speech?" Brother Ivory asked Brother Jahid-Ali.

"Naw, I can't take credit for that one. He wrote it."

Brother Jahid-Ali looked around and Denise's look-a-like was gone. He let out a sigh of relief. Now he could enjoy himself.

About an hour later, Denise got up to go to the ladies' room. When she got back to the table, Shelly was gone.

"Comrade, what happened to Shelly?"

"She left to go meet Comrade Kweli at her pad."

Denise frowned. "She could have said something before she left."

"She looked like she was in a hurry." Russell patted Denise's seat. "I'll get a cab if you need a ride."

"Thanks, but I drove." Denise sat down and lit another cigarette. She had a zillion things to do the next day, but felt like staying out a little while longer.

Russell put his around Denise's shoulder. "Like I was sayin' before you left, Maulana has good ideas, but some of them are counterrevolutionary."

"Oh really, what makes you say that?" Denise felt herself grow hot under the collar. If Russell said something bad about Brother Jahid-Ali, she was going to blow him all the way back to Frisco.

A woman came out of the ladies' bathroom. This time, Brother Jahid-Ali really believed it was Denise. Finally unable to control his curiosity, Brother Jahid-Ali got up from his seat. "Brothers, I'll be right back."

Denise looked up and saw a familiar face. A smile the size of the Grand Canyon spread across her face.

Russell saw Denise smile and followed her line of vision. "Denise, who is that?"

Without thinking, Denise responded. "Brotha, uh, I don't know. He looks like he belongs to the WEB organization." Denise shrugged her shoulders and pretended that she did not know the man who was making a bee line to their table.

Brother Jahid-Ali saw the look of recognition on Denise's face and then disappear. *Who the hell was she sitting with?* He almost stopped walking and then something inside of him broke loose. There was nothing that was going to keep him from his woman.

Denise rose from the booth and tried to head Brother Jahid-Ali off before he reached her table. She said a silent thank you to God for making Shelly leave.

"Niecie," Brother Jahid-Ali tried to bypass her to get to Russell. "Who's that?"

Denise cut him off and took a step back. "Brotha, have we met?" Her voice was curt.

Brother Jahid-Ali's face fell. "Niecie, why are you acting like you don't know who I am?" He didn't mean to raise his voice, but he couldn't help himself.

Russell took a step forward and Brother Jahid-Ali tensed up. In minutes, Brother Sphinx and Ivory flanked Brother Jahid-Ali on either side of him. Russell was clearly outnumbered, but that never stopped a Black Panther before.

"Brother, do you have a problem?" Russell spoke to Brother Jahid-Ali.

Brother Jahid-Ali pointed his finger in Russell's face. "No, but you might, if you don't sit down."

By now, it seemed that the only people talking in the whole restaurant were Russell and Brother Jahid-Ali. The tension was mounting in The Kyte and Denise was almost afraid to move. Brother Jahid-Ali was wearing a blue and black dashiki and Russell matched his stance in his afro, leather jacket, denim shirt and combat boots.

Denise winked at Brother Jahid-Ali. "You must have mistaken me for someone else." She was trying to tone the edge down in her voice, and cut some of the tension in the room.

"Yeah sista, you're right. I got the wrong woman." Brother Jahid-Ali's eyes burned. He turned on his sandled heels and headed for the door. Brothers Sphinx and Ivory fell into step behind him.

Denise let out an audible sigh.

"Denise, who was that?" Russell was standing at her side. "Do you want me to deal with him for you?" Russell said still in his menacing pose.

"No, Russell, I don't want you to do a thing. And, I already told you, I don't know him." Denise went back to the booth and sat down. She silently wished that Russell would disappear. Denise was certain that Brother Jahid-Ali misunderstood her sitting so close to Russell. All she needed was to get in trouble *again* behind Brother Jahid-Ali. Damn, she needed another cigarette.

"What's her problem?" Brother Jahid-Ali said out loud to no one. He made up a lie to Brother Sphinx and Ivory that he had some left over work to do at the WEB headquarters. After he dropped them off, Brother Jahid-Ali drove aimlessly around the city.

"What, she doesn't dig me anymore?" He gripped the steering wheel tighter and tighter. Before he knew it he was flying down Pacific Coast Highway, heading North to Point Dume.

Denise drove Russell to the apartment she shared with Shelly and her other comrades. Without shutting the engine off, she waited for Russell to get out of her Mustang.

"Denise, are you coming in?" Russell turned to face Denise in the car.

She kept her eyes forward. "Not yet."

"It's the middle of the night, where are you going?" He put his hand on her arm. "Are you upset about something?"

"No." Denise sucked in her breath. "Russell, I know that you mean well, but my daddy lives on the other side of town."

"Excooze me!" Russell got out of her car and slammed the door.

Denise didn't bother to respond, she just drove off.

Denise knew she was wrong for taking her frustration with Brother Jahid-Ali out on Russell. She'd have to make it up to him later. In the meantime, she had to find Brother Jahid-Ali and talk to him. He almost blew their cover. *What was her love thinking?*

Fourteen

"What have they done to you?" Brother Jahid-Ali searched Denise's eyes. They were standing face to face in the dark foliage of the Santa Monica mountains. The two lovers were both breathing heavily from the climb up the mountain to their secret meeting place.

"What are you talking about?" Denise shook her head in confusion.

"Niecie, did they make you forget about me?" Brother Jahid-Ali's eyes beseeched her.

"Oh no! No one could ever make me forget about you! I love you." Denise covered Brother Jahid-Ali's face with kisses.

"Niecie, who were you with at The Kyte? Is he your man or somethin'?" Brother Jahid-Ali demanded.

"His name is Russell and he is a friend of Shelly and Kweli's." Denise's eyes were wide with fear. She had never heard Brother Jahid-Ali sound so angry before.

"Some friend." He pulled away from her and turned his back. Brother Jahid-Ali stared at the black Pacific Ocean. He knew that he sounded like a jealous husband, but he couldn't help it.

"Don't walk away from me, brotha!" Denise jerked his arm hard. "Russell's a comrade from up North. I just met him."

"Oh really. Considering the two of you were all hugged up in the corner, if I didn't know better, I would've thought that he was your old man." Brother Jahid-Ali was breathing deeply.

"Baby, you know me better than that!" Denise pleaded with her eyes. "I think about you everyday. I miss you so much when we're apart."

"I know. I'm sorry. It's just . . ." He paused to kiss her. "It's just that I rarely get to see you and when I saw you with another man, I wanted to destroy him." His voice was strained with pent-up anger.

Denise held him tightly and stroked the back of his head. Her green eyes twinkled in the moonlight. "You almost blew our cover." She whispered softly into the night air.

"If anyone ever finds out, who knows what they'd do to us." Brother Jahid-Ali straightened up and pulled Denise closer to him. "That was a mistake. I'll never do that again." The tension in his voice had dissolved to tenderness. "I love you." He kissed her softly on her ear.

"How much?"

"This much." He caressed the back of her neck and bit her softly on her chin. Denise closed her eyes and gave into his kiss. She slid her arms around his neck. Brother Jahid-Ali removed his black and blue dashiki and laid it on the ground, then he gently guided Denise to the grass. She unzipped her leather jacket. Goose pimples spread all over her body and she thought that she would freeze to death, when Brother Jahid-Ali kissed her on her neck and rubbed her back. The sweet smell of his breath on her face, combined with the warmth from his body caused Denise to warm up immediately.

"How does that feel?" Brother Jahid-Ali seductively asked Denise.

"Righteous, brotha, just righteous." She swooned. Denise opened her eyes one last time to see the stars smiling down on her and her man. The love they made tonight would stay with them a lifetime.

Brother Jahid-Ali must have been reading her thoughts. He rolled her on top of him and began to kiss her passionately. His urgency startled Denise. She returned his fervent kisses. Brother Jahid-Ali unbuttoned her skirt and slid it down her legs. In another fell swoop, her velour shirt lay next to her leather jacket. He used his teeth to undo the black scarf that was tied around her neck. Denise helped him take off his slacks and played in his chest hair.

Brother Jahid-Ali kissed each of her nipples and Denise moaned softly. They had made love before, but something was special about that night. Denise couldn't put her finger on it, but felt somewhere deep inside of her that they might be running out of nights together.

He felt her slight hesitation and stopped kissing her. "What's wrong?"

"Nothing baby, just hold me."

He grinned at her. "I'll do more than that." Brother Jahid-Ali felt Denise relax and he rolled on top of her. He wanted the moment to last forever, so he began to kiss her sensuously from the top of her head to the bottom of her feet, all the while deliberately caressing her breasts and her stomach. When he couldn't take it any longer, he pulled her legs around his back and entered her slowly. Soon he was fully inside of Denise. She held on to Brother Jahid-Ali tightly. Their bodies culminated in a fiery rush of pleasure.

In the afterglow of love, Brother Jahid-Ali told Denise. "Niecie, don't ever leave me." His tone was serious.

"I'm not going anywhere." She was still caught up in their moment of unbridled passion.

"Never no matter what happens."

Denise came back to reality with a start. "You're scaring me."

"I'm not trying to scare you." He raised up on one elbow. "Just say that you'll never leave me."

"I promise. I won't."

"Niecie, I think that I'm gonna have a baby." Shelly rubbed her flat stomach.

Denise put down the papers she was grading. "Are you pregnant?"

"Not yet."

"What does 'not yet' mean?"

"It means that I am planning to have a baby for the revolution," Shelly said matter-of-factly.

"No, no, Shelly. I can't believe you fell for that jive, macho rhetoric!"

"It isn't rhetoric and I didn't fall for anything!" Shelly got defensive. "In order for the revolution to progress, we need soldiers. I'm just trying to do my part, that's all."

"Doing your part? Damn, Shelly, who is going to help you raise a baby?"

"Kweli, of course."

"Kweli won't even marry you. What makes you think that he will take care of a baby?"

"That was so cold," Shelly inhaled sharply. "We are not married because marriage is just the white man's symbol of proprietorship over women. Kweli is my old man, ain't no court of justice of the so-called peace going to tell us different."

"That's funny that you guys believe that, 'cause Huey's married, so is Bobby, Kathleen, need I go on?"

Shelly shrugged her shoulders. "I didn't say that I was going to marry Kweli, I said that he is going to be the father of my child."

"Does he know about this?"

"Yes. It was his idea."

"I should've known." Denise smirked. "Shelly, you are going to end up like the rest of the sista comrades with kids running around and no daddy to care for them. You don't have any money or did you forget that kids cost money?"

"I'm not like everybody else. Kweli loves me and he said that he would take of our little Mao."

"That is the most ridiculous thing I've ever heard in my life!"

"Forget it. Maybe if you quit being so damn relevant and gave a brotha a chance, you would see what I'm talking about!"

"Excuse me." Denise put her hand on her hip.

"Yeah, it's no secret that you don't have a man. Everyone's starting to say things about you."

"Oh really, like what?"

"Like the fact that you might like women or somethin'."

"Oh, so now I'm a lesbian because I won't sleep with any of these no good, uneducated, sexist pseudo revolutionaries."

"No, that's not it." Shelly was sorry she ever let those words pass through her lips.

"Yes it is and you know it!"

"Niecie, what was wrong with Russell? He was here over two weeks ago and you haven't mentioned his name once."

"He wasn't my type."

"Well, just exactly who is your type? Since we've been

in the party I've only seen you go out with a couple of comrades. You say that you are so busy with the school and trying to take over Kweli's position in the party."

"First of all, who I see is none of your damn business. And, second of all, I am not trying to take Kweli's job."

"I don't believe you." Shelly stood in front of Denise. "Tell me, sista Comrade, are you still seeing that brotha from WEB."

Denise did not look at her. "I don't know what you're talking about."

"Yes you do. I'm talking about that man that got you suspended during the early part of the summer. Now, do you know who I'm talking about?"

"I will tell you now, just like I told you then, that brotha is not my man!" Denise threw her hand up in the air. "Since you know so much, smarty, when would I have time to see him? Between trying to keep the school running and keeping up with the incompetent people who work for Kweli, when have I had time to even wash my car, let alone carry on a secret rendezvous with some brotha who is clearly the enemy?"

Shelly didn't answer Denise.

"Before you start pointing fingers at me, Shelly, you might want to check out who's been hangin' out in your backyard."

"What's that supposed to mean?"

"You're so worried that I'm trying to take Kweli's job, why don't you ask DeeDee how long she's been trying to take your man. If she hasn't already."

"That's a bold-faced lie, Denise and you know it!"

"Don't worry, Shelly. Time will tell who's lyin' and who's lyin' down with your man." Denise grabbed the papers in front of her. "Just 'cause you're unsure about your decision to have a baby, doesn't mean that I'm the one with the problem."

"Niecie, I'm having a baby for the struggle and I don't give a damn what you or anybody else thinks," Shelly shouted at Denise. She ran from the room, so Denise could not see the tears streaming down her face.

Fifteen

Revolutionaries committed to the struggle must travel abroad, Denise thought to herself. She was stretched across her bed studying the world map. For weeks now she had been considering taking a trip to Algeria or Cuba. Algeria popped into her head because Eldridge and Kathleen had gone there. Also, Franz Fanon had written about the indigenous people fighting the French imperialists. Later, after the split between Huey and Eldridge, she took Algeria off of her list of places to visit. Denise sided with Huey and figured that she might be accused of being a spy.

Cuba sounded like a reasonable choice. From all that she had heard and read about Fidel Castro, she thought that she might get more experience being the revolutionary that she already was. Denise really wanted to go to a country where all of the people were conscious, not just some of the people. It was hard being relevant in a society, where bourgeois Negroes and racist whites ruled the country.

Denise lay across the map. The world was so big and she was so small. Just one of a few persons sincerely interested in creating equity in the world. Initially, she embraced Marxism, only to learn that his doctrine regarding the proletariat did not include the slaves or the abject poor. He was writing about the working poor instead of the lowest of the low. While she agreed that the triangular structure of capitalism was the root of classism, she also believed that if the masses rose up together, then the ten percent at the top who controlled the ninety percent at the bottom would cease to exist. Outraged by the quasi-exclusive doctrine of Marx, Denise had become apolitical. Whether the Democrats or Republicans were in office, Black, brown, yellow, and poor whites remained at the bottom.

Days like this caused Denise to wonder if all of the fuss was worth it. So many people were part of the problem, they just didn't know it. Denise often felt overwhelmed, like no matter how hard she tried, people were just not going to change. They would continue to exist in their perfect little worlds, oblivious to all the social ills that pervaded the nation. There was also so much in-fighting between the various factions of the Black Power Movement that it was all Denise could do to keep from crying.

Denise got up and went into the bathroom. She threw water on her face and stared at herself for a long time. *Who am I to question the status quo? Who am I to demand that people, Black and white open their minds and hearts to the less fortunate in society?* She grabbed a towel and dried her face. *Maybe I should just quit.*

Then she would think about all of the children who died of poverty and ignorance, and her resolve returned. *Yes,* she said to herself, *I do have a responsibility to fight for the people.* She raised her fist into the air and saluted her reflection in the mirror.

With renewed enthusiasm, Denise ran into her room to finalize her destination. She had much to consider in planning a trip to a communist or socialist country. Once she arrived, the FBI and CIA would resume their surveillance of her activities. Lately, their tails hadn't been as frequent. Or, at the very least, Denise had gotten used to their presence and didn't think about it anymore. Her travel could result in her being exiled from the United States. As she turned this thought over in her mind, she wondered if it would be so bad to be expelled from good old America. She would miss her parents, though she had not spoken to them awhile. Every time she thought about contacting them, she remembered that they wouldn't dig what she was doing. Thinking about them made her sad. She wondered what her parents would say about her planning a trip abroad. Denise felt tears rush to her eyes. She inhaled. There wasn't time for tears. Denise pushed thoughts of her parents to the back of her mind.

Even though Shelly was still mad at her, Denise decided to invite her anyway. Maybe if she got away from Comrade Kweli, Shelly would wake up and forget about trying to have a baby for the revolution. Shelly was making such a mistake! Didn't she know that it was extremely difficult to raise a child alone? Shelly had read the Monyihan report. Shelly knew that Black women were blamed for the plight of the Black man and the high number of single parent households. By having a baby for the revolution, Shelly wasn't accomplishing anything, except becoming another statistic.

Somewhere along the way, Shelly had stopped living for the people and started living for Kweli. Even though Shelly really loved Kweli and Denise believed that he loved her, Denise still felt that a baby wasn't the answer. A trip abroad would give Shelly a new perspective on life. Maybe then she'd see that there was more to life than Kweli. As soon as Denise settled on a destination, she was going to run her ideas past Shelly.

The first of the year sounded like a good time to take the trip. The first marked a new beginning, a new moment in time. Hopefully, it meant that she and Brother Jahid-Ali could stop hiding their relationship. Sneaking around was really getting old and dangerous. There had to be a way for her to work for the people and love her man at the same time.

Brother Jahid-Ali was sitting at his desk at the WEB office. It was well after midnight and he could no longer concentrate on the speech he was writing. Every time he tried to write, his thoughts kept returning to Denise. At some point he was going to have to tell her of his suspicions. Twice in the last two weeks, he thought he saw men following him. When he turned around, the men continued walking as if they didn't even see Brother Jahid-Ali walking in front of them. Another time, he was driving home and could have sworn that a car was shadowing him. He made the block twice, before the car disappeared. It was a black sedan, sort of like an undercover police car. Funny, the vibe he got from the car that was dogging him wasn't a police vibe. The police in Los Angeles were so arrogant that they'd drive by a brotha and shine their high beams on him, just to kick their kicks. The car that followed him that night was more sinister, more calculating. Brother Jahid-Ali was fighting the rising paranoia he felt in his soul.

"Shelly, I'm very sorry about the other day." Denise was standing beside Shelly at the Black Panther headquarters. Shelly was typing a story that was going to be printed in the next day's edition of the *Black Panther* newspaper.

"Just forget it. I know that you didn't mean what you said." Shelly looked up from her typewriter.

"No, I meant what I said, though I realize that I should have chosen my words better," Denise said.

"You got that right." Shelly snapped. She was pushing the keys on the typewriter so hard that Denise thought that they were going to get stuck.

"I didn't come here to fight with you. I came here to apologize." Denise stuck out her hand. "I am very sorry for the things that I said about you having a baby for the revolution."

"Sh!" Shelly covered Denise's mouth. "No one else knows about this but you."

"You still haven't told Kweli?"

Shelly resumed typing. "No. I want to surprise him."

"He's going to be surprised all right," Denise muttered under her breath.

"What?"

"Nothing. Whatever you decide to do is your business." Denise tried to sound convincing. "Do you accept my apology?"

"Yes." Shelly smiled. "I'm glad that you came around, because I was getting tired of not speaking to you."

"So was I."

"So, what brings you here?"

"You." Denise read a few lines over Shelly's shoulder. " 'Black Panther Members Take Their Struggle Abroad." How ironic that Shelly would be submitting a story on the very subject that Denise wanted to talk with Shelly about. "What do you think about that?"

"I can dig it."

Denise pulled up a chair. "Do you ever think about going abroad?"

"Yep."

"Well, what's stopping you?"

"Money, for one. My man for another."

"What if we could secure the money?"

"From where?"

"It doesn't matter. Just what if I could swing the plane tickets, would you be down to go?" Denise was trying to entice Shelly.

"Where?"

"I don't know, Cuba or Angola."

"Hmm." Shelly continued pecking away at her story. "That solves one problem, but what about Kweli?"

"If he is as down for the struggle as he claims, he'll not only understand, but he will be here when you get back."

"I don't know, Niecie. I have to think about it." Shelly didn't sound too enthusiastic about Denise's plan.

"What is there to think about?" asked Shelly. "Either you are part of the problem or part of the solution."

"True. Why can't I be part of the solution in the States? Why do I have to go clear across the world to be part of the solution?"

"You don't have to go anywhere to make change. I was just thinking that it would be a good experience and it would broaden both of our horizons. So far, all we know about the struggles in other countries, is what we learned in the P. E. classes. Or, stuff that we heard from Huey and others who've gone abroad. As a teacher of Political Education for the kids and other adults, I think that my classes would benefit from first hand experience. Don't you?"

"Yeah. But—"

"Not to mention, your writing would improve. Just think how much richer your stories will be, when you are able to write in great detail about demagoguery in foreign countries. You will be able to link our struggle to the broader global struggle for equality for all people." Denise's sales pitch was strong.

"Now you sound like Malcolm."

"That's because Malcolm had vision. And where there is no vision, the people will perish."

Shelly did not answer right away. "What about Kweli? I love him. I don't want to leave him, Niecie." Shelly's face was full with love for Kweli.

"I'm not asking you to leave him." Denise tried a different approach. "I'm just asking you to expand your mind. Do you think that Kweli would not go to Angola or China because he was afraid that if he left you would love another?"

Shelly pursed her lip. "No. I would expect him to go."

"Why can't that same expectation be applied to you?" Denise could tell that Shelly's interest was peaked. "Women need to—"

"All right, Sojourner." Shelly teased. "I get your point. And for your information, the expectation does apply to me."

"Well, then, there doesn't seem to be a problem," Denise said smugly.

"Niecie, you don't have a man, so you don't know how I feel."

If only Denise could tell Shelly about the love of her life, Brother Jahid-Ali. Denise knew what it was like to love a man. Denise did not want to leave Brother Jahid-Ali, but she was confident that he would understand.

"Shelly, just think about it." Denise toned down her sales pitch. "I'm not trying to pressure you, I just think that it would be good for both of us."

"When is this trip supposed to take place?" Shelly tried

to sound casual. "And how long, if I decided to go, would we be gone?'

"I was thinking that the first of the year would be a good time to leave." Denise began counting on her fingers. "I guess once we get to wherever we go, we would stay a few weeks."

"A few weeks?" Shelly stopped typing altogether.

"I don't know yet. We'll figure it out."

"The first is still a few months away." Shelly hoped by then that Denise would change her mind.

"I know, but I've got to start planning right away." Denise was already thinking about what books she would need to read before they left.

"Niecie, how long have you been thinking about leaving?" Too late, it sounded like Denise had made up her mind. One thing about Denise, once she made up her mind, nothing was going to change it.

"When I realized that I couldn't save the world by myself."

Sixteen

Denise was eagerly awaiting Brother Jahid-Ali's visit to Point Dume. After the misunderstanding that went down between them at The Kyte, Denise wanted to meet with her man on a more consistent basis. They agreed to meet every Sunday night at midnight, no matter what.

Excited about seeing him again, Denise ended her P. E. class early and went to make a few purchases. The first item she bought was a double sleeping bag from Western Surplus. This surplus store was located on Florence and Western Avenue. It housed everything from artillery to guns to camping equipment to boating paraphernalia. Denise bought the thickest sleeping bag she could find. It was navy on the outside and a red flannel on the inside. The next time she and Brother Jahid-Ali made love under the stars they wouldn't get dirty, or find little rocks in their clothes.

After leaving Western Surplus, she went to the garment district on Los Angeles Street in Downtown Los Angeles. Winos and drunks lined the street in front of the mission on Main street. One block east of this was the garment district where the store owners were pleasant and the prices were cheap. Once Denise had gone down there with her mother and purchased a beautiful cream colored polyester dress.

As Denise went from store to store, she thought about her mother and their Saturday shopping sprees. They would get up early, go to breakfast and then hit the Crenshaw Shopping

Center. Denise left the mall with at least two bags of sweaters, socks, shoes, and of course, dresses. Her mother indulged Denise, because when her mother was a little girl, her family could not afford such luxuries. It was ironic that Denise would be shopping and thinking about her mother. In so many ways she was like her mother—slender, "good hair" and pretty eyes. Denise's new consciousness made her reject her inherited beauty. Yet, deep inside, Denise was happy that she favored her mother and grandmother so much. Maybe when she got home she would call her mother. Denise caught herself. It was a silly thought. She knew that as soon as she got back that she would not call home.

Denise bought a bright green tie-dyed back-out and matching shorts. Her purchase was so far from her stark Panther uniform that she laughed outloud. It didn't matter, she knew that Brother Jahid-Ali would dig anything she wore.

It was still warm when Denise pulled into the parking spot next to Brother Jahid-Ali's beige VW bus. He was standing a few feet in front of his bus with his back to her. She tooted her horn so that he knew she was there. When he did not turn around, Denise figured he was meditating and got of her car carrying the sleeping bag.

"Hey, daddy, you lookin' fine this August night." Denise slapped Brother Jahid-Ali on his behind.

He still didn't turn around.

"Baby, did you hear me?" Denise hugged him around his waist.

Brother Jahid-Ali rubbed her arms. "I'm fine honey, how are you?" His voice was muffled and his words sounded thick.

"You sound funny. What's the matter?" Denise turned him around.

No answer.

"Baby, what happened!" Denise brought her hand to her mouth and gasped in horror. Her purse and sleeping bag went crashing to the ground.

Brother Jahid-Ali's left eye was swollen shut and the other was red as a tomato. A trickle of blood slid down his chin. He wiped it away with the corner of his beige dashiki.

"I got jumped this evening." Brother Jahid-Ali shrugged his shoulders to dismiss the fight he had earlier that day. "It's nothing."

"Nothing!" Denise shrieked. "It looks like someone tried to kill you."

No response. He hugged Denise to him.

"Did someone try to kill you baby?" Tears welled up in Denise's eyes.

Brother Jahid-Ali couldn't bear to see the pain in her eyes.

"Answer me. Did someone try to kill you?"

He sighed heavily and wiped her tears. It was the inevitable moment of truth that he had to face. "Yes."

"Why would someone want to do that to you? We need to call the police." Denise was frantic. "They'll get to the bottom of this." She tried to drag him to the car.

"Niecie, you're a revolutionary and so am I. If I show up at the police station talkin' 'bout I got ambushed by God knows who, they will laugh and say 'good.' " Brother Jahid-Ali spoke sternly, despite the numbness in his lips.

"No, they won't!" She kissed his swollen eye.

"Niecie, for goodness sake. Dig it! You teach political education classes. Don't you teach your students that the pigs are not to be trusted?"

Denise held on to herself. "Ye—yeah. I do. But I feel like we've got to do something! We can't let them get away with what they've done to you." Denise stopped pacing. "You still haven't told me what happened to you?"

Brother Jahid-Ali noticed the sleeping bag on the ground for the first time. He bent over to pick it up, and grabbed his side. Denise reached for him. "I'll get it."

"No, I'm all right."

He groaned softly and stood up stiffly. Brother Jahid-Ali and Denise walked the short distance to their second spot. Once in the clearing, he untied the sleeping bag and spread it on the ground. "Sit down."

Brother Jahid-Ali tried to sit down without Denise's assistance. "Let me help you."

He wanted to sit on the blanket upright like a man, but the best he could manage to do was lie on his back. "Remember when you asked me if I killed those Panthers at UCLA?"

"Vaguely." Denise was gently rubbing his stomach.

"Well . . ." Brother Jahid-Ali closed his eyes. "Do you trust me?"

"With my life." Denise stared lovingly into his eyes.

"I didn't do it, Niecie," He grabbed her arm tightly. "I didn't kill those men, you've got to believe me."

"I do believe you." Denise's mind was racing. What did the deaths of Bunchy Carter and John Huggins have to do with him getting jumped? "You're not capable of killing anybody."

"Some people think that I had something to do with it." He was being evasive.

"Who?" Denise felt hysteria rising in her throat.

"Your organization, the FBI and who knows who else." Brother Jahid-Ali closed his eyes. "I didn't do it."

"Why do the Panthers think you did it?"

"I don't know." Again the evasiveness was smothering them.

"Talk to me. Tell me the truth."

"It might be because they need a scapegoat."

"But why you and not Sphinx or Ivory?" Denise was confused and very scared for her love's life. She knew that the FBI was ruthless and wouldn't waste an opportunity to do away with someone who was a threat to national security. The Panthers were equally a force to be reckoned with. Some of the members wouldn't think twice about dealing with an enemy of the party. Denise felt the bottom drop out of her stomach. If some of her overzealous comrades were after Brother Jahid-Ali, there's no telling what would happen to him. She had to save him.

"I am the number two man in WEB. The FBI thinks that if they get me, then they have Maulana Imhotep." He paused. "As for the Panthers, they have been looking for retribution for three years."

"What about those men who were convicted of killing Bunchy and John?" Denise was searching for a solution.

"What about them? Nobody knows for sure if they killed them." Brother Jahid-Ali inhaled deeply.

"That's ridiculous. What are we going to do?" Denise was trying to think of a plan. "We could go away. We could go to—"

"I'm not going to run like some sissy." He said gruffly. "Anyway, we aren't going to do anything. I am going to figure out what to do." Brother Jahid-Ali said with finality.

"Baby, I am your woman and we are in this together." Denise was equally as resolved.

"Look Niecie, this is my problem. I shouldn't have told you anything." Brother Jahid-Ali tried to turn over unsuccessfully.

"Yes, you should have told me everything. In fact, you should have told me a long time ago. Why did you keep this from me?" Denise stared hard into his eyes.

"I didn't want you to be involved," Brother Jahid-Ali said quietly.

"How could I not be?" Love flowed from her lips. "Ever since I got suspended, you have been a part of my life. You and Pauletta were my saving grace when my self-esteem was at its lowest. I get chills just thinking about how supportive and loving you were, even though I was an outcast from the very people to whom I had sworn allegiance." She gently wiped his forehead. "You lifted me up and entered my soul. How could I not return the favor? If there is an assault on you, then there's an assault on me." Denise spoke with conviction.

Brother Jahid-Ali cupped her face in his hands. "I don't want you to get hurt."

"I won't get hurt." She kissed his swollen lips.

He pulled her on top of him and held her closely. He groaned from deep inside. "Niecie, I love you so much."

After embracing for a few moments, Denise remembered Brother Jahid-Ali's side. "Baby, your side. I don't want to crush you."

He laughed heartily, though it hurt to do so. "You don't weigh enough to crush me."

Denise joined him in laughter. "Well, just in case, let me up."

Brother Jahid-Ali opened his arms and Denise rolled on to her side. "What do you think we should do?"

"I think that I need to act like nothing happened."

"Are you crazy? You just got beat within an inch of your life and you are going to carry on like nothing happened. What are you going to tell Maulana Imhotep? That you went bowling and the ball accidentally fell on your face?" Denise didn't understand men. Sometimes their machismo attitudes were more than she could take. "This is too much. I need a cigarette." She reached for her purse and pulled out her pack of Kool cigarettes.

"It will be best for me not to mention anything. I have to act like everything is cool, otherwise they will think that they got to me."

"But they did get to you."

"Mentally, Niecie. Sure, they whupped my butt, but they did not break me."

"I thought they were trying to kill you, not break you down." She was being flippant, because he didn't seem to understand the gravity of the situation. "You know that whoever these people are, they're not playing with you."

"I know. But, if I can show them that I can take it, then they'll have to come up with a better strategy."

"How does all of this affect my peace of mind?" Denise took a drag on her cigarette. "Every moment that we're apart, I'm going to be frantic. I need to see you everyday."

"That's impossible." He said gently. "Niecie, you've got to also act like everything is cool. If you don't, somebody might get suspicious."

She exhaled a long trail of white smoke. "Why would anybody suspect me? Nobody even knows that we're together."

"You really don't know who's been watching us." A cold, eerie sensation ran through his heart. "Sometimes I get scared and wonder if WEB is worth all the pain."

Denise pondered this thought for a minute. He was right. She really didn't know how closely the FBI's surveillance team had been watching her. Or which one of her comrades was following her. "I get scared, too. I often ask myself the same question. Is the danger really worth it? Is the struggle for liberation in America worth my life? And each time the answer is yes. Baby, I know you're scared, but always remember, you are not alone." Denise inhaled one last time on her cigarette. Then she stubbed it out in the dirt and snuggled up close to Brother Jahid-Ali. "If I can just know that you are all right, then I'll be okay."

He hugged her to him tightly. "Everything is going to be cool, I promise."

Seventeen

"Comrade Denise, I hear that you are turning out the baddest revolutionaries this side of China." Kweli unfolded what looked like a poster or a map.

They were at the Panther Headquarters. It was buzzing with activity as usual.

Denise smiled. "Comrade Kweli, what are you talking about?"

"The Freedom school of course." Kweli was going over a map of Los Angeles. "Do you see Pasadena anywhere on this map?"

Denise moved next to Kweli. "There it is."

"Where?"

"Just follow the Harbor Freeway North until it turns into the Pasadena Freeway."

"You found that so quickly."

"I am, well was, a Bruin and went to a few football games at the Rose Bowl in Pasadena." A look of nostalgia crossed Denise's face.

Noticing the change in Denise's expression, Kweli asked, "You don't miss that jive, do you, comrade?"

Though Kweli's tone was patronizing, Denise pretended she didn't care. "Not in a million years." She grabbed a red marker out of the pencil holder that was on the desk and drew a line connecting the Harbor Freeway with the Pasadena Freeway. "Why are you looking for Pasadena?"

"I have to rap to the sistas and brothas at Pasadena City College in a few days. I've never been to that campus before."

"Don't your trusted Comrades Leonard and Tyrone know how to get there?" It was Denise's turn to be patronizing.

Kweli avoided her gaze. "They probably do, but I like to know where I'm going, no matter who's driving." He began searching for a piece of paper. "You didn't answer me, how are things at the Freedom School?"

"The little revolutionaries are advancing quite well." Denise beamed with pride.

"What is the latest thing that they learned?" Kweli offered Denise a chair. "Have a seat."

"Thanks. We've been learning the differences between political systems like capitalism, communism and socialism."

"Tell me how you broke down such deep concepts to ghetto kids."

"To explain capitalism, I took a bag of cookies and spread ten of them on the table. Then I called five of the young soldiers to the front of the room. I gave two soldiers four cookies a piece. I gave the third child one; the fourth child and fifth children got to share one cookie. I whispered to the children who had the most cookies not to share their cookies with the other children, no matter what they said. Those were the only instructions I gave them. After a few minutes, the fourth and fifth children asked the other children for some of their cookies. When they all said no, the fifth child began to cry." Denise paused.

"I don't see what this has to do with capitalism."

"Let me finish. I asked the other children if I distributed the cookies fairly. They all yelled out "No!" Before I could even define capitalism, several of the other children began to say that the children with the most cookies were mean not to share their cookies with the other children. The point of this exercise was to show how unequal distributions of wealth, food, employment and shelter create discontentment. More importantly, I think the kids were able to understand that when all of the cookies are concentrated in the hands of a few, there is a problem."

Kweli applauded. "Did you also teach them that evil cancer known as capitalism is what founded this decadent nation?"

"Yes. I even went one step further and asked the young comrades how should they go about getting a fair share of the cookies?"

"Some said ask again nicely. Other comrades raised their fists in the air and demanded revolution." Denise laughed at the memory. "You should've been there!"

"Damn, I missed quite a lesson." Kweli made a mental note to visit the Freedom School.

"For communism, we—"

"That's okay, I would bet my last dollar that you got your point across. Speaking of points, what would you say if I took you out of the classroom and put you on my staff?" Kweli folded his hands on the desk.

"Ah, Comrade Kweli, stop jivin'." Denise didn't believe what he was saying.

Kweli looked her straight in the eye. "No, seriously."

"What would be my role?" Bemused, Denise pretended to go along with him.

"Well, since you are so good with the kids and in the P. E. classes, I was thinking that may be you should take your show on the road." Kweli reached into the top drawer of his desk.

"Come again?"

"I didn't forget our last conversation. Comrade, it's time. You could assist me with my speeches. I probably shouldn't say this, but some of the brothers don't quite get their facts straight. They are more interested in sounding tough and sometimes forget the topic. I need someone with bad research skills and someone who can write. Lately, I've been giving speeches to all white audiences . . . slang is cool for the people, but white folks don't always understand ghetto lingo." Kweli winked at her. "Ya dig what I'm sayin'?"

Denise didn't answer right away. "When do you need me to start?"

"Right now."

"Now?" Denise was surprised. "That's too soon. I need to wrap up with the school and find a replacement teacher." Her mind began to whirl. There were so many things that had to be done. There was no way she could leave her kids now.

"They're a bunch of teachers down there, why do you need to find a new teacher?" Kweli needed Denise bad and wasn't going to take "no" for an answer.

"Well, I want to feel comfortable that they are left in good hands." Denise made sure to choose her words carefully. She didn't want Kweli to think that there was dissension in the ranks at the Freedom School. More specifically, she didn't want to turn the education of the young revolutionaries turned over to DeeDee.

As if reading Denise's mind, Kweli responded. "Comrade DeeDee's there. She can take over."

Denise looked down at her hands. Here was her opportunity to tell Kweli exactly what she thought about that underhanded, conniving, two-faced hussy. Just as she opened her mouth, Denise remembered that DeeDee and Kweli were very close. How close she wasn't exactly sure, but if that witch DeeDee had her way, she and Kweli were probably closer than close.

"Yeah, she can." Denise bit her bottom lip. "There are just a couple of things that I need to go over with her."

"Hasn't she been teaching with you at the school?" Kweli was confused by Denise's hesitation. "Denise, you've been beggin' me for a chance ever since before you got suspended. Why are you actin' like you don't want it?"

"I do want this and I'm going to work with you. It's just that Comrade DeeDee doesn't take part in the teaching."

"She doesn't?" Kweli made notes of which street he needed to take to get to Pasadena City College. "I thought that was why she was there."

"Well, Kweli, we came to an agreement. Basically, I have been in charge of the curriculum and DeeDee has more or less been assisting me."

"If she has been assisting you, then it shouldn't be that hard for you to leave. Comrade DeeDee is a smart sista. Everything will be cool. Now let's get down to business. I need a speech written by the day after tomorrow. The subject is money. The party is hurtin' real bad for some cold hard cash."

Denise whipped out the tablet she used to make her lesson plans and began to take notes. "Kweli, you won't be disappointed!" She jumped out of her chair, ran over to Kweli and threw her arms around his neck. "I promise, you won't be sorry!" Denise pecked him quickly on the cheek

"All right, Comrade, let's get back to work." He couldn't help but laugh.

* * *

The next six weeks flew by like a lightning. Fall crept in and Indian Summer was in full force. September was hot, the leaves were falling and Denise loved it all. In fact, when she thought about it, this was the busiest and happiest she'd ever been since joining the Black Panther Party.

Each day Denise was up early accompanying Kweli to rallies and out late attending benefits given by celebrities to raise money for the Party. In the middle of the day, Denise would try to visit the Freedom School. It never failed but whenever she went to the school, DeeDee would be waiting for her with an attitude. No matter how negative DeeDee was to her, Denise did not let it damper her spirits or visits with the budding revolutionaries.

Denise was getting lots of encouragement from Kweli. Slowly but surely the other male comrades were starting to give her the respect that she deserved. Denise was so excited. Her new found position was great in all areas except one. With all of her responsibilities, she did not have time to plan her trip abroad. A couple of times she almost mentioned her plans to Kweli, but each time something came up. Oh, how she wished that she could speak with Pauletta. Pauletta would understand. Unfortunately, Denise had no idea as to how to find her. Denise heard that Pauletta had officially gone underground and joined the Black Liberation Army. Denise didn't know much about the BLA, but knew that Pauletta had a cool head and would be just fine.

Denise made a clandestine trip to the post office, near the Los Angeles airport. There was no one she could trust to messenger the letter over, so she had to slip out in the middle of the night. Denise mailed the note anonymously, so that no one would know that she was the sender. The note was mailed to Brother Jahid-Ali at the WEB headquarters. In her note, she told him that she could not meet him at Point Dume on Sunday. A few days later, he sent her a note saying that he loved her and that he really needed to see her.

On early Monday, Denise, Shelly and Kweli did not get home until two-thirty in the morning. It had been another long night. She began peeling her clothes off and thinking about her long list of duties for the next day. When Denise heard Kweli kiss Shelly goodnight, she gasped.

"Girl, what's wrong with you?" Shelly walked into the room they shared.

"Oh nothing." Denise remembered that she forgot to write to Brother Jahid-Ali and tell him that she would meet him later during the week. "I just remembered something I forgot to do."

Not noticing the pain on Denise's face, Shelly kept talking. "Elaine gave a helluva speech tonight didn't she?"

"Yeah. It was solid." Denise's thoughts were a mile away. What did Brother Jahid-Ali have to tell her? Something was beginning to give way inside of her. A cold chill ran down her spine. *What if he needed her?* Denise took a deep breath and went into the bathroom. She splashed water over her face. The cold water didn't soothe her like it normally did. Try as she might, she could not stop the panic that was rising in her stomach.

Denise went back to their bedroom and scribbled a few words on a blank sheet of paper.

"You're not about to write a speech at this hour, are you?" Shelly asked Denise. "Girl, you are too much."

"No. I'm just making a quick list of things to do tomorrow." Denise folded the note up and shoved it in her bag.

"Oh." Shelly turned off the light closest to her. "Then, get some rest."

"I am. I'm right behind you." Denise said a quick prayer for Brother Jahid-Ali and turned the light off.

One week, two weeks, then three weeks went by and no word from Brother Jahid-Ali. Denise went to Point Dume looking for him, but there was no sign of him. The last time she saw him, he had been beaten up pretty badly. Her worst nightmare was that Brother Jahid-Ali was somewhere lying in a gutter, helpless and bloody. Her imagination had taken on a life of its own.

Denise started experiencing a range of emotions. She sent two more notes. At first she was scared, then she got angry. The last few days, she was just a mess of confusion. It took all she had not to go to the WEB headquarters in person and look for him. There was no one she could talk to about this and Denise felt like she was dying a slow death.

To keep from going stir crazy, Denise attacked her duties with renewed zeal. She deliberately wore herself out during the day, so that at night she would crash. Denise did not want to dream. Dreams were dangerous and often filled with images of her and Brother Jahid-Ali in paradise together.

As the weather began to grow cold, Denise grew more and more edgy. She tried to act like everything was cool, but Shelly saw right through her.

"Niecie, can I ask you something?"

"Sure." Denise was working on a statement for the *Black Panther* newspaper for Kweli.

"What's his name?" Shelly put her hand on the paper that Denise was writing on.

"Excuse me?" Denise tried to move Shelly's hand.

"You heard me. What's his name?" Shelly was not giving up. Denise had a secret lover and Shelly was bound and determined to find out.

"Who are you talking about?" Denise said hastily. She hoped that if she sounded busy that Shelly would leave her alone.

"Niecie, I've known you for years and I know that look when I see it. I suspected that you were seeing someone, but I wasn't completely certain until now."

Denise tried to kept writing. "I don't know what you're talking about."

"Look at me and say that."

Denise faced Shelly and as calmly and convincingly as she could, she said. "I don't have a man." Denise almost succeeded, but Shelly made a silly face and Denise started laughing.

"I knew it! Who is he? And how come you haven't brought him around?"

Denise was busted. There was no way she could lie to Shelly. "I haven't seen him in a while." Denise said in a quiet voice.

"Why?"

"Haven't had time." Denise cleared her throat. "Uh, neither has he."

"Who is he?"

"He is the kindest, smartest, righteous brotha I know."

"Who is he?"

Denise's voice grew stronger. "He loves the people as

much as I do. He's eloquent, sincere and the voice of revolution. He's—"

"Cut the bull. What's his name?"

"Love." Denise felt a wave of relief overcome her. It was nice to finally be able to speak about the love of her life.

"Love?" Shelly thought hard. "That doesn't ring a bell."

Denise continued to let Shelly guess who it could be. In those few moments, Denise let her mind wander to Brother Jahid-Ali.

"Where is he?"

No answer.

"If you won't tell me his name, at least tell me where he is?"

Denise was stuck. If she told Shelly, she would be betraying Brother Jahid-Ali's trust, not to mention, she might be jeopardizing his life. If she didn't answer, Shelly would keep bugging her. Her decision was made. She would lie. "He's out of town."

"Where?"

"Does it matter?"

"Yes."

"Why?"

"I want to meet him."

"For what?"

"Because you are obviously in love with Mr. Love and I just want to see if he's better than that jive turkey Charles you used to date."

Denise laughed. "He's a thousand times smarter, cuter and definitely more relevant than Charles Jackson could ever be. Can you believe that I wanted to marry Charles?"

"No and I'm glad you got rid of that zero," Shelly said with a deadpan look.

"Girl, you got your nerve, what about Sean?"

"Oh yeah! I forgot about him. I heard that he's a news broadcaster in Maryland," Shelly said thoughtfully.

"Really? Good for him." Denise stood up and stretched. "Well, I heard that Brinkley is Chancellor of UCLA, can you believe that?"

"Somehow that doesn't surprise me. Niecie, do you ever miss those days? Life was so much easier and fun."

"It was easier because our conscious was asleep. We didn't know anything, so everything was fun."

"True, but you can't tell me that you didn't have a good time," Shelly insisted nostagically.

Denise pondered Shelly's question. Did she miss those days of sorority functions, football games and platforms? "I would be lying if I said that I didn't miss that time. But Shelly, my life has meaning now. I feel like I am making a difference. I just feel so much richer."

"I can dig it."

"If I tell you something, do you promise not to go blabbing to your boyfriend, Kweli?"

Shelly crossed her heart. "I promise. What is it?"

"I am starting my plans to travel abroad."

"Oh, no, not that again."

"I'm serious, Shelly. I can't wait."

They were both silent for a long minute. Shelly spoke first, "I've actually been giving thought to your proposed sojourn."

"And—?"

"And, I was thinking that if you don't have anyone to go with you, I'll go. That is, of course, if your man doesn't go. I am not going to be a third wheel."

"You wouldn't be! I'm so excited." Denise hugged

Shelly. "What a minute, what about Kweli? I thought you were afraid to leave him."

"Oh well, I got over that."

"Have you also gotten over your desire to have a baby for the revolution?" Denise was hoping for a miracle.

"No and if you want company on your trip around the world, I suggest you drop it." Shelly put her hands on her hips.

"I knew that that was asking for too much." Denise was happy to know that Shelly would be accompanying her on her trip. Now, if she could only get hold of Brother Jahid-Ali, everything would be perfect.

Eighteen

"Excuse me, is Miss Denise here?" A little boy about nine years old stood in the doorway of the Black Panther Office.

"Hi honey, I'm Denise." Denise motioned to the little boy to come inside.

He quickly walked toward Denise with a note extended toward her. "Here, this is for you."

"Thank you." Before Denise could offer the child something to drink, the boy ran out the door.

Finally Brother Jahid-Ali had contacted Denise. The note was short and to the point: "Meet me at midnight on Friday." Denise crushed the note to her chest. She was a little concerned that something might be wrong. It was Wednesday and they normally met on Sundays. Denise calmed herself down, it was nothing, she told herself, he just missed her.

Denise checked the master calendar on the far wall, above Kweli's desk. Friday was filled with the usual daily events, a noon rally at Cal State Los Angeles, a fundraiser at the Hollywood Roosevelt Hotel in Hollywood, and an after-hours planning meeting at The Kyte. Denise needed to think of an excuse to skip The Kyte and meet Brother Jahid-Ali.

* * *

"Guess what, Niecie?"

"What?" Denise was sitting on her bed staring up at her poster of Marvin Gaye.

"I'm pregnant."

"You are!" Dismay laced Denise's words.

"Yes and I'm so happy!" Shelly hugged herself. She danced around the room. "I want you to be the baby's Godmother. Kweli will probably ask Leonard to be the Godfather. I can't wait to tell everybody." Shelly stopped dancing and looked at Denise. "Niecie, what's the matter? Aren't you happy for me?"

"Yes, I'm happy for you. It's just that I thought you were going to wait?" Denise sat up. "How far along are you?"

"Well, I was, but then, well, it just happened." All of the wind had gone out of Shelly's sail. "I'm about six weeks pregnant."

"Does Kweli know?"

"No, but he will." Shelly sounded defensive.

"When?"

"I'm going to tell him Friday night." Shelly grew excited again. "I've got it all worked out. I'll invite him over and make him a romantic dinner. After dinner, we'll make love and then I'll tell him—just before he dozes off to sleep."

Denise winced. "Sounds good, except, you know that Friday night is planning night."

"Oh yeah, I forgot." Shelly slapped her forehead. "What time?"

"After we leave the Hollywood Roosevelt Hotel." Denise started counting on her fingers. "Probably around eleven."

"Where?"

"At The Kyte." Denise rubbed her eyes. "Shelly, how do you think Kweli is going to take the news?"

"He'll be happy. It shouldn't be that much of a surprise to him. We've been talking about needing soldiers to carry on the revolution."

"Right on." Though Denise disagreed with Shelly's logic, there was nothing she could do.

"Niecie, what's the meeting about?"

"The party needs to devise new ways to get members." Denise reached for her notebook. "Also, subscriptions of the *Black Panther* newspaper are back logged. A new method of distribution is desperately needed. And—"

"None of that stuff sounds that important," Shelly said seriously.

"Shelly, it's all important." Denise responded with an exaggerated flip of her hand.

"What I meant was, it doesn't sound like something you couldn't talk about on Saturday."

Denise could see a plan working in Shelly's mind. "True, I guess most of this can wait," Denise said as she flipped the page of her calendar.

"Good. Think of something to cancel the meeting."

Denise was excited. Shelly was giving Denise a window of opportunity to meet Brother Jahid-Ali. "I'll try, but you know that your man likes to stick to a strict schedule."

Shelly began to pace the floor. "Hmm. Too bad you guys have to meet on Friday."

"Yeah, it really is a shame." Denise tried to sound disappointed but hopeful. "Maybe the meeting won't last that long."

A devious look crossed Shelly's face. "I'll talk to Kweli and get him to cancel the meeting."

Inwardly, Denise cheered, but outwardly she responded doubtfully. "Good luck."

Before Shelly left the room, Denise blocked her path. "One more thing, even though I was initially against you having a baby, I respect your decision and I'm happy for you." They embraced.

"Yeah, well let's hope Kweli feels the same way." Shelly said. Denise detected a note of uncertainty in Shelly's voice.

"I'm sure that he will. Oh, I can't wait to meet my god-baby." Denise smiled at Shelly and whispered a prayer for the child. Religion was not taught in the Party. Actually some of the Comrades frowned down on Christianity, because of its connection to the pacifist Civil Rights Movement. Despite this, Denise still believed in God, and looked forward to being a godmother.

At last Denise and Brother Jahid-Ali met at Point Dume. It was late September and the once lush mountain hideaway had become a playground for red, orange and yellow leaves. A few clouds lingered near the moon and a lone coyote could be heard baying in the distance. Perhaps he yearned for his love the way Denise yearned for Brother Jahid-Ali. Ordinarily strange sounds scared Denise, but tonight the song of the coyote didn't bother her. She was with her man and nothing else mattered.

"Baby, I've missed you so much." Brother Jahid-Ali squeezed Denise tightly to him. "It's been too long."

Not wanting to spoil the moment, Denise nestled closer to him.

Something was nagging Denise's heart. "Sweetie, I know that we agreed not to discuss party business, but I've got to know something."

"I'll tell you anything you want to know." There comes

a time in every man's life when the woman he loves can have anything she wants. This was one of those times. He was prepared to give Denise the moon if she asked for it.

Denise took a deep breath. "I don't know how to ask this but do you know who the men are who shot Bunchy and John?"

Brother Jahid-Ali disengaged himself from her. He took a few steps away into the darkness.

"Did you hear me?"

"Yes, Denise." He said quietly.

"Yes, you know who did it or yes you heard me?" Denise's voice quivered when she spoke. A chill ran down her spine.

No response.

When he still did not answer, Denise grew nervous. "Honey, answer me . . ."

"That's the one question in the whole world that I cannot answer." His voice grew somber.

"Why not?" Denise joined him in the dark recesses of the trees.

It was so dark that Denise couldn't make out the features on Brother Jahid-Ali's face. "After I joined the Lions, I took an oath of secrecy."

"Is it that you don't trust me?"

"No, never!" Brother Jahid-Ali reached out in the darkness and stroked Denise's afro. "It's just that for your safety I cannot answer that question." He kissed her open palms.

Denise's chin dropped. He caught it before it hit her chest. "Baby, I need you to trust me on this. I would never do anything to jeopardize your life. You know that, don't you?" he asked, desperation dripping from his voice.

"Yes." Denise said softly.

"I might have to take a trip." He stepped into the clearing and stooped to pick up a rock.

"Where?"

"Far, far away from here." Brother Jahid-Ali threw the rock far into the distance.

"Why?" An uneasy fear began to grip Denise.

"Remember when I got jumped? Well, that wasn't the first time. My life is being threatened on almost a daily basis. I'm beginning to not even know the difference between my friends and my enemies. For the first time, life seems so very clear. There is no one I can trust, except you and I am afraid. I'm not afraid for myself. No, I'm afraid of what might happen to you."

Feeling as if she was missing something, Denise asked him again. "Why do you think that something is going to happen to me?"

"These people don't play. They will hurt the people closest to me, if they can't get me directly."

"Honey, no one even knows we're together."

"Pauletta does."

Denise shook her head. "She wouldn't tell a soul. Pauletta knows how dangerous it is for us to be together."

"Yeah, you're right."

"Brotha, who are these people? If you're talking about the F.B.I., they've been harassing revolutionaries for years."

"No. I don't think it's them this time." He said with a sarcastic chuckle. "I almost wish it was them—then at least I could sleep at night."

For the first time that evening, Denise took a good, hard look at Brother Jahid-Ali. His smiling eyes were so sad and his air had changed. It was almost as if she was standing before a complete stranger. Gone was his cool eloquence and in its place was a man who lived in fear. Just looking at him broke Denise's heart.

"Do you think it's my comrades?" She choked back tears.

Brother Jahid-Ali did not respond. Instead he changed the subject. "Let's talk about something else?"

"Don't shut me out. Talk to me. Tell me who you think it is." Denise pleaded with him.

Wiping the fear from her eyes, Brother Jahid-Ali answered her. "I'll make a deal with you; the next time we meet, I'll tell you."

"What's the difference between now and next time? Why can't you tell me right now?" She was getting angry, but it was useless.

"I just can't." He kissed the tip of her nose.

Resigned that he was not going to answer any more questions, Denise let the subject drop. Brother Jahid-Ali was not telling her something. Denise didn't know what it was, but she was determined to find out.

Shelly and Kweli were lying in Kweli's bed. Kweli's apartment looked more like the Panther Headquarters than a place to live. Paper, maps, posters and books were everywhere. He didn't bother to clean it, because he rarely ever slept there. Kweli used his pad for serious planning meetings or when he just needed a moment to himself. With membership rapidly dropping in the party, funds dipping dangerously low, and raids by the Los Angeles Police Department on other Panther residences, there were many nights he went home, put on Miles and just stared at the poster of Huey.

Kweli's bedroom was empty except for a huge king-sized bed that took up most of the floor. There was a small closet and an even smaller bathroom down the hall. He didn't complain. His apartment was in an unsuspecting neighborhood near USC and the Party paid his rent and beyond that, he didn't need much.

Kweli reached for his pack of cigarettes on the nightstand. After he pulled a cigarette out for himself, he offered Shelly one.

"No thanks." Shelly felt anxious. This was the moment of truth. Time to tell Kweli the good news.

In seconds the room filled with smoke. Shelly began to cough. The smoke was so overwhelming that it made her nauseous. She ran into the bathroom. When she reentered, Kweli was opening a window. "Since when did smoke start bothering you?"

"Oh, a few weeks ago." Shelly said weakly. She was still holding her stomach.

Kweli put his cigarette out. "Come to think about it, I haven't seen you smoke in a while. Did you quit?" He went over to her and helped her. "Lie down."

"Sort of." Shelly felt better. "Kweli, do you love me?"

"Yeah, you're my ol' lady. My number one fox. My numero uno." Kweli put emphasis on "uno." He plopped down on the bed next to her.

Shelly giggled. "Good, 'cause your number one is about to have a number two."

"A whoda?"

"Not a whoda, a number two, a baby, a warrior, a child to carry on the revolution." Shelly laughed outloud.

Kweli was stunned. "How? I thought that you were on the pill."

"I am. I mean, I was."

"Well, then what happened? Damn, I can't believe this!"

Kweli jumped out of the bed. "Shelly, I'm not prepared to be a daddy."

"But I thought that you wanted me to have a baby."

"I do, but not now." He lowered his voice. "The party needs me, Shelly. I don't have time to be a father."

Shelly curled up on her side and began to cry softly.

Realizing that he upset her, Kweli went to her and tried to hug her.

"Get away from me!" she screamed at him.

"I'm sorry. Shelly, please don't cry." Kweli tried to rub her back, but she pushed his hand away.

"Get away from me, Kweli! It was a mistake. I thought that you loved me, but I see that you don't." Her sobs grew louder. "You love your precious party more than you ever loved me. I'm so stupid! Niecie told me not to get pregnant. I should've listened."

"Niecie?"

"Oh forget it!" Still clutching her stomach Shelly started dressing. "You run around town in your black leather jacket and your combat boots like you own the whole damn world. You talk all that talk about reactionary Negroes not wanting to take responsibility for the community . . ." Tears were running down her face. "About how nobody wants to give a brotha a break; about how sistas need to have babies for the revolution to keep the struggle going; about how you owe it to Bunchy and John to keep the party strong." Shelly was huffing and puffing. "Kweli, you always have the answers . . . walkin' around here with your clenched fist raised high in the air, and you're afraid of a baby. I see now that all of that mighty rhetoric you spout ain't nuthin' but jive!"

Kweli was in a state of shock. He didn't know what to do.

"Get out of my way!"

Kweli stepped aside and let Shelly pass.

Shelly slammed into the apartment about the same time Denise's head hit the pillow. Shelly was crying wildly and bumping into everything on her way to the bedroom she shared with Denise.

Denise jumped up and ran to the doorway. "Shelly, you're gonna wake everybody."

"I don't care!" Shelly brushed past Denise. "I hate him."

"Who?" Densie asked, though she knew the answer to her own question.

"Kweli."

Denise joined Shelly on Shelly's bed. "What did he say?"

"He said that he didn't want to be a daddy." A torrent of tears ran down her face again.

"I'm so sorry." Denise put her arms around Shelly and began to rock her gently. "I'll help you raise the baby."

"Oh Niecie, I feel like such a fool."

"Oh, no, honey, you're not the fool. Kweli's the foolish one." Denise couldn't wait to get her hands around Kweli's neck.

Nineteen

The following morning, Kweli was abrupt and just down-right evil to everybody. No one knew what was wrong with him, except Denise and he made a point to keep his distance from her. It took all of the self-control that Denise had not to blast him in front of the other comrades. Maturity had taught her not to come between a man and a woman. Though Shelly cursed Kweli the entire night before, there was still the possibility of them getting back together. If Denise said something out of line and Shelly and Kweli got back together, Denise would be the one to end up alone, not Kweli. As pitiful as that sounded, Denise knew in her heart of hearts to stay out of Shelly and Kweli's relationship.

At the end of the meeting, Kweli asked Denise to stay for a minute. As soon as everyone left his apartment, he locked the door. "I guess Shelly is pretty upset with me."

Denise waved her hand in front of her face. "That's putting it mildly, don't you think?" Realizing that she had responded, Denise qualified what she just said. "Look you know she's mad at you, so don't be tryin' to drag me into your situation."

Ignoring Denise's earnest effort to not get in the middle of their problem, Kweli continued to speak. "I didn't know what to say. It was a surprise to me."

"A surprise? Weren't you the one who filled her head with all that mess about having a baby to save the future?"

"No," Kweli said innocently.

"Come on, comrade." Denise couldn't believe her eyes. Here was this grown man, a literal giant among men and he was acting like a little boy.

"Well, I didn't think she'd actually get pregnant." His tone changed to defense.

"Kweli, Shelly didn't get pregnant by herself." Denise reminded him. "It takes two to tango."

"Maybe it's not mine."

WHAP! Denise slapped his face. "Don't even try it."

"I'm trippin' . . . I didn't mean that. I'm sorry." Kweli absently rubbed the side of his face.

"I'm not the one you should be apologizing to."

"Yeah, well, I'll call her. Can you—"

"No." Denise zipped her bag. "That's between you and Shelly."

It was Wednesday and Kweli still hadn't called Shelly. In turn, Shelly was growing angrier and angrier by the minute. She called him every name but the son of God, stopped going to work at the Black Panther newspaper, and spent her days moping around the apartment. So far Shelly had missed two deadlines and was determined to miss as many as she could. Kweli, on the other hand, had become a drill sergeant and barked at everybody within his eyesight.

"Niecie, where are we going in Africa?" Shelly was going through the travel brochures that Denise had received from Triple A.

"I was thinking that we would go to Angola."

"Angola sounds nice." Shelly flipped through the brochure and looked at the map of Africa. She twisted the book to the right and ran her finger along the west coast of the motherland. "What about Namibia?"

"Hum. I don't know much about Namibia."

"It is south of Angola and north of South Africa. The Kalahria Desert sits to the east and the South Atlantic Ocean is on the west. Namibia is a little larger than half the size of Alaska and is home to precious minerals like diamonds, copper and uranium." Shelly smiled quite pleased with herself.

"I see that someone's being doing her homework." Denise was impressed.

"I've had so much time on my hands, and you've been so busy that I figured I'd begin preliminary plans for our trip." Shelly tried to sound excited, but her red rimmed eyes told of a different emotion.

Not wanting to upset Shelly by talking about her breakup with Kweli, Denise changed the subject. "How have you been feeling? Do you need anything? I've been running around so much that I forgot to ask if you've had morning sickness."

"Niecie, my physical health is just fine. It's my heart that's in knots. How could he do this to me?" Shelly patted her stomach affectionately.

"I don't know." Denise said pitifully. The conversation was growing awkward and Denise was running out of things to say. "Have you been to the doctor?"

"No, my appointment is Friday at one."

"Do you need me to go with you?"

"Naw, I'll be all right. My mama's going to take me." Shelly brightened a little. "She told everybody in my whole family and all the neighbors. She's already started making plans to be a grandmother. She wants the baby to call her

'Nana'." Shelly paused for a moment. Her voice dropped. "At least somebody's happy."

Just listening to Shelly was making Denise hate Kweli more and more. "That's cool that your mama is being so supportive. That's real cool."

Shelly got up and went to the bathroom. Denise resisted the urge to follow her. She knew that Shelly was going into the bathroom to cry. She felt so bad for Shelly. If only Kweli wasn't such a coward.

When Shelly returned from the bathroom, Denise was on her way out the front door. "Hey, Niecie, where are you going?"

"I'm going to check on my kids at the Freedom School. Do you want to go?"

"No, I'll just get in the way." Shelly plopped down on the couch.

"No you won't. In fact, it will do you some good to get out and get some fresh air."

"I like the smell of vanilla incense and cigarette smoke just fine." Shelly folded her arms across her chest.

"No you don't, Shelly. You hate the smell of vanilla and smoke makes you nauseous. Grab your jacket and let's go." Denise was adamant.

"You go on, I'll be just fine."

"Shelly, we've been friends a long time and I've never once asked you do anything you didn't want to do, have I?"

"No."

"All right then, trust me and get your jacket and let's go."

Shelly smiled. "All right, all right. You don't have to be so mean."

When they arrived at the Freedom School, DeeDee was

in front of the class teaching a lesson on Garrett Morrison, the inventor of the stoplight. Denise tried to be as inconspicuous as possible, so as not to interrupt the lesson. But as soon as Jamal saw her, he went flying into her arms.

"Comrade Denise, I've missed you so much."

When Jamal realized that the other male children were watching him. He took a step back and cleared his throat. "I mean, it's cool to see you."

Denise winked at him. "It's cool to see you too."

DeeDee was quite unamused with the spectacle. "Little brothers and sisters pay attention!"

"Ugh. Is she always like that?" Shelly asked.

"Yep." Denise pretended not to notice the irritation in DeeDee's voice. "Right on, Comrade DeeDee, that's keeping them in line." *Old witch,* Denise mumbled under her breath with a fake smile still showing on her face.

They spent about an hour at the school just observing. Just as they were leaving Kweli walked through the front door of the school.

"Oh God," Denise sighed.

"What?" Shelly looked up in time to see Kweli standing across the room. "Let's go."

"Follow me." Denise lead the way to the front door.

Kweli's eyes immediately locked on Shelly. There was only one exit and Kweli was blocking it. Denise tried to catch his glance, so that he would stop staring at Shelly, but he seemed to be mesmerized by Shelly's presence. As Denise approached the door, she could see that Shelly wasn't the only one who had had sleepless nights. Kweli looked almost haggard, like the wind had been sucked out of him. Denise continued past Kweli and onto the street. She looked behind her and Shelly was nowhere to be found. *Here we go,* Denise thought to herself.

Denise poked her head back through the door. "Shelly, are you ready?"

"Yeah, just a minute." Shelly didn't even look in Denise's direction.

Denise went back outside. It was getting cold and Denise was ready to go home. She couldn't hear what Kweli was saying to Shelly, but she saw Shelly's face soften. Two minutes later, Shelly leaned out the door. Kweli was a few feet behind her, out of earshot.

"I'll catch up with you later."

Denise could not read the expression on her face. "Are you sure?"

"It's cool. Kweli and I need to talk."

"Whatever you do, don't tell him about our plans to go to Africa." Denise's tone was firm.

"Why not?" Shelly's eye grew wide.

"I just don't think you should." Denise said gravely.

"Niecie, I love him." Shelly sounded sincere, but desperate.

"Okay, see you later." Denise gave Shelly a *I'm-not-too-sure-about-this-but-it's-your-life look*. Denise hoped that Shelly and Kweli worked everything out. She started the ignition of her Mustang, turned up the volume on her radio and drove home alone.

"Girl, he even goes with me to the doctor." Shelly was talking about her favorite two subjects: her baby and her man.

"He's supposed to."

Four months passed and Shelly still didn't look pregnant. "Kweli's so busy and everything—" Shelly continued to rattle on about Kweli this and Kweli that. Denise had tuned her out, though she threw in an occasional "Um hum" or "Really girl!" They went through the same routine almost every time they spoke. After Shelly and Kweli made up, Shelly more or less moved in with him.

"And did I tell you that he fixed up the apartment. It's bad. He bought some new posters and even a pair of baby combat boots. I never even knew that they made shoes so small. Niecie, you've got to come by."

"I will," Denise said over her shoulder.

"Oh and DeeDee gave me a tiny pick to comb his or her hair when they get old enough. Wasn't that sweet of her?"

"DeeDee?" Denise looked up.

"Yeah, she's been a lot of help. Always there if I need anything."

"Don't you think that's a little strange?" Denise's face was twisted in disgust.

"Oh Niecie, don't be jealous. I hate to bother you, since you're always so busy."

"I'm not jealous. I just think it's a little odd that DeeDee is tryin' to be your ace now, when before you got pregnant, she barely even spoke to you."

"Niecie, you can't hold a grudge against everybody. She's changed." Pregnancy apparently had softened Shelly's sensibility regarding women who were trying to get her man.

"Let's hope so." Denise shook her head. Something smelled fishy. "And I am never too busy for you. If you need something just holler."

"Well, I did call you a couple of times really late at night. Faye said that you weren't home. I guess you were out seeing that man you won't tell me about."

"Oh him."

"Who is it?" Shelly attempted to get Denise to answer her.

"Not this again." Denise rolled her eyes in exasperation.

"Maybe if you two quit hiding, you could get pregnant and then our babies could play together."

"Are you outta your mind? I'm not having any children anytime soon." Denise meant that. The world wasn't safe enough to bring a baby into. Besides she had too much work to do in the community.

"Whatever. You're saying that now." Shelly waved her finger in Denise's face.

"On to bigger and more realistic things, Shelly is it okay for you to travel?"

"I don't know."

"Have you asked the doctor?"

"I keep forgetting."

"The final payment is due in a couple of weeks."

"I know. I'll ask her at my next appointment."

Denise sensed a hesitation in Shelly's voice. "Shelly, you are still going, aren't you?"

"Niecie—"

Denise took a deep breath. "I should've known that he'd talk you out of it."

"Kweli didn't talk me out of anything. I'm grown and I make my own decisions." Shelly said with feigned conviction. "It's just that I'm four months pregnant and even if the doctor says it's okay for me to travel, Kweli doesn't think it's a good idea for me to be so far away, in case something happens."

As mad as Denise wanted to be, she realized that it was unrealistic for Shelly to travel while she was pregnant. Denise had been so wrapped up in trying to see Brother Jahid-Ali and covering all of the meetings that Kweli had missed, that it never crossed her mind that Shelly's pregnancy was not conducive to travelling abroad. "He's right."

"So you're not mad at me?" Shelly asked hopefully.

"Mad at you? Of course not. I hate to admit it, but Kweli's got a point. You should be close by."

"Why don't you take your man, uh, what did you say his name was again?"

Not falling for Shelly's trap. "I didn't and I think that I need to make this trip alone."

"Niecie, you are so brave."

"Either that or stupid."

Late one night, a week later, Denise went over to Kweli's to get Shelly.

"Niecie, where are we going?" Shelly was rubbing sleep out of her eyes.

"You'll see when we get there." Denise looked around and didn't see Kweli. "Where's your old man?"

"At a meeting," Shelly said confidently.

Denise did not comment, though she did raise an eyebrow. She didn't remember him having a meeting that night. Denise ignored the sinking feeling she had and ushered Shelly into the car.

"You sure do look cute." Shelly admired Denise's brown jeans, powder blue cotton shirt and matching brown silk scarf. The scarf turned her amber eyes hazel.

Denise blushed. "Thanks."

They winded down Pacific Coast Highway, popping their fingers and singing with the radio. "The Supremes we are not." Shelly said, now fully awake.

"That's because we are missing Diana."

On the way to Point Dume, Denise kept thinking about

Brother Jahid-Ali. Their last few meetings had been spo-
radic and very short. He was always in a hurry or talking
about leaving. He never said where or when, just that he
was leaving. Each time Denise tried to tell him about her
trip, but never got up the nerve. Brother Jahid-Ali would
cling to her so strongly when they were about to part, that
she was afraid to tell him about her plans. In a way, she
understood why Shelly was so eager to stay behind with
Kweli.

Finally tired of hiding her relationship with Brother Jahid-
Ali, Denise called Shelly at the last minute and told her to
get dressed. Denise didn't have time to tell him that she
was bringing someone, but she didn't think he'd mind, once
he saw that it was Shelly.

When Denise and Shelly reached their destination,
Denise blew the horn. This was her signal to Brother Jahid-Ali
that she was there.

"It's beautiful out here!" Shelly exclaimed. "Where are
we?" She twisted and turned in her seat.

"We are at the place the moon calls home," Denise said
figuratively.

Shelly turned to look at her friend. "Your man is here,
isn't he?"

Denise nodded affirmatively.

She stopped the car by the side of the mountain. "Shelly,
wait right here for a minute."

"Take your time." Shelly leaned the chair back in the
car and took in the view of white sand and ocean foam to
her immediate right.

With open arms, Brother Jahid-Ali welcomed Denise.
He kissed her long and passionately. It was several minutes
before their bodies parted. "Baby, why is the radio in your
car still on?"

"I brought someone to meet you," Denise smiled cheerfully.

Brother Jahid-Ali yanked a gun out of his pants pocket and pulled Denise behind him. "Is this a setup? Niecie, did you set me up?" There was panic in his voice.

"Oh no!" Denise's eyes flew open wide. "I just brought Shelly."

"Who the hell is that?" Brother Jahid-Ali looked perplexed.

"My best friend. She's pregnant, remember? I told you that the last time we met." Denise was trying to jog his memory.

Not believing her, Brother Jahid-Ali continued to question Denise. "Who else is with her and don't lie."

"Nobody, I swear. Honey, I didn't mean to frighten you." She stroked his arm. "I'm just sick and tired of sneaking around."

Brother Jahid-Ali relaxed a little.

"When did you get a gun?" Denise's eyes were transfixed on the shiny metal .358 magnum.

"I bought it the last time I got jumped." Noticing her expression. "Don't worry, I know how to use it."

Denise swallowed hard.

"Why didn't you tell me you were bringing somebody?"

"I didn't realize that I was going to until the last minute." Denise stared at his dashiki. "Take your dashiki off. She doesn't know who she's meeting, and I don't want her to figure out that you are the same man I was talking to at the Federal Building."

"Good idea." He removed his dashiki and put it in his bag. "If she's pregnant, she shouldn't be down there by herself. Go get her." Brother Jahid-Ali put the gun back into his pocket.

Shelly and Denise climbed to the spot where Brother Jahid-Ali was waiting.

"It's good to finally meet you. I'd say that I've heard all about you, but Niecie hasn't told me anything." Shelly folded her arms across her chest. "I don't even know your name."

Brother Jahid-Ali hesitated and Denise remained silent. Shelly looked at Denise and then Brother Jahid-Ali. Finally he spoke, "Carlton."

His answer surprised Denise. She didn't think that he'd ever use his given name again.

"Mine's Shelly." They shook hands.

"I know. Would you like to sit down?" He motioned to the blanket that was spread out behind him.

"No, I'm going to get back into the car and let you two love birds talk." Shelly winked at Denise and then whispered to Denise. "He's a stone fox."

Before Shelly could take another step, bright lights flashed through the bushes. Brother Jahid-Ali dropped to the ground, taking Shelly and Denise with him.

"Who's that?" Shelly asked.

"SH!" Brother Jahid-Ali hissed at her.

The lights continued to bounce off the trees right above their heads. Brother Jahid-Ali drew his .358 and crawled along the ground to the edge of the cliff. There was no way anybody was coming up where they were.

Seconds felt like an eternity. Shelly was frightened and had to go to the bathroom; Denise felt sweat run down her back. The four-door, black car cruised by real slow one last time and then it was gone.

"Let's go." Brother Jahid-Ali barked at Denise and Shelly.

"We just got here." Denise and Shelly said in unison.

"It doesn't matter. They might come back." His eyes had turned to stone.

Shelly scampered to the car and Denise unwillingly followed her. "When will I see you again?" Denise's eyes pleaded with Brother Jahid-Ali's.

"I don't know. Niecie, I'm leaving any day now and I want you to come with me." Brother Jahid-Ali said sadly.

"Where are you going?" She whined.

"I don't know yet." He responded quietly.

"I—I don't know what to say." Denise choked back tears.

"Say yes, baby. I need you." Brother Jahid-Ali clutched both of her hands.

"Brotha baby, you don't even know where you're going?" She tried reason.

"It doesn't matter." He attempted to smile. "As long as you're with me, I will be in the right place."

"What about Maulana Imhotep? What about—?" Denise was desperate. "Why do you have to leave?" She said through tears, she didn't even feel.

"Forget about him." Brother Jahid-Ali spoke with authority. "Answer me. Niecie, are you coming with me or not?"

Denise felt confused and a little dizzy. "Everything is happening at once."

Brother Jahid-Ali pulled her within inches of his face. "If you love me, meet me here at exactly 1 A.M. next Friday. Niecie, I'll wait until one-o-five. If you are not here, I'm gone. Do you hear me, baby? I'm gone." He kissed her one last time. "It's either them or me." With that parting statement Brother Jahid-Ali ran to his VW bus and revved the engine.

"Niecie, get in the car. Get out of here." He yelled out of the window.

Denise was rooted and couldn't move. Scenes of her life began to flash before her eyes, making her unable to think clearly. She felt like someone had snatched the world out from under her.

Shelly gently pulled Denise into the car. "Niecie, we've got to go," Shelly said softly.

Denise sat like a zombie the whole trip back to Los Angeles. Shelly tried to talk to her, but Denise was as cold as ice. The only thing Denise said over and over was "He's gone and I never got to tell him about Namibia."

Saturday night. Kweli was walking down dimly lit Vermont Avenue toward his car. It was the end of a long day, and he couldn't wait to meet Shelly at The Kyte. Kweli did not usually travel alone, but since he was going to meet his lady, he didn't think that he needed a bodyguard. On his way to The Kyte, he made a quick detour to the Headquarters. Kweli realized that he had left a small gift for Shelly in his desk drawer at the office. The gift wasn't much . . . just a picture he had blown up of Mao Tse Tung. He and Shelly wanted to name the baby Mao, if it was a boy, and Alma, if it was a girl. Alma was Kweli's mother's name. Before he reached his car, a figure stepped out of the shadow and blocked his path.

"Why did you put a hit out on me?" Brother Jahid-Ali pushed Kweli a couple of steps back.

"What?" surprised at first, Kweli gave a start. "I don't know what you're talking about," snapped Kweli.

"You know damn well what I'm talking about, Kevin!" He grabbed the lapels of Kweli's leather jacket. "Some of

your men have been following me, trying to kill me."
Brother Jahid-Ali eyed him suspiciously.

"Well, if it isn't Jahid-Ali, or is it Carlton these days?"
Kweli snarled. "If I wanted you dead, you would've been
a long time ago."

"I didn't kill those men and you know it," Brother
Jahid-Ali said with conviction.

Kweli shrugged Brother Jahid-Ali's hands off of his
jacket. "That's what you say."

"What happened to us? We used to be brothers."

"That was a long time ago."

"It feels like yesterday."

"Man, you must be jivin'. You turned your back on me,
Carlton." Kweli paused. "We left home together, we
dreamt of making it in California together . . . Man, it was
us against the world. Seemed like the moment we got to
Los Angeles, you changed."

"What do you mean, I changed?"

"Right after we joined WEB, it was like something came
over you. I can't explain it."

"I guess I got caught up in Maulana Imhotep's message."

"And he ain't nothin' but a shrivelled up fraud."

Brother Jahid-Ali remained silent.

"Ain't you going to defend your mfalme?" Kweli
taunted.

"No." he said quietly. "Things changed." Brother Jahid-
Ali looked Kweli square in the eyes. "I owe you an apology
for turning you away that night. I'm sorry. I was so caught
up that I mistook my own brother for my enemy."

Kweli was quite moved. "Don't sweat it." His tone had
softened. "I should actually thank you."

"Thank me? For what?" Brother Jahid-Ali was confused.

"You, well, Maulana Imhotep, forced me to take a long hard look at myself. I understood from that moment on that I was the only person I could trust." Kweli's words hurt Brother Jahid-Ali. "That was the night I became a man."

"You always did read people better than I did." Brother Jahid-Ali chuckled wearily.

"I know about you and Denise," Kweli said quickly. "Man, don't try and deny it."

"How long have you known?" Brother Jahid-Ali asked gravely.

"For a while."

"How come you haven't said anything."

Kweli lit a cigarette, "Want a square?"

"No."

"There hasn't been a reason for me to say anything." Kweli inhaled the smoke deeply. "On the one hand, I think it's cool. You and Denise are kinda made for each other. She's opinionated and outspoken. You used to be kinda soft. Even when we were kids, you were always taking up for the rejects. Remember that time we were playing baseball and nobody picked Walter on his team because snot was always hangin' from his nose?"

Brother Jahid-Ali laughed at the memory. "Yeah."

"Remember we ended up having to delay the game because you refused to play unless Walter was on our team. I was so mad at you. But since you were the best pitcher out of the bunch, there was nothing I could do."

Brother Jahid-Ali picked up the story. "Walter gave up so many runs that day! He made us lose."

"That was the last time Walter ever played with us."

Kweli mused. "I wonder what ever happened to old snot-nosed Walter."

"My mama said that he's finishing medical school," Brother Jahid-Ali answered.

"Solid."

"Carlton, how are your folks?" Kweli felt like they were kids again.

"Ever since I refused to go to Vietnam, my father hasn't spoken to me." It broke Brother Jahid-Ali's heart. He and his dad had been so close. "I talk to mama pretty regularly. What about you? How are your parents and sisters and brothers?"

"Everybody's fine. My mama and daddy still think I'm going to be a preacher."

Both men laughed.

"Kevin, I love Denise."

"That's obvious. Man, the risks you take to meet her!" Kweli shook his head. "Dangerous."

"We've been careless."

"You need to be *careful*. Maybe even stop seeing her for a little while." Kweli said conspiratorially.

"Excuse me?" Brother Jahid-Ali was thrown for a loop.

"Carlton, let's just say that people are looking for you."

"So you *are* behind the threats."

"No." Kweli flicked an ash into the street. "I'm just sayin' that y'all need to cool it."

Brother Jahid-Ali collected his thoughts. "If anything happens to her, I promise—"

"Nothing is going to happen to Denise. You've got my word." Kweli fished in his pocket for another cigarette. "Brotha, I can't protect you."

"I know you can't."

"You should lay low."

Brother Jahid-Ali nodded in agreement. In six days, that's exactly what he planned to do. "I can't leave without her."

Kweli turned fierce eyes on Brother Jahid-Ali. "Carlton, you've got to. She's my right hand, the party needs her."

"So that's why she's protected . . . to be your flunky. Kevin, you still don't know the difference between a servant of the people and being served by the people."

"What in the hell is that supposed to mean?" Kweli's eyes flared.

"It means that living for the people is serving, not getting other people to do all your work, while you take all the glory."

Tension began to engulf them. "You don't know what you're talkin' about."

"I'm right and you know it. Man, you're still the same self-centered punk you were when we were kids."

"That's right, chump, put me down. Just a minute ago I was your brother from around the way. Now, I'm just some punk." Kweli sucked his teeth. "We'll see what kind of punk I am when they catch you."

"They who?" Brother Jahid-Ali asked.

In the distance, three men were walking toward Kweli and Brother Jahid-Ali. Noticing the men first, Kweli stepped to him. "My boys are almost here. If I was you, I'd split."

Tired of running, Brother Jahid-Ali stood his ground. "Kevin, here's your opportunity to get me. Why don't you just turn me in?"

"Carlton, you don't get it. I'm trying to give you your life." Kweli took two steps back and looked at his friend. "Do you want Denise to be a widow of the revolution?"

Kweli had touched Brother Jahid-Ali's soft spot. "No."

Twenty

"Comrade, where have you been?"

"I, uh, haven't been feeling well." Denise said from behind dark sunglasses. It was Tuesday and she had been unable to get out of bed since Saturday. She could do nothing but sleep. Each time she woke up and tried to dress herself, her mind returned to Brother Jahid-Ali's parting words. *If you are not here, I'm gone.* Didn't he know that she just couldn't up and leave? There was no way she could leave her comrades and her parents.

"Soldiers don't get sick." Kweli smirked. He was pacing back and forth in front of her.

"It will never happen again," Denise said dryly.

"Comrade, we really needed you on Saturday at the planning meeting. Where were you?"

"I told you, I was sick." Denise refused to be intimidated. Her life was hanging in the balance.

"Were you hungover?" Kweli was trying to embarrass her in front of the other comrades. "I know that you don't want to get suspended again for being missing in action. So, just admit that you were loaded and this meeting can get started."

"You know what, I already told you I was sick." Denise coughed in his face.

Kweli was pressing his luck. "Shelly said that you two

went to The Kyte. I didn't see you guys there. So, where did you really go?"

Denise rubbed her face and continued to speak in a monotone. "We just stopped there briefly and then we took a drive."

"Where to?"

"Just around." She looked out of the window.

"Around where?" Kweli barked trying to jolt her into telling him where she and Shelly had gone.

"I needed to run a couple of ideas by you," Denise pointed at him. ". . . but since you weren't home, Shelly volunteered to go with me." Denise put the ball back in Kweli's court. "Where were you?"

"The Kyte."

"Really, about what time?" She adopted his accusatory tone.

Kweli returned to his desk and nervously said, "Oh it was before you and Shelly got there. Then we, I mean, I stopped by the office." He cleared his throat and averted his eyes.

Denise knew he was lying, but didn't get into his business. Kweli was Shelly's problem.

The meeting started but Denise didn't hear a word. She only spoke when spoken to and then, kept her comments to a minimum. Though she spent most of the meeting in and out of a daze, she couldn't help but feel that someone was staring very intently at the back of her head. Finally, unable to take the feeling of being violated, she turned around to see Comrade DeeDee glaring at her. *Ah ha,* Denise thought to herself, *Kweli was with her last night.*

* * *

When the meeting ended two hours later, DeeDee approached her.

"I don't believe that you and Shelly were just driving around, Comrade."

"What is the problem DeeDee, did someone steal your broom?"

"As a matter of fact, I have a piece of wood that none of your books, college girl, could ever tell you how to use." DeeDee said smugly. "You're a liar, Comrade. I've never liked you and I told Comrade Kweli that. I even recommended that he suspend you for insubordination."

Denise removed her glasses. "Somebody needs to suspend you for being so nosy. I'm going to give you a word of advice and I'm only going to say this once; If Shelly and Kweli break up because of you, you might think about getting going underground, dig?" Denise slapped her own cheek in mock concern. "Oh, I'm sorry, did I say 'underground', I meant back to the hell you came from, because only *real revolutionaries* go 'underground'." She snarled at DeeDee. "You'll never be that deep."

"Are you threatening me, Comrade?" DeeDee tried to act unaffected by Denise's words, but it was obvious that she took Denise's words seriously.

"Nope, those are just the facts." Denise smiled. Threatening DeeDee actually lifted her spirits.

"Comrade Denise?"

"What now, Kweli?" Denise dispensed with the titles. Kweli wasn't worthy of even being called dog.

"Where are you going?" He sounded patient.

"If it's any of your business, I'm going home."

"Then where?"

"To Mars where I can get some respect," Denise said smartly.

"Comrade Leonard is going to accompany you to Mars, if you don't mind."

"I do mind."

Kweli shrugged his shoulders. "Comrade Leonard, escort Comrade Denise home."

"I swear." Denise headed for the door.

"We don't want anything to happen to you. This is a busy week for us. Please cooperate Denise."

"Whatever."

That was the first incidence of Kweli mandating that a comrade be with Denise everywhere she went. At every meeting, every rally, fundraiser and when she went home. Even if she drove herself, a comrade was always trailing in a car right behind her. She already lived with three people, now she was living with four.

As Friday approached, Denise was growing more and more anxious. With her tail, she was unable to send a secret message to Brother Jahid-Ali. *What was she going to do? He wouldn't just leave her, would he?* And why was someone always following her. Kweli was up to something. Either he was afraid that she was going to tell Shelly about her suspicions about DeeDee or was he after Brother Jahid-Ali? Did he know? When she thought about it, she hadn't seen or talked to Shelly since the week before. No, no Shelly couldn't have, wouldn't have. Would she?

Denise had to ditch her tag-along comrade. She was running out of time and she had to find out if Kweli was the one who put the word out on her love. This possibility took the place of the hesitation she felt a week earlier when Brother Jahid-Ali asked her to choose between him and the Panthers. Denise had her answer. There was no way she'd live another day without him.

* * *

Brother Jahid-Ali had packed his few belongings in the wee hours after he saw Denise. As much as it was killing him, he made no attempt to contact her. In fact, Brother Jahid-Ali carried on like nothing had happened. No one at WEB, not even Maulana Imhotep, knew about the attempts that had been made on his life. Kweli was right, revolutionaries had no one to trust but themselves.

Friday. Brother Jahid-Ali headed out to Point Dume for the last time. It was only eleven thirty, but he didn't have any other place to go. When he came to the winding road that lead to their secret rendezvous spot, he drove very slowly. He was on the lookout for someone who might have possibly been following him. Brother Jahid-Ali also wanted to inhale every aspect of the drive. This would be the last time he drove this way. The December sun had set long ago and the air was quite chilly. He didn't mind the cold. He rolled the window down in his VW bus and let the air blow against his face.

His mind was on Denise. Brother Jahid-Ali loved her so much. He began to visualize their life. It wouldn't be much at first, but he would work hard to make sure that she never wanted for anything. He still didn't quite know where they were going. For some reason, Mississippi kept calling him. May be he would take her there . . . just for a little while. He grew comfortable with the thought. He hadn't brought a woman home to meet his family in years. They would like her. *No,* he told himself, *they would love her.*

"Shelly did you tell Kweli about Brother Jahid-Ali?"
"Who?"
Denise forgot that he told Shelly his given name. "Carlton."

"No."

"If you didn't who did? No one knows about him, except one other person and now you."

"I haven't told Kweli anything, I swear to you."

"Shelly, Kweli has had somebody tail me all week. Doesn't that seem odd to you? Did he say anything to you about not trusting me?"

"No, in fact, I thought you guys had been busy all week."

"We have been, but no one has had to stand guard over me before now. Something doesn't make sense."

"Niecie, I swear on my child's life that I didn't tell Kweli anything." Shelly rubbed her swollen stomach. "I don't know why he's having you followed."

Denise was perplexed. "Somethin's not right."

"What are you going to do?"

"I'm leaving." She stood up. "I'm meeting Brother Jahid-Ali tonight and we are leaving."

"Now it all makes sense. All of the nights I couldn't find you; why you wouldn't date anyone else. Niecie, why didn't you tell me?"

"The last time I told you I saw him, you dimed on me. I couldn't take that risk again."

"Are you sure you're doing the right thing?"

"I can't picture life without him, Shelly. I love him, you of all people should know where I'm coming from."

"I do, girl. I do." Shelly knew the depth of Denise's emotion

"Before you go, Niecie, I want to tell you something. If the baby is a girl, her middle name will be Denise—Alma Denise."

"That's sweet." Denise inhaled sharply to keep from crying. "I gotta go."

Shelly extended her hand to Denise. "What are you doing?"

"I'm giving you our secret handshake."

Denise gripped Shelly's hand.

Together they sang in unison, "The bonds of sisterhood will bridge any distance."

Then, they embraced.

Denise passed Kweli on her way out of the door.

"Oh Niecie," Shelly called after her. "You forgot your bag."

Denise turned around and stared at the black leather bag with the black panther stitched on it. "Shelly, that's not mine."

Shelly examined the bag closely. "Whose is it? And how did it get here?"

"Ask your old man," Denise called out.

"D.D. . . . D.D., Comrade DeeDee?" Shelly was saying out loud. "Wait a minute. Kweli, I know that this bag does not belong to Comrade DeeDee."

Kweli eyed Denise before he answered Shelly. "How would I know whose bag it is?" His tone was defensive.

"Maybe 'cause I found it on the floor in our bedroom!" Shelly was screaming at him. "Kweli, how could you?"

"What did you tell her?" Kweli hissed at Denise.

"I didn't tell her anything, you just told on yourself." Denise felt triumphant. He was finally caught.

"Answer me Kweli, how could you do this to me?" Shelly was yelling at the top of her lungs for the whole block to hear. "After I supported you . . . believed the lies you told me . . . I'm even having your baby! Why can't that be enough?"

"It was a mistake." Kweli responded miserably. "I'm sorry. She doesn't mean anything to me."

"I can't believe this!" Shelly was still holding DeeDee's purse in her hand. "I trusted you." She threw the bag at Kweli's head. He ducked.

"Let me explain."

Denise longed to stay for the fireworks, but Brother Jahid-Ali was waiting for her. It was eleven forty-five. If she hurried, she could be at Point Dume by twelve thirty.

Thinking that she had lost her tail, Denise drove directly home. She made it and shoved clothes, toothbrush, albums and book of poetry into a duffle bag. Denise stood in what had been her room for almost four years and quietly closed the door behind her. Through the closed door, she could feel Marvin Gaye's eyes on her. "I'm sorry, Marvin, I can't take you with me. Know that you are always in my heart, right next to Brother baby." Denise was almost home free when Leonard met her at the door.

"Going somewhere Comrade?" His eyes were menacing.

"Yes, I'm taking a little trip for Comrade Kweli." Denise glanced down at her watch to see that it was midnight.

"I wasn't aware of any trip." Comrade Leonard used his whole body to block the doorway.

"It came up at the last minute." Denise was figuring out whether or not she could take him. Comrade Leonard was a few inches taller than her, but with a hard enough shove, he would be out of the way.

"I don't believe you." He glowered at her.

"I don't care what you believe, it's not my fault that Kweli doesn't tell his subordinates his every move."

Denise tried to walk around Comrade Leonard.

"You're not leaving until I speak with the Captain."

Before Denise could respond, the phone rang.

Denise answered it on the first ring. "Hello." Her heart

was pumping. It was twelve o' three. Time was slipping by.

"Denise, you need to get over here as fast as you can." Kweli sounded strange.

She thought it was a trick. "Why?"

"It's Shelly. Something happened. The ambulance is on the way."

"What did you do to her?" Denise was kicking herself for leaving his apartment earlier.

"Nothing. We were arguing and she went into labor." Kweli sounded afraid. "Hurry, Denise."

"Labor? It's too soon! Oh my god, she's only four months pregnant." Denise dropped the phone and ran to the door.

"Where are you going?" Comrade Leonard yelled.

She ignored him, got into her car and zoomed to Kweli's apartment.

"The baby's coming!" Sweat was pouring down Shelly's face. "Oh, it's coming." Shelly was squeezing Kweli's hand.

Kweli was a nervous wreck. "Where is that damn ambulance?"

Denise held Shelly's left hand and tried to calm her down.

"Denise, she's bleeding." Kweli looked down at Shelly's legs. "Isn't that too much blood?" Shelly's white and gold flowered dress was drenched with blood.

"Give me that towel!" Denise barked at Kweli.

Kweli did as he was commanded. "I don't know what happened. We were arguing, then the next thing I know, she fell on the couch clutching her stomach."

"Shut up."

"No, Niecie, it's not his fault." Shelly panted. She tried to hold Denise's gaze.

"Shh, save your strength."

Kweli was trying his best to soak up the blood with the towel.

"He-he didn't . . . not his fault." Shelly's voice was growing faint and her eyes were fluttering.

"Hold on Shelly, the ambulance will be here any minute." Denise mopped the sweat on Shelly's brow. "Kweli, go see if the ambulance is here."

He was immobilized. "Kweli, get up and see if the ambulance is here."

Kweli was crying into his hands. "It's all my fault. I'm sorry, Shelly. I'm so sorry. Please don't die. I love you so much—"

"Nobody is going to die, except you, if you don't go and check on the ambulance," said Denise through clenched teeth.

Still unable to move, Kweli cradled Shelly's head in his arms. "Denise, we're losing her."

"No we're not." Denise continued to hang on to her friend.

But Kweli was right. Shelly's eyes rolled to the top of her head and her breathing stopped.

Denise called Shelly's name; pushed down on her chest; tried CPR and nothing worked. The paramedics were coming in the door. Too late, Shelly was gone.

"Ma'am, we need to get there." The first paramedic said to Denise.

She reluctantly moved out of the way.

Kweli tried to attack the second paramedic. "What took you so long?"

"We got here as fast as we could sir." The man wanted

to avoid a confrontation. "Please sir, let me get to your wife."

"Shelly was not your wife!" Denise screamed in a rage. With both fists she pounded on Kweli's chest. "You killed her! You killed her with your macho talk of revolution. Murderer!"

"I'm sorry. I—I—" Kweli was choked up again and sobbing. He was trying to hug Denise, but she jerked away from him.

"Save it for God 'cause he's the one you're going to have to answer to. Not me." Refusing to cry, Denise put a finger in Kweli's face. "I hope you're happy. Now you and DeeDee can be together."

"No it's not like that, Denise. I love Shelly." Kweli broke down completely. "What am I going to do?"

Denise backed away from the scene in front of her. The clock on the wall said twelve forty-five. There was no way she would make it to Point Dume in time, but she was going to try.

For the first time ever, Brother Jahid-Ali doubted Denise's love for him. In fifteen minutes he was leaving. He thought surely she would be there by now. Maybe something happened. He didn't know what to do. As he weighed the pros and cons of staying until after one o'five waiting for Denise, a car drove by.

"She's here!" Relief flooded his whole body. "I knew you'd come." Brother Jahid-Ali ran down the hill to meet her, when he noticed that the car kept going. Instinctively, he pulled his .357 magnum from his jeans. To his horror, it was the same car that passed by the week before. The black sedan made a u-turn. Brother Jahid-Ali dived into the bushes.

The car slowed and then stopped. From his vantage point, he could not see who was in the car. After several minutes, the car drove on. Brother Jahid-Ali remained crouched down in the foliage for another five minutes. It was minutes to one, but he couldn't wait. The risk was too dangerous.

He carefully slid through the bushes and crawled on his stomach to the passenger side of his VW bus. He gently opened the door and got into the car. Brother Jahid-Ali waited on the floor of his van another two minutes, hoping that Denise would drive up before he pulled off.

The minutes ticked by at an excruciatingly slow pace. There was no way for him to determine the time in the darkness of his van. His left leg was beginning to cramp under the weight of his body. Brother Jahid-Ali was afraid to move a muscle, yet the cramp in his leg was getting sharper and sharper. He would eventually have to move to keep from losing all feeling in his leg.

Denise checked her watch at the stoplight on Sunset and Pacific Coast Highway. It was one o'clock on the dot. Damn! She only had five minutes to reach a destination fifteen minutes away. For a moment Denise thought about turning around and going back. *Going back to where?* She had no place to go. Well, there was one stop she needed to make. Denise had to notify Shelly's mother of Shelly's death. In all the craziness, she panicked and completely forgot about Shelly's mother. Her heart began to ache as she thought of her friend being covered and rolled away by the paramedics.

The light turned green, Denise was frozen at the wheel. Should she go back and tell Shelly's mother in person? Or, should she keep on schedule and try to meet Brother Jahid-Ali. "Oh God, tell me what to do." A few seconds later, a horn blared behind her. That was her answer. Denise pushed the peddle to the metal and raced to Point Dume.

The black sedan drove past the beige VW bus slowly a second time. Brother Jahid-Ali clutched his gun and clicked the safety off. The black sedan made a u-turn in front of his van and shined the bright lights on it. He heard a car door slam and heavy footsteps coming toward his van. Sweat beads ran down Brother Jahid-Ali's face and into his eyes, almost blinding him. He took three deep breaths to steady his wildly beating heart. He raised his gun to his face. He made a promise to himself: there was no way they were going to take him alive.

The footsteps got closer and then suddenly retreated. Brother Jahid-Ali could only hear muffled voices. He could hear a radio or walkie-talkie. Police! That's what made the footsteps retreat. The police's announcement came over the loud speaker.

"It is after curfew. Vacate the premises." The voice boomed over the car's megaphone. "We will be returning in three minutes. If anyone is here when we return, you will be cited and your vehicle towed."

Brother Jahid-Ali could hear the sedan speed past his bus. This was his cue to get behind the steering wheel. *Where was Denise?* The question echoed in his head as he watched the police drive in a circle making the announcement twice more and then driving off into the darkness. He was so happy to see the cops, he didn't know what to do. Their presence saved his life and bought him some more time to wait for Denise. Brother Jahid-Ali figured that was the last he would ever see of the black sedan. His rejoicing was short lived when he heard the low rumble of a car pull up behind him. Brother Jahid-Ali slid to the floor of his van. "Damn! They're back."

The beige VW bus was parked in the same place it always was. There was no one inside as far as the driver could see. With ease the car slowed to a stop directly behind the VW bus. With the motor running, the driver grabbed a small bag, got out of the car and creeped up to the passenger's side of the bus. The window was rolled up and the bus appeared to be empty. As the driver turned the handle to be certain, the door flew open and the muzzle of a silver .357 magnum stared Denise in the face.

"Niecie! Oh my god. I thought you were one of the men trying to kill me." Brother Jahid-Ali fell back on the seat panting with relief.

Denise, who was still frozen, said, "It didn't look like anyone was in the van." Her voice was shaking.

"I was hiding on the floor." Brother Jahid-Ali pulled Denise into the van. "I didn't think that you were going to come."

Denise threw her arms around him and he pulled her into the bus. "I was so afraid that you left without me."

"Never, Denise, I would never leave you." Brother Jahid-Ali said sincerely. He kissed her softly on her lips. He felt wetness on his face. "Niecie, why are you crying?"

"The most terrible thing happened." The tears she had been holding back, poured down her cheeks like rain.

"What?" He asked concerned.

Denise choked on her sobs.

"Baby, tell me. The police will be here any moment."

"It's Shelly . . . she's dead."

"Dead? How did that happen?"

"She miscarried and bled to death." Denise buried her head in his shoulder. Her body shook with pain. "I didn't know what to do."

"Where is she?" Brother Jahid-Ali took control of the situation. "Do we need to go to her?"

Denise wiped her eyes with the back of her hand. "No. Kweli is with her. I do need to call her mother, though."

He gently pulled away from Denise, so he could close her door. "As soon as we get out of here, we'll stop at a phone."

"I feel so bad . . . for running out like that." Denise looked down at her hands. "I just didn't know what else to do. I felt like I had no one to turn to, except you."

"Don't worry about anything. I'm sorry for the loss of your best friend. In a different but similar kind of way, I know how you feel." He briefly thought of Kweli and what he must be going through. "Shelly knew that you were there for her."

"You know, she said that she loved Kweli right up until the end." Denise said in sad amazement. "After everything he'd done to her, she loved him no matter what."

Brother Jahid-Ali didn't know what to say.

Denise straightened up. "Do you think that Shelly will forgive me?"

"Of course. You were her best friend, her sister, her comrade." Brother Jahid-Ali said confidently. "Baby, I'm not trying to rush you, but we can't afford to run into the police or those other men."

Denise smiled sadly. "I'm ready."

Brother Jahid-Ali searched Denise's eyes for certainty.

"There will be no turning back." He wanted Denise to be sure that she knew what she was in for.

"I know. I don't care." Her teary eyes held the depth of the love she felt for him. "I would follow you to the end of the earth."

"No you wouldn't, 'cause I'd be following you." He leaned over and kissed her one last time before starting the engine. "Niecie, I love you."

Brother Jahid-Ali started the engine and jammed the clutch into first gear. Denise wiped her eyes one last time and looked over at her man. Yes, she thought to herself, she had made the right decision.

The two lovers drove off into the darkness, with only the moon and Shelly as silent witnesses of the two of them ever having been together.

About the Author

Neffetiti Austin has her master's degree from UCLA in African-American Studies, with a specialization in Women's Studies and U.S. Political History. A person of diverse talents, Neffetiti has worked on everything from assembly campaigns to community based organizations, a soul food restaurant, and as an academic counselor. She is a member of Alpha Kappa Alpha Sorority, Incorporated, and is very active in the community.

Look for these upcoming Arabesque titles:

December 1996

EMERALD ENVY by Eboni Snoe
NIGHTFALL by Loure Jackson
SILVER BELLS, an Arabesque Holiday Collection

January 1997

ALL THE LOVE by Bette Ford
SENSATION by Shelby Lewis
ONLY YOU by Angela Winters

February 1997

INCOGNITO by Francis Ray
WHITE LIGHTNING by Candice Poarch
LOVE LETTERS, Valentine collection